"The culture of death is conquered each time that a woman says 'yes' to the life of her unborn baby! In the novel *Life's Choices*, the protagonist is an eighteen year old woman who boldly and emphatically chooses to defy death by choosing life! I encourage everyone to read *Life's Choices* and rejoice each time a choice is made to conquer the culture of death!"
> —Father Frank Pavone, National Director,
> Priests For Life, Staten Island, New York

"Prison ministry and pro-life intervention share a core value for those whose lives have brought them to desperation or hopelessness. Both inmates in prison and pregnant women who have already chosen abortion or are considering it need the compassionate arms of Christianity to come alongside and love them. How shall they choose? Carlos made mistakes that threatened his freedom on the outside and the fresh start he had begun. Friends gathered round him and prayed for his well being. Lourdes responded to volunteers on the sidewalk and trained staff in the pregnancy help center. Testimonies inspired her to choose adoption rather than abortion. In both, the answer is relationships forged by caring, hands-on Christians. In *Life's Choices*, Paul Turk masterfully weaves parallel plots to their joyous intersection."
> —Judy Madsen Johnson, Author, *Stories from the Front
> Lines: The Battle Against Abortion*, Oviedo, Florida

"*Life's Choices* is a book which is both entertaining and enlightening. Paul Turk provides great insight into often misunderstood pro-life help. He gives detailed descriptions of what goes on at Sidewalk Prayer outside of abortion mills, the purpose of Crisis Pregnancy Centers and how they can help, and the in's and out's of adoption. Mr. Turk uses his fictional novel to promote a culture of Life. I highly recommend this book."
> —Yoli Cory, Hiawassee, Georgia

"*Life's Choices* is an easy read and an eye opener to the citizen who has not yet crossed paths with the pro-life movement. I recommend this novel if you are looking for a real life view of choices we face in today's culture."
—Mary Rodriquez, R.N., Program Administrator, Birthline/ Lifeline Pregnancy Care Centers, Delray Beach, Florida

"Paul Turk's latest novel, *Life's Choices*, is a gripping, thought-provoking story that you will not want to put down until the conclusion. It is a riveting narrative, with a likeable circle of friends, who exhibit godly character and a real compassion for others. The book will make you wish you had friends such as these, even though many led criminal lives before having life-changing experiences. It makes you want to live in Paul Turk's world, where life is all about how you can help others and bring joy to their lives. *Life's Choices* is a book about second chances and are presented from a Christian perspective. His legal knowledge enriches the story, while bringing courtroom scenes to life. Paul Turk's fiction inspires, draws you closer to God, makes you feel cleansed inside and fills you with hope."
—Kathy Johnson, Esq. Attorney and Author of
Starlette Universe: Eva from E-ville,
Delray Beach, Florida

"I heartily recommend *Life's Choices* for any reader who is looking for a story filled with legal suspense and a pro-faith, pro-life message. Paul Turk manages to weave together a tale of how our life choices can impact our families, our future and even our freedom. With hard-hitting courtroom scenes and a story that is warm, encouraging and true-to-life, he exposes the weighty issues at play, but demonstrates the mercy and grace of God at work. *Life's Choices* is a wonderful read for the community of faith, but also for anyone who is confronted with this issue. It will challenge your thinking, but mostly, it demonstrates that there is always hope."
—A. Wayne Gill, Esq., Attorney, minister and
author of *The Runner*, Lake Worth, Florida

4-25-15,
John and Sharon,
Thanks for your support! I hope you both enjoy my book. God Bless!

Paul Turk

Life's Choices

Paul Turk

*"You formed my inmost being; you knit me in my
mother's womb. I praise you, so wonderfully you
made me; wonderful are your works!"*
Psalm 139, Verses 13-14

Publisher Page
an imprint of Headline Books, Inc.
Terra Alta, WV

Life's Choices

by Paul Turk

copyright ©2015 Paul Turk

To order additional copies of this book or for book publishing information, or to contact the author:

Headline Books, Inc.
P.O. Box 52
Terra Alta, WV 26764
www.PublisherPage.com
800-570-5951

Publisher Page is an imprint of Headline Books

ISBN: 978-1-882658-24-4

Library of Congress Control Number: 2015933772

PRINTED IN THE UNITED STATES OF AMERICA

This book is dedicated to all of us, who make many choices in life on a daily basis. May God and Jesus Christ guide us in our choices.

1

As Carlos Delgado slowly opened the door to Rough Riders Bar in the northern section of West Palm Beach, his eyes darted around in search of a familiar face. Although there were a number of people in the building, the dimly lit room made it difficult to recognize any one. He pulled his cell phone from his pants pocket and saw it was 11:00 p.m. There had to be someone he knew here. Usually, on a Saturday night, plenty of acquaintances were there to share a beer or two. Delgado closed the door and carefully made his way to a part of the bar where there were several empty stools. As he sat down, he looked up and down the room, but he saw no familiar faces, other than the bartender, "Big Jake" McCloud. At 6'7" and 350 pounds, the nickname was more than appropriate. Big Jake noticed Delgado sit down and made his way to Carlos, nervously tapping his fingers on the counter.

"All right, hold your horses, Delgado," bellowed McCloud. "You want the usual?"

"You got it. And hurry it up 'cause I'm thirsty." Delgado smirked at Big Jake, who saluted Carlos in mock fashion. After the barkeep poured him a draft beer, he placed it in front of Carlos, who rubbed his hands together in anticipation of the frosty delight.

"That's more like it, Big Jake." Delgado raised the mug, nodded at McCloud, and drank a sizeable portion of the brew in a matter of seconds. Five minutes later he was finished and motioned to McCloud for a refill. Big Jake quickly complied with Delgado's request.

"You weren't kidding, Delgado; you are thirsty tonight. I've never seen you down a beer so fast." McCloud smiled at Carlos.

"You're right. I guess not seeing anyone I know and can talk to helped me polish off the first one pretty fast. Where are Davis and Peters? They're usually around on a Saturday night."

"Both of them were here earlier. I think they left around ten. They didn't say why, and I didn't ask. After all, I'm not their keeper."

"I know, Big Jake," answered Delgado in a gruff voice. "I'm just wondering why they aren't around."

"You'll have to find out from them." McCloud appeared annoyed and quickly moved down the bar to wait on other customers.

As Delgado watched Big Jake entertain other patrons, he felt a strong push on his shoulder. He quickly spun around to see who it was. His mouth hung open when he recognized the encroacher. Before Carlos could respond, William Jones, an ex-inmate who had served time at Newtown Correctional Institution while Delgado was also incarcerated there, launched into a verbal assault on his prey.

"Look who's here. If it ain't Carlos Delgado in the flesh. The last time I saw you was when you came into Newtown with the so-called Christian prison ministry team. As I recall, I was about to pop you out in the yard before that skinny, choir boy minister stepped between us. You sure were lucky not to have gotten a good beatin'. And you would have deserved it." Jones couldn't contain the evil smile that erupted across his lips.

Delgado felt the anger rising from within him as his memory quickly raced back to that day of confrontation. He recalled how he almost caused the prison ministry team to be ejected from Newtown. Carlos quickly decided against getting into another fracas with Jones.

"Listen, Jones. I came in here to have a couple of beers, not to get into any arguments, so please leave me alone and let me enjoy my drink."

Carlos turned around to face the bar and could no longer see Jones. Without saying a word, Jones spun Delgado's bar stool around and viciously sucker punched him on the side of the face. The force of the blow knocked Delgado off the stool onto the floor. Big Jake saw the hit being delivered. He ran from behind the bar to where Jones stood over Carlos taunting him.

"Are you out of your mind, man? What do you think you're doing getting into a fight in my bar? I warned you before about acting up in this place. Now get out of here and don't ever come back!" Big Jake was livid. He picked Jones up by the back of his collar like he was a rag doll and quickly pushed him out of the bar. One of the patrons held the door open as McCloud threw Jones out of the bar with such force that he fell to the ground. Jones got up and ran away without saying a word. Big Jake watched his hasty retreat and when he could no longer see Jones, went back into the building.

A couple of the customers helped Delgado to his feet. The side of his face was already puffy, and a black eye was imminent. Delgado appeared groggy, and his vision was distorted.

"You okay, Delgado? I'm sorry this happened. That guy Jones is a bad dude. I've had problems with his mouth before, but, he's never hit anyone. He won't be let back in here." McCloud appeared genuinely concerned about Delgado's physical state. Perhaps more from an owner's liability standpoint than from a humanistic aspect.

"I'm okay," growled Delgado. He was seething. "There's only one thing I want to know."

"What is it?" responded Big Jake.

"Where does the no-good jackass live?" Delgado stared intently at McCloud as he waited for the answer.

"Why do you want to know?" A look of concern crossed Big Jake's face.

"Why do you think I want to know? I'm gonna pay him back for what he did to me. There's no way he's gettin' away with sucker punching me." Delgado shook his head from side-to-side trying to get rid of the cobwebs he felt from the attack.

"I don't know where he lives. And even if I did, there's no way I'd tell you. It would only lead to a lot more trouble. Go home and take care of yourself."

"I guess you won't tell me, so I'll find out myself. When I do, Jones will pay the price."

Delgado stormed out of the bar without saying another word. He was immediately followed by one of the customers who had helped him get up from the floor.

"Hey, buddy. Wait up."

Delgado turned around to see who called him. "Yeah, what is it you want?" He stopped while waiting for the response. A frown crossed his face.

"My name's Johnnie. I'm one of the guys who helped you up after Jones hit you."

"Don't think you're gonna get a thank-you. I'm not in the mood to appreciate anything right now."

"Hey, man, that's not why I came out here. I heard you ask Big Jake where Jones lives. I know the answer, and I'm here to tell you."

"And why are you gonna tell me? What's in it for you?" Delgado looked skeptically at this stranger.

"I'm gonna tell you because I can't stand Jones. He hassles me all the time with his big, bad attitude. I'd like to see you put him in his place. Not only for you, but for me as well."

"All right. So where does Jones live?"

"In an apartment building about a half a mile from here. The street number is 115 McNear Street. His apartment number is 103." Johnnie looked anxiously at Delgado, waiting for his response.

"How do you know?"

"Because I live in the area."

"All right, man. Thanks for the info. I'll go pay him a visit now and see if he's home. It will be too bad for him if he is."

Johnnie's face lit up in anticipation of Jones taking a beating that Johnnie felt would be well deserved. Delgado turned away without saying another word and marched off in search of Jones.

Delgado slowly walked to Jones' apartment building. It was pitch-black and no one was in sight when he arrived. It was a three-story building with a front-door entryway. Delgado walked up the steps to the front door and tried it. He was in luck. It was open. Carlos went inside the building. Again there was no one to be seen. He quietly made his way down the hallway, looking for Apartment 103. When he reached his goal, he saw the door, slightly ajar. He couldn't believe his good fortune. Little by little, he pushed the door open and went inside.

2

"Good mornin', everyone. It's good to see all of you so bright and early on a Monday morning." Robert Williams looked around. His irrepressible smile lit up the meeting room at First Baptist Church in Pahokee. "I don't think we all know each other so I'd like to go around the room and have everyone introduce themselves. But first, I want to ask Pastor Gilbert to lead us in an opening prayer."

Gilbert quickly shot out of his chair. "Thank you, Robert. I'm going to introduce myself now to those who may not know me because after my prayer to the Lord, I'm turning this meeting back over to Robert. After all, he's our leader on this most worthy cause. My name is Anthony Gilbert, and I am the pastor at this church. Please bow your heads while we pray."

The minister took a deep breath. Then he began a heartfelt prayer. "Dear Lord, we give You thanks for bringing all these devoted people together today to work on an important mission. All of us are committed to doing our utmost to stop abortions, and we seek Your help in accomplishing our objective to save the lives of unborn children. Please guide us in our actions, and help us to be persistent in attaining our goal. In Jesus name, we pray." After Pastor Gilbert finished his prayer, he sat back down and nodded at Robert, who immediately took the cue.

"Thank you for the wonderful petition to Jesus, Pastor Gilbert. I'm not goin' to waste any time tellin' everyone who I am because I know all of you, but my beautiful wife is here, and I know some of you haven't met her, so I'd like to ask her to start us off." Robert winked at his spouse. She arched her eyebrows and shook her head in response to Robert's statement.

"My name is Coral Williams and the first thing I'm going to say is when my husband refers to me as his beautiful wife, I know he's looking for an extra-special dinner." As Coral smiled at Robert, the room erupted in laughter.

Robert slyly grinned at Coral. "Guilty as charged," he admitted.

Coral quickly became serious as she continued on. "Laughter is a good thing, but I know we're all here for an important purpose. The reason I'm here today is to support my husband and all of you in his attempt to have our churches come together to help prevent abortions. Thank you." She glanced at the woman sitting to her left.

"I'm Sister Agnes, and I'm from St. Juliana's Catholic Church in Belle Glade. I am very thankful to you, Robert, for putting this meeting together. Action like this is desperately needed." Sister Agnes nodded at the man in the chair next to her.

"My name is Pastor Paul Demus. I'm from St. Peter's Lutheran Church in Loxahatchee, and I fully agree with Sister's sentiments."

"Well, I also believe in the necessity of this program. My name is Pastor Ed Jonas from St. John's Methodist Church in Wellington," said the man sitting next to Pastor Demus.

"The Episcopalians agree as well. I'm Pastor Bob Jamison from St. Mark's Episcopal Church in

South Bay. What about our friends from the non-denominational Christian church?" Jamison looked over at the couple sitting near him.

"We're all on the same page, Pastor Jamison. My name is John Edwards and sitting next to me is my wife, Lorraine. We're from First Calvary Church in Royal Palm Beach." Lorraine smiled at the group.

"Excellent," said Robert. "It looks like we're off to a great start. Now, there's one other person we haven't gotten to yet, and I would like the pleasure to introduce her because she is our speaker today."

Robert looked across the table at a middle-aged, blond woman who grinned from ear-to ear. He gestured at her as he spoke. "Maria Rodgers is the Program Administrator for Choose Life Pregnancy Care Centers. She's here today to make a presentation about her organization, and most importantly, to tell us how we can help Choose Life in fulfilling its mission."

Robert sat down, and Maria quickly bounded out of her seat. Her enthusiasm was unmistakable as she began to speak. "Thank you so much, Robert, for having me here today. And thanks to the rest of you for taking time out of your busy schedules to listen to me."

Maria took a deep breath and launched into a heartfelt synopsis of Choose Life's history and mission. "As Robert mentioned, I am the Program Administrator for Choose Life Pregnancy Care Centers. We started out ten years ago with one office located in Boynton Beach. At the time, we had half a dozen employees and ten to twenty volunteers. Since then, we have opened two more locations – one in West Palm Beach and the other in Palm Beach Gardens. And next month we're opening a new office right here in Pahokee. Our paid staff is now at twenty five, and our volunteer count ranges from fifty to sixty. I've been the Program Administrator for five years, and my primary work office is in Boynton Beach, although I travel among all our locations on a regular basis."

Rodgers glanced around the room and saw she had everyone's undivided attention, so she continued on in whirlwind fashion. She truly was a woman on a mission.

"The name of our organization emphasizes our goal – to help pregnant women in Palm Beach County choose life, rather than abortion. As an integral part of our values, we treat each person with dignity and respect. We believe every child is a unique and unrepeatable miracle. Pregnant women, especially those who are considering abortion, need compassionate and loving support."

"To provide support, there are a number of free services we offer. Among those are pregnancy tests, obstetrical ultrasounds, counseling and information, referrals for prenatal care, and adoption information and referrals as an alternative to abortion. We also provide education classes and informational sessions on parenting, breastfeeding, and Biblical teachings emphasizing the Gospel and a culture of life rather than a culture of death. Additionally, for those women in need of financial assistance, diapers, clothes, cribs, car seats, and other essential items are also available."

Suddenly, Rodgers stopped talking. She cleared her throat. There was something she wanted to emphasize, but it momentarily escaped her. Then she realized what it was. "I mentioned we provide obstetrical ultrasounds. And I cannot stress enough how important they are. I have witnessed on hundreds of occasions that when a mother sees an ultrasound image of her unborn child, she chooses life!"

Applause filled the room. Tears welled in Robert's eyes as he spoke in a quiet voice. "It sounds like ultrasounds are really a key part of your program, Maria."

"Yes, they are, Robert. And that's one of the reasons why I'm asking for your help. We need an ultrasound machine for our office opening in Pahokee next month." Maria grimaced as she continued. "The machines are expensive."

"How expensive?" asked Sister Agnes.

"The one we're looking at costs nearly forty thousand dollars, but the beautiful thing about the machine is it allows the mother to see a wonderful picture of her baby."

"So, you're in need of funds to purchase the ultrasound, Maria?" asked Pastor Jamison.

"Yes, we certainly are," sighed Maria.

"Well, we have a large congregation base at our church," replied John Edwards. "I'm sure we can help raise some funds." Several of the other participants echoed similar sentiments.

"That would be such a blessing," responded Maria. She cupped her hands over her face in reaction to the favorable responses.

"Maria, I want to talk in more detail about how we can raise money for the ultrasound machine," said Robert. "But before we do, tell us how else we can assist Choose Life?"

"In addition to needing money to purchase the ultrasound, Choose Life relies on the generous financial contributions of donors, without which we would not be able to offer services free of charge to our clients. There is also a need for more volunteers, especially at the Pahokee office to be opened."

Robert and Coral exchanged glances as Maria continued. "And we're always looking for referrals. Is there someone any of you know who needs help making the decision of her life? But the most important thing we need is prayer. Whenever I make a presentation, I always ask everyone to please pray daily for the success of Choose Life and for our society to return to a culture of life."

"We all certainly can and will do that individually, Maria," said Pastor Jonas. "But what about group prayer? I've driven by abortion centers and watched people across the street praying for an end to abortion. I understand those type activities have sometimes resulted in mothers who were going into the abortion center from not having an abortion."

"You're absolutely correct, Pastor Jonas," replied Maria. "There are different church groups which organize those kinds of pro-life events."

Jonas wasted no time in responding. "Recently, there was an abortion center opened in the Wellington area. I'd love to see members of our congregation go out to the center and pray for an end to abortion, and to pray for the mothers going into the facility to have a change of heart and choose life for the baby. I realize there are rules and procedures to be followed, but I'm sure we can get some guidance from the groups who are already participating."

"You sure can, Pastor Jonas," said Sister Agnes. "My church and other Catholic churches in our Diocese take part in such events and we have a strict written code we follow when we are at those facilities."

"Excellent. It looks like we're off to a great start today." Jonas folded his arms across his chest.

"Yes, we are," replied Robert, "but, we must keep the momentum going. Now I'd like to discuss how we can."

For the next hour, all the participants at the meeting engaged in a spirited dialogue regarding how their churches could assist Choose Life in its mission. They left with optimistic feelings that in some way their congregations would help in promoting a culture of life.

3

Carlos Delgado walked into the Palm Beach law offices of Taylor, Archibald, & Hughes and glanced at his watch. It was 9:10 a.m. He desperately hoped John Taylor would be there and available to meet with him. The receptionist looked up and greeted him with a warm smile.

"How may I help you, sir?"

"My name is Carlos Delgado. John Taylor is a friend of mine. I don't have an appointment, but I'd like to talk to him if he's here."

"Mr. Taylor's secretary is out of the office today, and I don't know his schedule. Let me go back to his office and find out whether he can see you." She quickly opened the door behind her and disappeared from sight as the door closed. Delgado nervously awaited her return. As the door opened, and she came back into the lobby, Carlos took a deep breath and bit his lip in anticipation of the news.

"Mr. Taylor said he would be out in ten minutes. Please take a seat while you're waiting. May I get you a cup of coffee?"

"No, thank you."

Delgado sat down and waited. Twenty minutes later, he was still waiting. He was a nervous wreck. He couldn't believe Taylor wasn't here yet to see him. Five more minutes passed by. He started slapping his hands on the sides of the chair he sat in when the door suddenly opened. At last, Taylor appeared.

"Hi, Carlos. Great to see you. Sorry it took so long, but I couldn't get the lawyer I was on the phone with to shut up. You know how long-winded attorneys can be."

John's smile was returned with a look of fear and hopelessness. He immediately knew something was wrong. "You don't look well, my friend. Let's go back into my office and talk about what's bothering you."

Delgado silently followed John into his office. John closed the door and motioned for Carlos to take a seat. After he sat down, Carlos held his head in his hands and began to sweat.

John took a deep breath. In a quiet tone he said, "Tell me what's going on, Carlos. I see how upset you are."

Delgado nervously shook his head from side-to-side. "I can't believe what I got myself into Taylor! I just can't believe it!" Then there was silence. John patiently waited for Carlos to continue.

"I always said after I got released from prison there would be no way I would ever go back. But now, I'm afraid I'm goin'."

"What in the world are you talking about, Carlos?" Although bewildered, John felt Carlos' sense of panic. He was deeply afraid for his friend, for whom John struggled so hard to keep on a straight and narrow path.

"Let me ask you this first. Is anything I say to you confidential?"

"Are you coming to see me for legal advice?"

"Yes."

"Then anything you tell me is privileged and confidential."

"Okay." Delgado looked John straight in the eyes. "Did you read today's paper?"

"Yes. Why?" John was totally perplexed.

"Did you notice the article about the guy the paper said was the victim of a vicious attack who was found unconscious in his apartment?"

"Yes, I did. What's this all about?"

"What it's about is the guy's name is William Jones. Do you remember a couple of years ago when I went into Newtown with you and the rest of the prison ministry team for the retreat, and almost got into a fight with him?"

"How could I forget?" John's heart raced. He now suspected what was coming.

"Saturday night at the Rough Riders Bar, the creep snuck up on me and started insultin' me when I was mindin' my own business. Then when I asked him to leave me alone and turned away, he spun me around and sucker punched me. I fell off the bar stool, and while I was still on the floor, the bartender threw his butt out of there. After I got my senses back, I found out from one of the other customers where he lived, so I headed to his apartment to pay him back for what he did to me."

John quivered inside. He wanted to stop and ask Delgado why he had done something so stupid, but he knew from his years of experience in the legal profession that he couldn't. It would only serve to further intimidate Carlos. Instead, John remained silent and let Delgado go on with his story.

Carlos looked like he might start to cry. This was a side of Delgado John had never seen. "Anyway, when I get to his building the front door was unlocked, so I went to his apartment. As I got in front of his door, I saw it was open a little, I pushed it more and went in. After I walked in, I saw someone lyin' on the floor but couldn't tell who because it was too dark. There was a light switch I turned on, and then I could see it was Jones. He was on his stomach and the back of his head was bleeding."

Delgado stopped talking. It became more and more difficult for him to continue.

"Take your time, Carlos. When you're ready, let me know what happened next."

"What happened next should never have happened, Taylor." Delgado was becoming increasingly irritated. "I was stupid. Instead of just getting' out of there, I went up to Jones and tried shakin' him to see if he was okay. He didn't move. Then I heard a scream. I looked behind me and saw this woman standin' near the doorway watchin' me. I didn't know who she was. I panicked and ran out of the apartment. On the way out I bumped into her, and then just kept goin'. I never stopped runnin' until I got home."

"Are you telling me you had nothing to do with hitting Jones?"

"That's what I'm telling you."

"Then why did you run away?"

"The woman's scream really scared the hell out of me. I just took off without thinkin' about it."

"You realize how bad this looks?"

"Of course, I do," Delgado angrily replied. "I haven't been able to sleep the past two nights. Then when I saw the article in the paper this morning, I really freaked out. I decided I needed to talk to you immediately. Thank God you were here. Is there anything you can do to help me?"

Carlos was becoming more and more despondent. John exhaled deeply and pondered his response.

"I can't help you by personally representing you. Criminal law is not an area of law I practice and you need an experienced criminal defense lawyer on your side. I can help you find someone."

"What about that guy who represented you in your DUI case? You always said he was a good attorney."

"You're talking about Donald Brisbane. He's not an option. He was appointed a circuit court judge last year."

"There's got to be someone else?" Delgado sighed and looked down as he waited for the answer.

"There is. I have a close friend who is one of the top criminal defense lawyers in Florida. His name is Jack Randolph."

"One of the top criminal lawyers in Florida?" cried out Delgado. "How in the world do you think I can afford him, Taylor?"

"Let's not worry about it right now. Jack owes me some favors, so I think we can work it out. Let me call him and see if he's available. If he can see you now, I'll take you to his office. This can't wait."

"I know it can't. Do it."

John immediately made the call. Fortunately, Randolph was available.

Fifteen minutes later, Carlos and John sat in Randolph's office. Carlos was undergoing a barrage of questions. It was nearly two hours before Randolph was finished. Delgado was impressed with both his physical appearance and demeanor. Randolph was a big, strapping guy and a no-nonsense sort of person. Delgado's perception was Randolph really knew what he was doing and was excellent at his job. Carlos started to relax a little bit. The change in his demeanor wouldn't last long.

"Okay, guys. I've got what I needed from Carlos. It's time for Carlos and me to head over to the Sheriff's Department. Let me tell you what we're going to do."

Delgado swallowed hard as he waited for Randolph's advice. What was going to happen to him? He cringed at the thought.

4

"Lydia, open the door. Hurry up." The pounding on the door grew louder with every second of delay.

"Hold on, Lourdes," rang out the frustrated response. As Lydia unlocked and opened the door, she hollered out, "Why didn't you use your key instead of banging like … ." The question was never finished. Lydia saw her younger sister crying uncontrollably. She quickly ushered Lourdes into the apartment and took her to sit on a couch in the tiny living room.

After she sat next to her, Lydia gently stroked Lourdes's head. "The news at the doctor's wasn't what you hoped for, was it?"

"No, it wasn't! I can't believe I'm pregnant! Lydia, what am I going to do?"

Lourdes desperately searched Lydia's eyes. Lourdes was no longer crying, but Lydia could see and feel the panic flowing from her sibling. Lydia knew she needed to do her best to calm Lourdes down. She took a deep breath and reflected on what she should say.

"I'm sorry I couldn't be there with you today, but I just got home from work. I know we both wish Mom was here. She always knew what to do. So let's pretend I'm Mom and see if I can't help you like she would."

Lourdes nodded in agreement. "That would be good. I miss her so much. I can't believe it's already been a year since she died. How I wish the car accident never happened." Tears again rolled from Lourdes' eyes. Lydia took Lourdes' hands into hers and began to speak slowly.

"Lourdes, I know this is awfully hard on you. You just graduated from high school six months ago, and you're only eighteen years old, but you've got an older sister who loves you very much and will do anything possible to help you through this."

"Thanks, Lydia. I don't know what I would do without you." Lourdes leaned over and hugged Lydia as hard as she could.

"Probably a lot better. You know what a dictator I can be."

A smile sprang across Lourdes' lips. Lydia seized the moment to move on with the conversation.

"Now tell me what Jose said when he found out. I assume you already talked to him."

"Yes, I did, and the discussion wasn't good."

Lydia saw the mountain of anger rising from within Lourdes. She held her breath as she waited for her sister to continue with the story.

"He was a total jerk. He told me I'd better have an abortion. And if I didn't, I was on my own. He made it perfectly clear to me he wants nothing to do with this baby. In fact, he even threatened to leave Belle Glade and go live with his brother in Texas if I decide to have the baby. I don't know what I ever saw in him."

Although Lydia agreed with Lourdes' comments about Jose, she decided not to say anything in response. Instead, she calmly told her sister, "Let's not dwell on Jose. It's obvious from what he said you'll never receive any support from him, financial or otherwise. At least not voluntarily."

"What's that mean?"

"I'm talking about if you decide to have the baby, and he won't help you out by paying child support, you could sue Jose to force him to contribute to the expenses for the baby."

"Lydia, suing him would be like trying to get blood from a turnip. Besides, I think he's totally serious about going to Texas if I choose to have the baby. And I don't feel like chasing him around trying to get money out of him. Even if he did make some money, I'm sure he'd do his best to hide it."

"Okay, so we're done talking about Jose. Have you thought about what your next step should be in coming to a decision about whether or not to have the baby?"

"No, I guess I was hoping for better news. Sitting here talking this through with you makes me think of all the problems I would have in trying to raise a child by myself. This isn't going to be an easy choice." Lourdes exhaled deeply and put her head against the back of the couch. She couldn't believe the nightmare she had gotten into.

"It will be hard to make a decision, but you've got to consider all your options."

"Thank you all for coming to our Bible study class tonight. I hope you enjoyed it." Robert looked around the social hall at First Baptist Church in Pahokee to gauge the reaction to his comment. He wasn't disappointed.

"We sure did, Robert," shouted out Loretta Watson from the back of the room. Her reaction was echoed by the other dozen people who attended the class.

"Well, then, I look forward to seein' you all again next week. Same place, same time." Robert flashed his trademark smile. Everyone other than Coral Williams slowly left the room.

"Great job, Robert. You have a way of explaining Our Lord's words so they really hit home with people. I'm very proud of you."

"Thank you, darlin'. Hearin' you say that makes me happy to be an evangelist for Christ."

Robert opened up the cabinet where he put his cell phone and turned it on. He noticed he had a voice mail, and listened to it. Coral could see the look of concern on his face.

"What's wrong, Robert?"

"John Taylor left me a voice mail. I could tell by the tone of his voice something is bothering him, but he didn't say what it was. If you don't mind, I'd like to see if I can reach him now."

"Of course I don't mind. Go ahead."

Robert dialed John's cell. It was quickly answered.

"Robert, thanks for calling me back. I really need to talk to you." Robert felt John's anxiety.

"What's goin' on, John? It sounds like there's a big problem."

"There is. It's Carlos Delgado."

"Oh, boy. What kind of a mess did he get into this time?"

"A huge one. He's been charged with aggravated battery."

"What?" Robert was stunned. "Tell me what happened."

"It's a long story. Let me give you the short version for now."

"Go ahead."

"Do you remember William Jones from Newtown Correctional?"

"I sure do. That guy was a bad dude. Always looking for a fight with somebody."

"Well, he was released from prison, and he ended up getting into a fight with Carlos at a bar."

"Dear Lord. I can't believe what you're telling me!"

"I couldn't either. Carlos is the one who told me what happened. According to him, Jones sucker punched him and knocked him on the floor. Jones ended up getting thrown out of the bar by the bartender, which should have been the end of it. But Carlos, being the hothead he is, finds out where Jones lives and goes to his house to pay him back."

"Oh, no." Robert bowed his head, and his body trembled.

"Carlos tells me when he got to the house, the door was partially opened and he went in. Then he says he saw Jones down on the floor. He goes over to him and shakes him to see if he's okay. Jones didn't move. Then Carlos hears a scream from a woman standing behind him near the doorway. He panicked and ran away."

"What happened to Jones?"

"He didn't die, and they just removed him from the critical care unit."

"Thank God for that."

"You're right, but Jones is in bad shape. It looks like he might have some permanent injuries."

"Who's representing Carlos? You're not, are you?"

"No, but I managed to have a friend of mine, who's a great criminal lawyer, take on his defense. His name is Jack Randolph, and he's been doing a terrific job. In fact, he got Carlos out of jail on bond, but he is under house arrest."

"What's that mean?"

"He has to wear an electronic monitoring device at all times, and he can only leave the house under limited circumstances. He's also being closely monitored by the Sheriff's department, but he is allowed to have visitors who have been approved go to see him, and you're one of them."

"What do you want me to do?"

"That's one of the reasons I'm calling. Carlos asked me to contact you and ask if you would come to see him. He also told me to tell you everything we talked about. Do you want to see him?"

"Of course. I'll go as soon as I can. Someone needs to tell me how."

"I'll have Jack Randolph call you with the details. I'm sure he's going to tell you anything Carlos and you talk about is not privileged and might be inquired into by the State Attorney who's handling this case, so be careful. Everything I've said to you, other than Carlos being a hothead, is what Carlos has told the Sheriff's office, and what he asked me to say to you."

"I got it, John. I'll be waiting for Mr. Randolph's call. I want to do whatever I can to help Carlos."

"Thanks, Robert. Jack will be in touch."

Robert put his cell into his pocket and looked over at Coral, who had been sitting down reading her Bible. She saw his exasperated demeanor and made a comment.

"Something is terribly wrong, isn't it?"

"Yes, and we need to pray about it right now."

5

As Carlos Delgado opened the front door to his house, he was delighted to see who was there.

"Robert Williams, you big hulk, it's good to see you." Although Carlos was no small guy, his 6'0", 200 pound frame was dwarfed by the 6'9", 310 pound man whom Delgado always had a name for.

"It's good to see you too, Carlos." Williams quickly shot out his hand. Although he wanted to give Delgado a hug, Robert knew what an aversion Delgado had to such forms of physical contact.

Carlos quickly led his guest to the living room. As they sat down on the couch, Robert commented on the great job Delgado did in fixing up his home.

"It was a lot of work, but it added value to the house. I'm sure glad I spent the time and money because I had to use this place as security for the bond I posted to get out of jail."

Delgado let out an enormous sigh and shook his head from side-to-side. Robert was deeply contemplative about what he would say. After an uncomfortable silence, Williams decided to break the ice.

"John told me a little bit about what's goin' on, but I don't know the full story. I'd like to hear it from you. Your lawyer said anything we discuss is not confidential, so keep that in mind when you're talkin' to me."

"I'm not worried about what I say to you. I already told the police the whole story."

"Okay. Go ahead."

"I'm sure you remember that bum, William Jones, from when we were in prison at Newtown."

"I do, and he was a bad guy, but be careful about the names you call him. It could come back to haunt you."

"Yeah, I know. My attorney has already told me the same thing, so I'll try to be careful with the name callin'." Carlos hesitated for a few seconds, and then continued. "I was at the Rough Riders Bar on a Saturday night havin' a couple of brews and tryin' to chill out."

Robert wanted to stop Carlos and ask him what in the world he was doing at a bar at night, especially when the two of them talked several times about the dangers of his becoming involved in a confrontation with other bar patrons. However, he quickly decided not to interrupt Delgado and make it seem like he was being reprimanded.

"I'm mindin' my own business when Jones sneaks up behind me and starts with the insults. I knew he was lookin' for a fight and tried to avoid it. I was actually bein' nice to him. But then he sucker punches me and knocks me to the floor. After that, he's standin' over me tauntin' me when the bartender came and threw him out." Carlos took a deep breath before continuing.

"When I was outside, another guy from the bar came and told me where Jones lived, so I decided to go there and have it out with him. Please don't lecture me. I know now how stupid I was for doin' that, but at the time, all I could think of was payin' him back."

"I wasn't goin' to lecture you." Robert looked at Delgado with caring eyes. Carlos felt his concern, and deeply appreciated it.

"Good. After I got to his building, I saw the door to his apartment partially open. I went in and saw him on the floor on his stomach. I walked over to see what was wrong and tried to wake him up. I couldn't, and then I saw a wrench on the ground next to him. I don't remember if I told Taylor about the wrench or not, but I did tell my attorney and the police about it. Anyway, stupidly I picked up the wrench and then I heard a scream from the doorway. I guess I never closed the door after I went in. When I looked back, I saw this woman, and she just kept screamin'. So I threw the wrench down and ran out as fast as I could. I never stopped until I got home."

Carlos looked at Robert to gauge his reaction. It didn't take long.

"So you're tellin' me you never hit Jones."

"That's right. Do you believe me?" Delgado anxiously awaited the response.

"I believe you. And with the Lord's assistance, I think the jury will also." Robert's sincere tone helped bolster Delgado.

"Thanks, Williams. I sure hope the Lord will help me out on this one. I really need it."

"You do, and I'm here to support you in any way I can. If you don't mind, I've got a few questions I'd like to ask you."

"Fire away."

"What's goin' on with your job?"

"God's been with me. I told my boss, Steve Ramrell, about my arrest and that I didn't do what I've been charged with. He believes me. I guess him bein' a prison minister has somethin' to do with takin' my word."

"Great news! And you're right, God is with you, and He will always be with you."

Carlos hung his head and quietly said, "Thanks for the encouragement, Williams. I really need it. That was the reason I wanted to see you now." Although Delgado was not able to verbalize it, he cared greatly for Robert and viewed him as a source of peace and comfort.

"You're welcome. John told me you were under house arrest. What's that like?"

"Not only will I tell you. I'll show you too." Delgado lifted his pant leg up and revealed the electronic monitoring device attached to his ankle. "How do you like my bracelet?" Delgado quipped. "Because I'm an ex-con and was sent to prison before for battery on two guys, the system is takin' pains to watch my every move. But it's better than bein' in jail. I think my lawyer did a great job in gettin' me bonded out, no matter what the terms. I hope he keeps it up."

"Yes, it sure is better than bein' in jail. Where are you allowed to go?"

"To and from work, to the gas station for gas, and to the grocery store for food. No alcohol allowed. And I can be surprised at any time with a visit from a probation officer to check up on me and do drug testing." Delgado hesitated a few moments. "I almost forgot that I can go to church within five miles from here. I'd go to yours, but it's too far away. There's really none around here that I'd care to go visit."

Robert wasted no time in responding. "I'll tell you what, Carlos. If you can't come to my church, I'll bring church here to you."

"What's that mean?" Carlos frowned as he asked the question.

"It means I'll come over every Sunday afternoon, while you're under house arrest, after the services and Bible study at my church are finished. We'll study the

Bible together and talk about whatever is on your mind. Is that somethin' you'd like to do?" Robert's sincere smile caused Delgado to be amazed at his friend's selflessness.

"I would, but that's a long drive for you to go back and forth from Pahokee to West Palm. Plus, it's Sunday afternoon. You really ought to be with your wife. You comin' out here today on a Saturday afternoon with all you have goin' on really is a great thing, but I hate takin' any time away from you and her on Sundays."

"Don't worry about Coral," replied Robert with a sly smile. "She sees more than enough of me. I'm sure Coral won't have a problem with me comin' here to spend time with you and talk about Jesus and His Word."

"Well, if it's okay with you and her, it sure works for me."

"Great. We'll start next Sunday. You still have the Bible I gave you, right?"

"Yes."

"Wonderful. Let's talk about what you can be studying between now and then."

"Man, you sure don't waste any time, do you?" Carlos was impressed.

Robert grinned as he said, "Not when I'm doin' the Lord's business."

As Robert drove back to Pahokee from West Palm, Coral finished her volunteer shift at the Pahokee Choose Life Pregnancy Care Center which recently opened. This was her first time serving at the center. She committed to be at the office to help on Saturdays from 9:00 a.m. until 1:00 p.m. Maria Rodgers was also at the center today, along with two staff members and another volunteer. All the others had left, and Coral and Maria were alone in the building.

"Coral, you did a great job manning the front desk today, especially for your first time here. I'm impressed."

"Thanks, Maria, but I couldn't have done it without your help. And the other staff members were terrific as well."

"Yes, we're fortunate to have a great staff. Now tell me what you thought about the clients who came here."

Coral searched for the right words to convey her feelings. "At times I felt overwhelmed. Seeing the women who came here searching for help with their pregnancies made me feel God's presence. I'm glad I can assist in some small way."

"There's nothing small about your assistance, and as time goes by, and you get more experience, you'll be able to do more things."

"Sounds great. I look forward to it."

"By the way, I haven't shared with Robert or you yet some terrific news I found out a couple of days ago." Maria was filled with joy.

"Don't keep me in suspense," laughed out Coral. "What is it?"

"You remember when we met at First Baptist Church and I talked about how we needed forty thousand dollars for an ultrasound machine for this office?"

"I sure do."

"Well, with the help of all the church representatives who were at the meeting, and some other generous benefactors, we now have enough money to buy the machine." Maria was thrilled to share the information.

"Praise the Lord! How wonderful." Coral embraced Maria.

"After the machine arrives, I'll have you come in and help when we use it to show one of the mothers the picture of her baby. I think you will be amazed at the effect it has on her."

"I can't wait. And I can't wait to go home and tell Robert. He will be so delighted."

6

"Lydia, I really appreciate you coming with me today. I don't think I would have been able to go by myself." It was 3:30 p.m. on Saturday, and Lydia was driving Lourdes from their apartment in Belle Glade to a medical office in Wellington. Lourdes had scheduled an appointment to obtain information regarding a possible abortion of the child she was carrying.

"You know I'll always be here to help you in any way I can, Lourdes."

"Yes, I do."

As Lydia turned into the driveway leading to the building they were headed to, they noticed a sizeable number of people near the road praying. There were two large signs the sisters could see. One of them said, "Pray To End Abortion." The other sign read, "Choose Life – You Have Options." Lydia looked over at Lourdes but said nothing. Lourdes closed her eyes and remained silent. Lydia continued on to the medical office, and the women exited the car and went inside.

While the siblings were inside the office, the group of people outside continued to pray the rosary. There were a total of thirty people present, and they were being led by Sister Agnes from St. Juliana's Catholic Church in Belle Glade. Coral Williams had come with her from Belle Glade, after Coral had finished her volunteer shift at the Choose Life Pregnancy Care Center in Pahokee.

As they finished the rosary, two other groups arrived to continue the prayer service. The first contingent was from First Baptist Church in Pahokee, and numbered twenty-five. Robert Williams was among them, and he was their leader. The other people who had come were from St. John's Methodist Church in Wellington. There were fifteen individuals present from St. John's, and they were led by Pastor Ed Jonas.

"It's great to see so many coming to replace us," beamed Sister Agnes.

"It sure is, and I'm glad my husband is one of them," replied Coral. "Sister, I'm going to stay and ride back with Robert. He'll take me to St. Juliana's to pick up my car. Thanks for bringing me here."

"You're welcome, Coral. Are you planning on coming again next Saturday afternoon?"

"Yes, I am, and next week I'll drive, if that's okay with you?"

"It certainly is. I'll see you then."

Sister Agnes and the other parishioners from St. Juliana's said their goodbyes and headed home. Robert wasted no time in having the two new groups begin their mission.

"Pastor Jonas, if it's all right with you, I'd like to offer an opening prayer."

"Absolutely. Thank you, Robert."

The group circled up and held hands. Robert bowed his head and began to pray fervently.

"Lord Jesus, we humbly come before You and ask that You hear this prayer to assure life for the unborn so they too may share the joy of life and the beauty of Your love. We pray that those women who are troubled and in doubt about what to do with their pregnancy may have the strength and grace to trust in Your will.

We also pray that parents put themselves aside for the good of their babies. And we pray for mothers and fathers who are considering abortion to realize there are alternatives and they make use of the help available to them in choosing life over death. In Jesus name we pray. Amen."

"Amen," rang out the impassioned response.

As the group continued on with more prayers, Lydia and Lourdes returned to Lydia's car. Visibly shaken, Lourdes let out a deep sigh.

"Lydia, I don't know what to do. I'm so scared." Tears flowed down her face.

Lydia reached over and squeezed Lourdes's hand. "I know you are, but at least you found out you're fourteen weeks pregnant, so you've still got more time to decide."

"Yeah, but it took me well over a month to get here from when I first heard from my doctor I was pregnant. I can't bear the thought of raising a baby at this point in my life, but I'm not sure I can go through with an abortion."

As Lydia approached the turn near where the church groups were praying, Lourdes rolled down her window. "Stop for a minute. I want to ask them a question."

"Are you sure?" Lydia was uneasy with her sister's request.

"Yes. Please stop now, Lydia."

Lydia quickly came to a stop. They were only fifty feet away from some of the people praying. Coral saw the women and immediately went over to the car.

"Is there something we can help you ladies with?" asked Coral in a caring tone.

"I don't know," answered Lourdes. "I saw your sign about choosing life, and there are options. I'm trying to decide what to do about my pregnancy. I'm only eighteen and have no husband or boyfriend.

"And I'm fourteen weeks pregnant. We just came out of the medical office behind you to get information about having an abortion." Lourdes was becoming more and more emotional as she continued. "What information do you have about options?"

"Hold on a minute, honey. We've got different brochures with us that will explain some of your alternatives." Coral hustled over to a table and came back with a stack of materials. She handed them to Lourdes.

"There's a bunch of information there about Choose Life Pregnancy Care Centers. Several of those brochures deal with the option of adoption rather than having an abortion. Where do you live, honey?"

"In Belle Glade."

"Recently, Choose Life opened an office in Pahokee, so it's not far from where you live. I'm a volunteer there on Saturday mornings. The office staff is very understanding and compassionate. I've seen a bunch of moms who are thankful they went there, and decided to have their baby instead of aborting the child. Why don't you come out on a Saturday morning? I'll introduce you to the staff, and then we'll show you around and answer any questions you have." Coral smiled sweetly at Lourdes.

"I'll think about it. Right now, I don't know what to do. I'll look at the brochures you gave me and see if I want to come in. What's your name?"

"Coral Williams. Let me write down my cell number in case you want to reach me."

Lourdes handed Coral one of the pamphlets. Coral wrote her name and cell on the front and gave it back to Lourdes.

"Do you mind telling me what your name is, honey?"

Lydia didn't want her sister to answer the question. Before she could tell her not to, Lourdes blurted out, "I'm Lourdes Castillo, and this is my sister, Lydia."

"You're not going to use what my sister told you about who we are to hassle us, are you?" asked Lydia in an annoyed voice.

"Of course not. I wanted to know your names in case your sister decided to call me so I would know who I was speaking with. I won't give your names to anyone and I won't try to contact you. I'll wait to hear from Lourdes, if she decides to get in touch with me."

"Fair enough," responded Lydia.

"Thank you for trying to help me. I need more time to think about what I'm going to do."

Lourdes stuck her hand out and shook Coral's hand. Then Lydia drove away.

Coral wondered if she would ever hear anything from Lourdes. She hoped she would. When Coral returned to the group, she told them what happened without revealing the sisters' names.

Then Coral offered up a prayer that life would be chosen over death by this young woman. It remained to be seen how the petition would be answered.

7

"Don't look so worried, Josh. Everything's goin' to be fine. The Lord is here with us." Robert Williams grinned at his young friend, Josh Wilbur. The two of them, along with twelve other prison ministers, were at Newtown Correctional Institution for a two-day retreat. It was Saturday morning at 7:30, and the group was anticipating the arrival of the ninety inmates signed up for the event. Most of those inmates already attended a four-day weekend where they had been introduced to and were a part of the prison ministries program designed to lead them to a closer relationship with Jesus Christ. The purpose of this weekend was to encourage them to continue on with the faith foundations the ministry team helped establish in the four-day mission. For the few residents who did not previously attend the four-day program, the hope was these two days would propel them to go to a future one.

"I know everything will be great, Robert. I'm a little nervous about saying the wrong thing. After all, this is the first two-day I've attended, and I'm on my own in a group with seven or eight residents. When I came here for the four-day retreat over a year ago, I had John Taylor and a senior team member taking the lead. There's no such luxury now, especially with John not being here because he's out in California taking depositions."

Josh stretched his arms up in the air over his head. Robert felt his anxiety. He quickly made a comment. "John told me what a great job you did when the two of you were here together. I know you'll do the same today." Before Robert could continue, the door opened and the inmates began coming into the room. There was a feeling of electricity in the air, and Josh's concerns evaporated.

As the residents came in, many of them stopped to hug the outside team members. Old and treasured acquaintances were being renewed and re-fortified, not only for the benefit of the inmates, but for the ministers as well. There were two of the team members in the front of the room playing musical instruments and singing. Three of the inmates who arrived quickly joined them. The room was alive with praise and worship. After a few minutes, Robert Williams stepped up to the podium. He was the team leader for the weekend. Robert raised his right hand above his head. The signal was the call for silence throughout the course of the retreat. The room quickly quieted down.

"Good mornin', brothers," bellowed out Robert.

"Good morning," shot back the quick and exuberant response.

"It is a pleasure to be with you all so we can praise Our Lord and Savior, Jesus Christ, for all the wondrous and mighty things He has done in our lives." Robert was alive with the Holy Spirit.

"Amen," hollered out much of the crowd. Applause and cheers filled the room.

"Everyone please take a seat." Within seconds the one hundred plus men sat down and eagerly waited for Robert to begin the weekend. They weren't disappointed.

"Brothers, many of you know me because I was a resident of this establishment for ten years. For those of you who don't, my name is Robert Williams, and I am very grateful to be your team leader for the weekend." Robert's introduction was interrupted by applause. After it quieted down, he continued.

"I want to talk for a few minutes about the theme for our weekend and how it will be structured. But first, I want to open with a prayer. Please bow your heads." All the men followed his request.

"Heavenly Father, we come before you today seeking Your guidance and assistance. Please help all of us to always maintain our faith in Your goodness, and to trust in You, no matter what difficult circumstances we may be faced with. Please help all of us to demonstrate our faith in You by working for the good of Your Kingdom. Be with us this weekend as we come together as Brothers in Christ to encourage and build each other up so that we may overcome the snares of the evil one. Thank you for all the blessings you have given to each man in this room. In Jesus' name we pray. Amen."

"Amen."

Robert's ubiquitous grin came alive. "We've got a great program lined up for the weekend. We'll be focusin' in the Bible on James and his teachings. There will be a series of eight talks of about ten to fifteen minutes each. After each talk, we'll split up in small groups of about seven or eight men to discuss what the speaker said and to share our thoughts about his talk. In between the talks, we'll have plenty of time to play some music. And we've got breaks this mornin' and afternoon for snacks, coffee and soft drinks. We'll go this mornin' until around 11:00 when the residents need to head out for lunch. Then we'll resume in the afternoon until around 4:30. Tomorrow, we'll start up at the same time and follow the same schedule in the mornin' until the lunch break. Then in the afternoon, the inmates will be in charge of handlin' the monthly reunion between the inmates and the outside team members." Robert stopped and looked around. "So, are you ready to get goin'?"

"Yes," rang out the loud and unanimous reply.

"Good. It won't take long to get started because I'm the first speaker." For the time being, Robert's smile disappeared. He was totally immersed in the talk he was about to begin.

"James was a true disciple and servant of God and Our Lord Jesus Christ. His words about perseverance under trials ring out as loudly today as they did two thousand years ago. James tells us the person who perseveres under the trials he or she is faced with will receive the Crown of Life which our Heavenly Father has promised to those who love Him." Robert stopped and looked around the room. Then he took a deep breath and resumed.

"There isn't a man in here who hasn't faced many trials in his life. I'm not just talkin' about the court trials you lost that got you in here." Robert was dead serious in his remark and everyone knew it. There was no laughter, only anticipation of what was coming next.

"I mentioned earlier for those of you who don't know me that I was an inmate at this prison. I want to share with you the circumstances in my life that caused me to be sentenced here. It's still not easy to talk about it, but with God's grace, I'll get through it."

Robert bit his lip and continued. "Fifteen years ago I had a wonderful life. I was happily married, with a great job, and was blessed with a seventeen-year-old son who was a joy to be around. He was smart, had a good heart, and was a star athlete on his high school football team. Then one night the unthinkable happened. When he was leavin' a church dance with a bunch of his friends, three guys drove by and started firin' shots at random. My boy was struck in the head and killed instantly." Robert stopped and struggled to regain his composure. The room was totally silent.

"A few weeks later, the shooters were found. Ultimately, they were convicted and sentenced to life. Their only motive was to kill someone. As it turned out, that was only the beginnin' of my trials. I was unable to deal with my boy's death. My Momma had raised me to be a God-lovin' man, but I began to hate Him. I ended up divorcin' my wife and became a drunk. I lost my job and everythin' else. Then I committed the crime that landed me in here. One night I got totally smashed by drinkin' a liter of whiskey. Then I made my next mistake of drivin' drunk. I caused a wreck and killed a man. There was no point to a trial, so I pled out in exchange for a ten year sentence. My life was one huge mess, and I sure wasn't persevering under the trials I had been confronted with." Robert shook his head from side-to-side.

"It took me a very long time after my son's death to turn back to God. But with the help of many different people, including a lot of men in this prison who had turned their lives over to Christ after their incarceration, I slowly but surely came back to my faith. When I reached out to Jesus, and asked for His forgiveness, I began to persevere through the trials that had come my way. I'm still able to do that today, by relying on Jesus Christ who strengthens me to do all things. That's my message to you men. Fight the good fight, and persevere through your trials by turnin' to Jesus and askin' Him to sustain you. He won't say no. By doin' so, you will receive the Crown of Life when you go on to your Heavenly reward. God bless you all. Now please bow your heads and reflect on what I spoke about, and how it may apply to your lives. In a few minutes, we'll break up into small groups to discuss this talk."

Robert had purposely asked the men to bow their heads and reflect on what was said at the end of his talk to diffuse any applause. The weekend was not about receiving personal praise. It was about honoring Our Lord and seeking His assistance in overcoming the tough times in everyone's life. Each of the other speakers would conclude their talks in the same manner.

Two minutes later, Robert asked the men to break up in small groups of seven to eight inmates with one outside team member participating with each bunch of men. The chairs were quickly placed in circles. All of the inmates wore name badges, as did the outside team, so they could see each other's names. Josh found himself with seven inmates, only one of whom he had previously talked with. As the outside team member, he was expected to facilitate the discussion, and lead it if necessary. Josh silently prayed for the right words in fulfilling his mission. Then he flashed a smile and began the discussion.

"I'm glad to be with you guys this morning."

No reaction. "Wonderful," he thought, but he overcame his anxiety and wasted no time in continuing.

"Robert sure gave us a lot to think about, didn't he?" He looked around and hoped for a response.

After a few more seconds, inmate John Moore replied. "You're not kidding. And I thought I had it rough. I knew Williams when he was in here, but I didn't know what happened to his family and to him. Whew!"

The other residents nodded in agreement. Moore continued talking. "I've had my own trials to go through since I was a little boy. My dad took off on us when I was four, and my mom was left alone to raise six kids. Then when I'm sixteen she dies and all the kids are split up among different relatives. That was the beginning of the life of crime I got into. I did all kinds of bad stuff, including robbing banks. Ten years ago, when I was nineteen, I got sentenced to thirty years. I still have twenty more years to go."

Moore watched the group to see if they were listening. They were, so he continued. "I was like what Williams talked about after mom died. I hated God, didn't really even believe in Him, and when I got sentenced to thirty years, I despised everyone on this planet. But after a few years in here, being filled with bitterness and rage, and not even wanting to live anymore, I knew I had to find a better way."

Then, looking directly at Josh, Moore said, "So five years ago, I signed up for one of your four-day retreats figuring I had nothing to lose. Besides, I wanted the good food all you guys bring in here." The comment caused the other inmates to echo their agreement.

"When I attended, at first I wasn't too taken in by what was going on. But around the third day, things really started to change, especially after I read all those messages of encouragement you outside guys brought in from people at their churches. It started to dawn on me I needed to try to get Christ back in my life. Since then, I've been going to all the faith-based programs this prison offers, and it's made a big change in my life.

Although I still have some pretty bad days, I am able to persevere with the help of Jesus by going to Him in prayer and asking Him to strengthen me as Williams talked about."

"You're lucky, Moore. I'm not doing well at all in that department," said inmate Joe Baron. "For me, it's one bad day after another. The gangs in this prison can suck the life right out of you, with their ridicule and threats. And you've always got to watch your back because you might get a good beat down physically too."

Baron's tone was despondent. Josh wanted to respond in some way, but he knew nothing about life in a prison. He decided to go at it in another way.

"What can you guys suggest to help Joe?" Josh glanced at the residents in his group to see if anyone would make a recommendation.

Moore came to the rescue. "Are you attending any of the faith-based programs they offer here?"

"No."

"Why not?"

"Because I didn't think they would do much good. I've never been to a four-day retreat before either. I came this weekend because of the snacks and drinks I heard were served. But now that I listened to Williams talk and to what you said, I'm starting to think maybe it would be good for me to go to some of those programs."

"No question about it, Baron," chimed in inmate Anthony Johnson. "They've helped me out a lot, and you can start making more contacts with men who have either turned their lives over to Jesus, or who are doing their best to make it happen. Attending some of the faith based events will help you take your mind off the gangs. Instead, you can become a member of Christ's gang."

Johnson smiled. His response caused Baron to return a grin of his own before he replied, "Maybe I will. I've got nothing to lose."

"But you've got a lot to gain," said Johnson.

Josh silently thanked the Lord for this moment. There would be many more such encounters among the men before the weekend concluded.

8

On Sunday, the morning session at Newtown flew by. The inmates returned from their lunch and settled in, along with the outside team. Chip Daniels, one of the residents, stood at the podium and raised his hand above his head. The room quickly quieted down.

"Good afternoon, brothers. I'm the leader for our monthly reunion today with the prison ministry team, and I've got some great news! Before we begin our regular program, we have an awesome event which is going to take place in a few minutes right outside this room. Fifteen inmates will be baptized for the first time by either a Catholic priest or other clergymen, and everyone here has been cleared to attend the ceremony. So let's follow officer Sanders out the door to the area where the baptisms will be held."

Daniels looked at Sanders, who motioned for everyone to follow him. All the men rapidly filed out of the room. Although it was sunny and bright outside, it was a cold winter's day by Florida standards. It was only fifty degrees, and the blustery winds made it seem even colder. Robert walked next to Josh. The smile on Robert's face grew larger when they reached their destination and he saw a familiar and beloved face.

"Father James Anderson, what in the world are you doin' here?" Robert was puzzled but delighted. He quickly reached Father before he could respond and hugged him, although not with as much force as he wanted. Robert knew the priest was getting up in age, and Robert didn't want to hurt him. After Robert let go, he introduced Josh to him, and Father Anderson then answered Robert's question.

"I'm here to baptize a few of the residents. I found out a little while ago from Chip Daniels, while your team was out at lunch, that you were here for a two-day retreat and would be back this afternoon. What a great surprise to see you. It's been too long." Father Anderson let loose with his famous Irish grin.

"It has been too long. Are you down here from Syracuse now for the winter?"

"Yes, I am, my boy. I arrived last week, and I'm loving it. Except today, it's a little too cold. It almost feels like I'm back up north."

Before Robert could reply, Daniels hollered out they were ready to begin the ceremony. The fifteen inmates being baptized were all lined up, ready to be immersed in a large wooden tub filled with water. The three men whom Father Anderson was to baptize went first. Father performed a traditional Catholic ceremony on the three to the great applause of the prison ministers and inmates who were watching. After he finished, Father Anderson approached Robert.

"I've got to leave. I have an appointment to see two sick friends who are both in the same hospital. I'll be in West Palm for two more months. Let's get together for dinner, and please bring your wife."

"It's a deal. I've got your cell. I'll call you next week, and we'll set a day and time."

"Wonderful!" exclaimed the priest. "I can't wait. It was nice meeting you, Josh."

"Same here, Father. Take care."

After Father Anderson left, Robert and Josh continued to watch the other inmates be baptized by various ministers. When the men came out of the tub, with just shorts and a T-shirt on, they all quickly retreated to a restroom inside the building to put on warm and dry clothes. After the ceremony concluded, the men who attended the retreat started to make their way back to the room where the reunion was being held.

"What a blessed ceremony, Robert. I can't believe what I witnessed. To see fifteen inmates being baptized in a maximum security prison is awesome. The Lord sure was here with us."

"He sure was, Josh." Before Robert could continue, they were stopped by an inmate who sneered at Robert. Josh couldn't believe the size of this guy. He was even bigger than Robert, and was covered with tattoos.

"Well, if it ain't Robert Williams. I heard you were here with this bunch of Christian wannabe prison ministers. I guess you're keeping yourself out of trouble seeing as how you're in here without the prison blues you used to wear." The inmate's disrespect and contemptuous attitude was obvious. Josh cringed and hoped nothing serious would develop.

"That's right, Fuller. I'm staying out of trouble," answered Robert in a low-key and matter-of-fact tone. "And I hope you're doing the same."

"Don't worry about me, Williams," roared out Fuller in an angry voice. "I'm still one of the top dogs around here, just like I was when you were here. By the way, I saw an article a while back about Carlos Delgado being arrested and charged with aggravated battery. You know anything about that?"

Robert hesitated and thought about his response. He knew he needed to be careful with what he said. "I've seen Carlos. He says he didn't do it, and I believe him."

"That's a bunch of bull. You'd believe anybody. That's one of your problems, Williams. Delgado is guilty as hell, so, I guess it won't be too long before he ends up back in here. When he does, he better do what I tell him or he'll pay the price." Fuller let loose with an evil laugh and walked away smirking.

"Who is that guy, and what in the world was that about?" asked Josh.

"He's a bad dude, Josh. His name's James Fuller, and he's a lifer. He's been in prison for twenty years with no chance of gettin' out. When I was here, he was the leader of one of the worst gangs, and it seems like he still is. He's the kind of guy the inmates need to keep away from if they want to stay out of trouble."

"I can't believe the size of the man. He's bigger than you, Robert!"

"Yeah, he is, and he likes to throw his weight around. We need to pray for his conversion over to Jesus."

"Sounds like an impossible task."

"Nothing is impossible with the Lord's help. After all, our God is a God who delights in impossibility."

"You're right. I need to keep focused on that thought."

9

"John and Anna Taylor, it's so good to see both of you. It's been way too long." Coral Williams wasted no time in greeting each Taylor with a hug. It was Saturday afternoon around 1:55. The Taylors just arrived at the area nearby the abortion clinic in Wellington to join the others who were participating in praying outside the facility for an end to abortion.

"You're right. It has been too long since we've gotten together," replied Anna. "John and I have been meaning to come out here to pray. I'm glad we made it today while you're here."

Anna looked around at the people who were present. There were more than thirty. "You've got a good sized group here today, Coral. I don't think I know any of them. I don't believe they're from our parish."

"You're right. Most of them are from St. Juliana's in Belle Glade. We're being led today in the rosary and other prayers by Sister Agnes from St. Juliana's. Do you two know her?"

"I've never met her," answered John.

"I haven't either," responded Anna.

"Let me make a quick introduction because we are about ready to start praying. Are the two of you staying for a full hour?"

"Yes," said Anna.

"Great. When the next team comes in an hour from now, we leave. Let's catch up a little bit in the parking lot."

"Sounds like a plan," replied John with a smile.

Coral led the Taylors to Sister Agnes, who warmly welcomed them. Then Sister Agnes immediately began speaking to the group.

"It's time to start. This morning, we'll first pray the rosary, and then continue with some other prayers until our replacements arrive."

It was close to an hour later when the rosary was concluded. Sister Agnes then recited a series of short prayers and was now ready to close with a final one.

"Heavenly Father, we praise You for the gift of life which You have so abundantly provided to all people. Unfortunately, there are many who do not recognize Your blessing, and choose to end the life of a precious baby while in the mother's womb. We pray the Holy Spirit will come down from Heaven and instill in the hearts and minds of all those considering the abortion of an infant the wisdom and courage to choose life over death. And by doing so, may your generous grace remain with, protect, and guide the mother, father, and child all the days of their lives. In Jesus name we pray. Amen."

"Amen."

The next prayer group arrived. The Taylors and Coral met in the parking lot and began an animated conversation.

"So where's the big lug you're married to?" asked John with a mischievous grin.

"He was here earlier today with a bunch of people from First Baptist Church of Pahokee. This afternoon he's working on a house renovation project in Clewiston."

"Sorry, we missed him, and he'd be tough to miss," John quipped. "I take it Robert is staying very busy."

"You have no idea. His carpentry business has taken off, and he's very involved with the church. We don't see each other enough, but when we do, it's definitely quality time. I'd rather see him keeping busy, than moping around because he doesn't have enough to do."

"I know exactly what you mean, Coral," laughed Anna. She looked at John, who rolled his eyes in response. "What about you Coral? Is everything going well?"

"Yes, it is. I'm not as busy as Robert, but I still have a lot on my plate. My job at the preschool in Pahokee takes up thirty hours a week. And I help out at St. Juliana's as well as Robert's church whenever I can. Plus, last month I started volunteering on Saturday mornings at the Choose Life Pregnancy Care Centers office in Pahokee. I am really enjoying that!" Coral was alive with enthusiasm.

"That's terrific!" Anna was thrilled Coral was so joyful.

"And how is school going for you, Mrs. Taylor?" Coral arched her eyebrows as she waited for the response.

"Wonderful! I'm still teaching fifth grade, and loving it. This year I've got thirty-three students in my class, but with the help of my assistant, we're keeping up with those kids."

"And you, John, how is the law business? Busy as ever I suppose."

"It sure is. We recently took on two new partners, so there are five now. And we're up to ten associate attorneys. We're keeping our staff very busy. Things are good in the law practice."

"I saved the best for last. How are your three adorable children doing?"

John looked at Anna and held out his hand for her to respond. He knew better than to try to take over her territory.

"The kids are a handful," replied Anna with a giant smile, "but a very blessed one. Jean is nine now and in fourth grade. Renee is seven and in second grade. And Laura is three and in preschool. With all the running around we have to do with them, they're keeping us young, that's for sure."

"I bet they are," answered Coral wistfully. She thought about how much she would like to have a child of her own. Then she glanced at her watch. "I can't believe what time it is. I've got to get going because Robert and I are going out to dinner this evening, and I still have a bunch of things to do."

Suddenly, a thought came to her. "Wait a minute. Do you know who we're having dinner with tonight?"

"No." Anna smiled as she answered.

"Of course you don't," laughed Coral. "It's Father James Anderson. I know what a good friend he is to each of you. Why don't both of you come with us?"

"We'd love to," said John. "Unfortunately, we've got to take a rain check because Anna and I are hosting a dinner for my office this evening. Please give our regards to Father, and tell him I'll call him next week."

"I sure will. Have a great time tonight."

"You and Robert as well with the wonderful man you'll be with." Anna smiled as she waved goodbye.

Several hours later, Robert, Coral, and Father Anderson, sat on the outside patio of Bradford's Restaurant, located on the Intercoastal Waterway off of Flagler Drive in West Palm Beach. Father Anderson and Coral each sipped on a glass of wine, while Robert enjoyed his favorite concoction – lemonade and sweet tea. They started to discuss the Pilgrimage to the Holy Land that they, and twenty others, made almost two years ago. Father Anderson was the spiritual leader on the trip.

"I still have many vivid and blessed memories of our time together on the Pilgrimage. You really made everything come alive for us, Father. Your descriptions of how Jesus had walked the paths we followed, as well as your daily homilies, were inspiring." Coral beamed as she spoke.

"I couldn't agree more," added Robert. "I sure would like to make that trip again. Would you be up for another visit?"

"I'm always up for another visit. We'll just wait and see what God has planned for us." Father winked at Robert, and all three laughed.

Father Anderson changed the topic. "Coral, when Robert called me to set up this dinner, he briefly mentioned you were volunteering for a pro-life organization. I'd like to hear more about it."

"You better be ready for a long story, Father." Robert glanced over at Coral and grinned. "But it's a really good one."

"Don't pay any attention to my husband. I won't go on for more than half-an-hour or so." Now it was Coral's turn to smile.

"Hey, I asked for it, so fire away." Father intently eyed Coral.

"I'm volunteering for Choose Life Pregnancy Care Centers at their Pahokee office, and I love it. At first, I was working at the front desk, and I enjoyed helping the women who came in with the paperwork. But, recently, the office manager has me interacting more with the mothers. I counsel them and provide information about all the services available to help in their decisions. I've also been able to observe on several occasions when a mother was having an ultrasound. The office recently purchased a great machine, and it makes such a difference when the women can actually see a picture of their infant. It definitely makes them want to choose life."

Suddenly, Coral stopped talking and looked down.

"What's wrong, Coral?" Robert knew his wife was stressed and was puzzled by it.

"I'm feeling a little jealous about the clients having a baby. I know I shouldn't be. I guess it's because I never had a child, and I never will be able to after the hysterectomy I had years ago. But that's all in the past. Anyways, Father, I feel very blessed to be a volunteer for an organization with such an important mission."

"You sure are," responded the priest, "and our Lord is certainly very proud of you for the wonderful work you're doing."

"Thank you, Father," replied Coral in a soft tone.

Father Anderson sensed it was time to change the focus of the discussion. "Robert, how's it going with your carpentry business?"

"Wonderful. Jesus has blessed me mightily. I've gotten so busy I had to hire a full-time assistant. We've got jobs lined up for the next two months."

"That's great news. What's happening with your work at First Baptist Church?"

"Pastor Gilbert has me very involved. On Sundays, I lead a Bible study group. Durin' the week, I'm usually there once or twice to either help out with different programs the Pastor puts on, or to do some repair work. We've still got a lot of fixin' up left after the tropical storm last year. I enjoy it all because I know my work is for the Lord."

"That's terrific, Robert," replied Father Anderson. "And there's something else I really admire about the two of you."

"What's that?" Coral eagerly waited for the answer to her question.

"It's really inspiring to see the two of you relate so well to each other's churches. You are Catholic and attend St. Juliana's, and Robert is Baptist and goes to First Baptist, but both of you are totally supportive in your faith walk with each other."

"Actually, Father, Robert comes with me to Mass at St. Juliana's, and I attend the services with him at First Baptist. We both get a lot out of being together to honor Jesus at both churches."

"We sure do," echoed Robert.

"How great is that?" Father Anderson remarked. "You two are an example of how all Christians should come together to honor Jesus. After all, Christ is the cornerstone of Christian faith and the building block we must rely upon. Whenever the Christian community does not remember that simple truth, we begin to divide according to human standards and against His will. I believe we should pray for the Holy Spirit to descend upon all Christians so we may always be our Lord's loyal, hopeful, and loving people. When we see the best in each other, no matter what denomination of Christianity we follow, Jesus is very joyful for His children."

"I'm with you, Father," declared Robert.

"Me too," added Coral.

"Father, there's an issue I'd like your advice on."
Robert looked pensive.

"Of course. How can I help?"

"I know firsthand what a great prison chaplain you were from our contact at Newtown. I've sort of taken on that role with a guy who was an inmate when I was there. He was released a couple of years ago, but recently he got himself into a world of trouble. He's been charged with aggravated battery and faces serious prison time. Although he's out on bail, he's got some strict terms to deal with and can't leave his house much except to go to work, or a few other limited places, so I go to see him every Sunday, to try and counsel him. I have him read different parts of the Bible and discuss them with him. I also work with him to talk about whatever may be on his mind, but I'm not sure I'm havin' much of a positive effect. He hasn't told me not to come see him, but I question whether my visits are positive. Do you have any suggestions how I might better help him?" Robert looked the priest squarely in the eye.

"Knowing you, Robert, I'm sure you're doing a terrific job. From everything you told me, it sounds like you're on the right track. So stay the course. It may take some time for your friend to come around, but eventually with Christ's help, I believe you'll see a change. Don't give up, no matter how difficult the circumstances may become."

"I won't, Father. I won't."

10

"Good to see you again, Tom. I really need your help on one of my cases." Jack Randolph rose from his chair and firmly shook Tom Peters' hand. It was Saturday morning, and Peters just arrived at Randolph's law firm. Randolph's office was large and tastefully decorated, not at all flamboyant. It matched Jack's personality.

"I'm always available to help you, Jack," responded Peters with a smile as he sat down on one of the oversized leather chairs positioned in front of Randolph's desk. "What's going on?"

"I'll tell you what's going on," replied Randolph as he shook his head from side-to-side. "I'm representing a guy named Carlos Delgado, who's been charged with aggravated battery. He's an ex-felon, and is looking at very substantial jail time if he's convicted. The facts are terrible for us, but he absolutely insists he didn't do it and refuses to plead guilty to avoid a trial. I've been a criminal defense attorney for thirty years, and this may be the most difficult case for me to win that I've ever taken on. What makes it even harder is I believe this guy when he tells me he's innocent. Trying to prove it to a jury, however, is going to be a monumental task. I need your help. By far, you're the best private investigator I've worked with."

"I appreciate that," answered Peters with a sly grin, "but I'm a little gun shy with the introduction you gave me. So give me the long version of what's happened here so I can take some notes." Peters quickly pulled a legal pad and pencil from his briefcase.

For the next hour, Randolph expertly imparted to Peters everything he needed to know about the case in order for Peters to start his investigation. When Jack was through, Peters let out a long and emphatic whistle.

"Well, now I know why you said this case was such a hard one for you to win. I think it's a really tough situation for me to help you with, but I'll give it my best shot."

"I have no doubt you will. That's why you're here. But I still have another matter to discuss with you." Randolph let out a deep sigh.

"I'm afraid to ask what it is, but I think I already know. It's about my fee, isn't it?" Peters anxiously waited for the answer.

"Yes, it is. And it's not just your fee, but mine as well. I was referred this case by John Taylor. You must know him?"

"Yes, I do. I've worked with him before. He's an excellent lawyer and a great guy."

"John has quite a long and checkered history with Delgado. I won't go into all the details, but the bottom line is they're now close friends. John asked me to take this case on at a reduced fee. Delgado's got a good job, as I already mentioned, but there's no way he can pay full rates. I owed John some favors from a couple of lucrative cases he referred me, so I agreed with Delgado to bill for my time at one-half my normal rate. I also agreed to take payment from him for some of those bills on an extended time basis." Randolph saw the look of concern on Peters' face.

"Don't worry, Tom. I'm not asking you to do the same thing."

"I'm glad to hear no reduced hourly fee is involved. It's not that I don't want to work with you again, but I am busy with a bunch of other cases which pay my full rate."

"I appreciate that. Here's the deal. I told Taylor I needed to bring in a private investigator, and it would be costly. We talked about how Delgado could never afford to pay those fees on top of my bills, even at my reduced amount, so John agreed to pay up to $20,000 in defense costs for a private investigator. Taylor won't pay more than that, and frankly Delgado is lucky to have such a good friend to cover those costs. So, can you work on this case at your normal rates with a fee not to exceed $20,000?"

Peters thought long and hard about the answer. "My hourly rate is $200. That leaves me with being paid for one hundred hours. Based on everything we talked about, I know my time will easily exceed that amount." Peters stopped for a few moments as he continued to ponder his decision. "Taylor's not asking for me to be paid on extended terms, is he?"

"No, he's not. You can submit monthly bills to me, and Taylor will see you're paid for each statement within thirty days, up to the amount of $20,000. Once you reach that, no more money comes your way."

"Okay. As long as I am paid promptly for each bill up to the $20,000, I'll do it."

"Excellent," replied Randolph with an exuberant smile. He rose from his chair and firmly shook Peters' hand.

"All right, Jack. Let me out of here, so I can start to work on what we talked about."

"No problem. Besides, Delgado is coming to see me in twenty minutes to talk about the case. Now I can give him the news you're on the team."

A short time later, Delgado sat down in Randolph's office. Carlos wasted no time in immediately speaking his mind. "Although I really don't want to be here, at least you got the judge to let me come to your office instead of you showin' up at my house. I'm startin' to go nuts bein' there all weekend long."

Carlos was already exasperated. Randolph knew he was in for a rough meeting. He quickly decided to bring up what he hoped would be positive news to hearten Delgado.

"I've got some information for you which is very beneficial to our case."

"What's that?" Delgado quickly shot out.

"I met earlier this morning with Tom Peters, the PI I talked to you about, and he's agreed to work on the case. He's great at what he does. I see his involvement as being very helpful for your defense."

Before Randolph could continue, Delgado cut him off. "If you say it's very helpful, I'm sure it is. But as I asked you when you said you were goin' to talk to the PI, how in the world am I supposed to pay him? I know you gave me a break on your fees and when they're paid. But, I can't afford to cover anyone else." Delgado scowled at Randolph.

"Don't worry, Carlos," answered Jack with a grin. "It's being handled."

"What do you mean?" asked Delgado in a skeptical tone.

"I mean John Taylor has agreed to pay up to $20,000 of Tom's fee for working on the case."

Carlos was stunned. "What are you talking about? I never heard anything about this before."

John and I had several discussions about the need for a private investigator on your case. He knew you couldn't afford one, so he offered to pay up to the $20,000 amount."

"I can't believe it. How come nobody told me about this?" Delgado glared at Randolph as he waited for the answer.

"John didn't want you to know about it unless we got an investigator to agree to the fee. Once that happened, I was free to tell you about the deal."

Carlos was clearly shaken by the news. "What happens if Peters' fee goes above the $20,000?"

"Tom has agreed there will be no charges to anyone for more than the $20,000."

Delgado was sweating and wiped his forehead with the back of his hand. In a quiet voice he said, "Williams is always tellin' me the Man upstairs hasn't forgotten about me and is always watchin' over me. I guess he's right."

"I think Mr. Williams is right, and there are a lot of other people on earth trying to help you as well."

"I know that, Randolph. You're one of them. I probably never said it before, but I appreciate it. Thank you." Delgado's demeanor had completely changed. He bowed his head humbly.

Randolph seized the moment to move on to a difficult topic, a subject which was sure to cause Carlos a great deal of angst. "You're welcome. There's something else we need to talk about."

Delgado sensed Randolph's mood swing and quickly looked up. He waited for Randolph to continue.

"Yesterday afternoon, I spoke with the Assistant

State Attorney who's handling your case. He asked me to talk to you about a plea deal they're throwing out on the table."

Carlos let loose with an exasperated sigh. "Go ahead and tell me what it is. Let's see if the Man upstairs is watchin' out for me now."

11

"Good morning, it's great to see you. I'm happy you're here." Coral Williams scrambled out of her chair and quickly made her way around the counter to where the young woman was standing. It was Saturday morning at 9:00, and the Choose Life Pregnancy Care center office in Pahokee had just opened. Coral gently shook Lourdes Castillo's hand.

"Is your sister here with you?"

"Yes, Lydia's parking the car. She'll be right in."

"When you called me yesterday and said you wanted to come to Choose Life's office to talk about alternatives to having an abortion, I was excited."

Before Coral could finish talking, Lydia walked into the office. She heard what Coral said to her sibling and quickly responded.

"I don't mean to be rude, but Lourdes hasn't decided what to do about her pregnancy. We're here to get information only." The tone of Lydia's voice made it clear she would be a major factor in Lourdes' decision.

"I understand," replied Crystal in a conciliatory voice. "I'm glad Lourdes is considering all her options."

"Okay, I want to be sure we're on the same page." Lydia was appeased by Coral's respect for the purpose of their visit.

The front door opened again. Maria Rodgers walked in. Coral introduced the three women to each other. Then Coral addressed the Castillo sisters.

"I called Maria yesterday after I spoke with Lourdes and told her the two of you wanted to come into our office today to discuss possible alternatives to an abortion. As the Program Administrator for Choose Life for the past five years, she can speak with the two of you in detail about the choices available to Lourdes."

"Good," said Lydia. "Is there somewhere the three of us can talk in private?"

"Of course," answered Maria. "Let's go to my office."

"I'd like Coral to be with us for the meeting," Lourdes meekly replied. "If that's okay?"

"Of course, it is," responded Maria.

"And I'd love to be there." Coral smiled sweetly at Lourdes.

The four women went to Maria's office, and she closed the door. After they were all seated, Maria saw how nervous both Lourdes and Lydia were. She decided to begin the conversation.

"First, I want to say how pleased we are the two of you are here to discuss alternatives to having an abortion. Second, I want to assure both of you we will in no way exert any pressure on Lourdes to make a specific decision on what to do with the baby. We will likely make a recommendation, but the choice is entirely up to you, Lourdes, along with whatever input Lydia gives you."

"Thank you. That makes things easier." Lourdes was on the verge of tears. She quickly grabbed her sister's hand and squeezed it tightly.

"How far along are you in your pregnancy, Lourdes?" asked Maria.

"I'm eighteen weeks right now. I know from speaking to the staff at the abortion clinic if I decide to have an abortion, it needs to be performed within twenty-three weeks. I realize there's not a lot of time left if I choose to go that way." Lourdes exhaled deeply, as she continued grasping Lydia's hand.

"I see the father of the baby is not here today. Will he be involved in any way with the decision to be made?"

"Absolutely not," snapped Lourdes. "All he's done is to insist I have an abortion. He won't talk about any options. In fact, he's told me several times if I choose to have the child, he'll take off and go live with his brother in Texas." Lourdes was angry, and Maria was determined to calm her down.

"I see that happen a lot, Sweetheart. You can't control what the father does, but I want to let you know I'm asking these questions because I'm trying to get a sense of what your best alternative to abortion may be." Maria's calm and matter-of-fact tone was working to defuse Lourdes.

"I appreciate it. Thanks." Lourdes gazed directly at Maria with a look that revealed the depth of conflicting emotions she was experiencing.

"How old are you, Lourdes?"

"Eighteen."

"Have you graduated from high school?"

"Yes, last year."

"What are you doing now?"

"After I graduated from high school, I started working at Crystal Sugar Corporation in Clewiston as a secretary. I'm also taking some night courses in business management at the community college in Belle Glade."

"Do you like your job?"

"It's okay, but I don't want to be a secretary forever. It doesn't pay enough. There are some pretty good benefits. In fact, I talked with the office manager about what expenses would be covered if I have the baby."

"What did the office manager tell you?"

"Most of the doctor and hospital bills would be paid, but I'd still be looking at paying several thousand dollars, which I can't afford."

"Where do you live?"

"Lydia and I rent an apartment together. Between the two of us we barely make enough to pay our bills. There isn't much extra cash coming in."

"And where do you work, Lydia?"

"At the drugstore in Belle Glade. I'm one of the day shift supervisors."

"What about your parents? Are they living in the area?"

Lydia and Lourdes anxiously looked at each other. Lourdes quickly decided she would respond.

"Our Dad took off on Mom and us five years ago. We haven't heard from him since. And, unfortunately, last year Mom was killed in a car accident." Tears welled up in both sisters' eyes.

Coral looked over at Maria, who quickly made a comment. "We're so sorry to hear about your mom's passing. It must be very hard on you ladies. Do you have any other family members in the area?"

"No. It's just the two of us," answered Lydia.

"So, if you decide to raise this baby, it would be the two of you taking care of the child."

"Yes, that's right, Ms. Rodgers," answered Lourdes, "but I don't think that's fair to Lydia. After all, she's only twenty and is working hard to support herself."

Lourdes hesitated for a few moments and looked down. Then she glanced up and said, "And to be honest with both of you, I don't think it's fair to me either. I'm not ready to be a single parent, and I can't afford the expenses, even with Lydia's help. I know that makes me sound selfish, but that's how I feel." Tears again formed in Lourdes' eyes.

"Sweetie, that doesn't make you sound selfish," said Coral. "You're being realistic, and by being here to discuss options to abortion, you obviously have a concern for your baby." Coral reached over and squeezed Lourdes' hand. Her gesture was returned with a smile.

"I agree with Coral," added Maria. "And from everything I heard having the baby as a single parent would not make sense for either you or the child." A big smile came over Maria's face. "But you have the option of having the baby and giving it up for adoption."

"If I choose to have the baby and give the child up for adoption, can you tell me what my rights are as the birth mother?"

"Absolutely," answered Maria. "As the birth mother, you have the right to choose the adoptive family. You also have the right to choose how much contact and information about the baby you want in the future."

"What does that mean?" asked Lourdes.

"The adoption process has changed. There are recently developed options for mothers placing their babies for adoption that help to create a loving transition from the birth mother to adoptive parents." Before Maria could go on, Lourdes interrupted her.

"Tell me what the options are. I don't know anything about this whole process."

"That's understandable. Most people do not realize there are four types of adoptions. One is where the mother makes an adoption plan with a close relative. Based on what you said, that wouldn't work because there are no relatives."

"Correct," said Lydia.

"The second option is a closed adoption where no information is shared between you and the adopting family. No communication is expected. A third option is what's called a semi-open adoption. Under that alternative, you and the adoptive family maintain contact through an agency or attorney by pictures and correspondence. Usually, there would be no direct contact with the child or adopting family. The fourth option is called an open adoption. Under that scenario, you and the adopting family exchange contact information and have a trusting and flexible relationship. You and the adoptive family work out the best times to get together. It's important to realize any of these arrangements must be in writing and approved in court by a judge, but there is a lot of flexibility involved in the process."

Lourdes was deep in thought about the information communicated to her by Maria. After a few more moments, she posed another question.

"What if I decided to have the baby and go forward with an adoption, can I later change my mind?"

"Yes," answered Maria. "An adoption is not legally binding until you have signed the legal documents at least 48 hours after the baby is born."

"Does the father of my baby have the right to stop the adoption? I know he never would because he wants nothing to do with the baby, but I'm curious."

"Based on what you told me, I don't think it would be a difficult matter to have the father's rights involuntarily terminated."

"You've given me a lot to think about with adoption," said Lourdes.

"We talked about a lot, but I have one other thing for you to consider. Tomorrow at 9:00 a.m. at First Baptist Church in Pahokee there will be a church service where three speakers associated with our organization will be talking about adoption. Do you know where the church is located?"

"No, I don't," said Lydia.

"I don't either," said Lourdes.

"To be honest with you, our family has never been church-going people," said Lydia. "I'm not saying we're atheists, but attending church services has never been something we've done."

"I understand," replied Maria. "The reason I'm bringing this up is because you would have an opportunity to hear firsthand from three different people whose lives have been very positively affected by the adoption process. I think listening to them may be helpful to Lourdes in making her decision about the baby." Maria held her breath as she waited for a response. She wasn't disappointed.

"I'd like to hear them talk," replied Lourdes. "Tell us where the church is."

Coral gave the women directions to First Baptist. After Lourdes and Lydia left, Maria and Coral said a prayer the sisters would come to listen to the speakers.

12

"Good morning, everyone. My name is Lisa Long. First, I would like to thank Pastor Gilbert for allowing John, Anthony, and me to be here at First Baptist Church in Pahokee to talk to all of you." Long momentarily turned around to see the other two speakers who sat behind her. Both smiled. It helped to diffuse the tension they each experienced. Today was the first time any of the three had spoken in public about adoption. The several hundred people present added to their anxiety, but the nervousness would soon disappear as the messages were delivered.

Robert and Coral Williams and Maria Rodgers sat in the same row near the front of the church. Coral had not seen Lourdes or Lydia and wondered if they were here. She turned around and saw them coming in from the rear of the building. The sisters quickly took a seat in the back row. "Don't turn around," Coral whispered to Maria. "The girls just came in." Coral grabbed Maria's hand. Maria couldn't contain the smile erupting across her face.

Long continued on with her story. "The reason the three of us are here is to speak briefly about the wonderful things we've all experienced with adoption being chosen as an alternative to abortion. Fifteen years ago, my husband and I adopted a beautiful baby girl. I was unable to have children, and we both desperately wanted a baby. We looked into the adoption process and were able to find a child to adopt. The birth mother was single and only nineteen. She did not feel she could raise a child by herself, but didn't want to abort the baby. The mother moved away from Florida shortly after our daughter was born, but over the years we have maintained contact by pictures and letters through our attorney who arranged the adoption."

Long's eyes lit up. "We have been blessed by God with our daughter, Sara, who is a sophomore in high school. She gets good grades and is active in sports, but the most important thing is how Our Lord turned the three of us into a family that truly loves and cares for each other. Quite frankly, we never stop thanking Him for bringing us together. We also thank Him that the birth mother had the courage and compassion to go forward with the baby being born instead of aborted. I can't imagine what life would be like without Sara." Long bowed her head, then looked directly at the congregation.

"That's all I have to say. After the services, the three of us will be available to answer any questions you may have. John is going to speak next."

John sprang from his seat and stood at the podium. He grinned as he looked out at the congregation. "Good morning, everyone. My name is John Carroll."

"Good morning," rang out the hearty response.

"It's great to be here today. Like Lisa, my family has also been blessed mightily by adoption. When we adopted our son, we already had two children. Janet was seven and Kristen was five at the time. After Kristen was born, my wife had a hysterectomy for medical reasons. We were unable to have any more children, but we both wanted a baby boy so badly. And so did our daughters. We looked into adoption and were able to arrange through an adoption agency for our baby boy to come into our lives. That was five years ago. Our son's name is John Carroll, Jr. He's named after his dad." John laughed as did the audience.

"Our situation with the birth mother is different from Lisa's. At the time, the mother was single, and the father wanted no part of his son. She wasn't able financially or emotionally to care for her baby by herself, but she did not want to abort him. Today the birth mother is married to someone else and has two children with her husband. Although she gave up the baby for adoption, she wanted to maintain contact with her son. We entered into what is called an open adoption. What that means is our family and the birth mother have contact with each other on a regular basis. In fact, John Jr. spent last weekend with the birth mom and her family for the first time. Their time together turned out well for all. God is so good!"

"Amen," came out the loud and unanimous reply.

"Lisa told you how blessed her family was and is because of the adoption. So is my family as well as the birth mother's family. Johnnie started kindergarten a few weeks ago. What a ball he's having. And speaking of balls, I recently got him a baseball and bat. He's doing great! I can't wait to see him play center field for the Florida Marlins." Carroll put his hands together as though he was holding a bat and swung hard. The congregation loved his gesture. After the laughter subsided, he concluded.

"We are all grateful to Jesus the birth mom chose life over death for little Johnnie. I don't know what any of us would do without him. Now, Anthony has some thoughts he wants to share."

John and Anthony shook hands as John sat down. Anthony got up from his seat and walked to the podium. A beautiful smile crept across his very youthful face.

"My name is Anthony Davis. My story is not the same as Lisa's and John's, but equally as blessed. I'm eighteen years old and a senior at Pahokee High School. And I'm a defensive back on their football team."

"Go Blue Devils," shouted out several members of the congregation.

Anthony gave thumbs up to the group and continued. "My story about adoption is different from the others. In my case, I'm the one who has been adopted. My mom and dad adopted me when I was born. My birth mother was also a single mom who couldn't and didn't want to care for me, but Praise the Lord, she chose not to have an abortion. So here I am eighteen years later. In the flesh!"

Anthony flashed his beautiful smile. The audience laughed and clapped. Lourdes and Lydia looked at each other. Lydia saw the gamut of emotions engulfing her sister. She wrapped her arm across her sibling's shoulder. Lourdes put her head down on Lydia.

"My mom and dad have been absolutely wonderful to me and so have my two sisters and one brother. I'm the youngest, and I try my best each day to treat my parents and all my family with respect and kindness. Sometimes I fall short, but they're always there to pick me up and support me. We are all so blessed, just as Lisa and John told you about their families. I give thanks to God every day for the wonderful life I have." Suddenly, Anthony became emotional and stopped speaking. Then he exhaled deeply, and went on.

"There's one thing that still bothers me. I don't know who my birth mom is. I would like to know her, but she didn't want to have any contact with me or my parents. Maybe someday, with God's help, I'll get to meet her. I would like to tell her how much I appreciate her bringing me into this world and not aborting me. Thanks for listening to all of us. God Bless."

Anthony sat back down. Everyone in the Church stood up. The loud clapping was complemented with fervent cries of "Praise God" and "God bless you all." The three speakers were thrilled at the reaction.

Pastor Gilbert walked over to the podium to briefly speak. "I want to thank all of you for attending our services today. And I especially want to thank these three God loving people who are an inspiration to us all. Our Lord has blessed all of you in great ways, and your talks today about adoption as an alternative to abortion have been wonderful testimonies to the love each of you have for God and others. Lisa, John, and Anthony will be in the back for a few minutes if anyone has any questions."

The congregation began to leave the church. Coral and Maria looked around for the Castillo sisters, but they were nowhere to be seen.

"I think Lydia and Lourdes have left," said Coral. "I sure hope what was said today will positively impact Lourdes so she doesn't choose abortion."

"Me, too. We'll keep praying about her decision and hope for the best."

"Yes, we will."

Robert, Coral, and Maria stopped in the back to chat with some of the people leaving. As the three of them exited the building, Coral noticed Lourdes and Lydia were out in the parking lot talking with Anthony Davis.

"Oh, my gosh!" exclaimed Coral, as she pointed at the three of them. "I can't believe it!"

"What's goin' on?" asked Robert.

"Those two young women talking to Anthony are the sisters I've spoken to you about. Maybe Anthony's testimony really struck a chord with Lourdes, and she'll decide to have the baby." Tears flowed down Coral's face.

"Sweet Jesus, be with those young ladies," responded Robert, "and help them choose life for the baby."

13

It was Friday at 7:00 p.m. Private Investigator Tom Peters worked hard following leads to obtain information to help in the defense of Carlos Delgado. He just arrived at the apartment building where William Jones lived. Peters knew Jones had not returned to his apartment yet, for he was in a rehabilitation center. Peters also knew Jones would be discharged in a few days, so he desperately wanted to wrap up his investigation in this area before Jones returned. Earlier in the week, Peters visited the apartment building and interviewed several persons. One of those was Latoya Johnson, the woman who had seen Delgado kneeling over Jones and begun screaming. Tonight, Peters was first looking for Johnnie Morrison, the man outside Rough Riders Bar who told Delgado where Jones lived. Peters learned from one of the people he talked with what Morrison's last name was and where he lived. Morrison's apartment building was across the street from Jones' residence. Peters walked across the road to where a group of men sat on the front steps of the building. Several of them were drinking beer. As Peters approached, he was carefully watched with a great deal of suspicion. Peters knew he was being closely scrutinized, but was determined to get the information he needed. His years of experience as an investigator, as well as his prior military background, allowed him to maintain a calm and comfortable demeanor, no matter what the circumstances.

"Hello, guys," said Peters as he walked to where the men were sitting.

"Who are you, and what do you want?" asked a young-looking, thickly muscled man. He sipped on the can of beer in his hands as he waited for the answer.

"My name is Tom Peters. I'm a private investigator, and I'm looking for Johnnie Morrison. I just want to talk to him for a few minutes."

"What did Morrison do now?" asked the same man, with a grin on his face. The rest of the group laughed.

"Mr. Morrison didn't do anything. I just need to ask him some questions about an altercation that took place over at the Rough Riders Bar a few months ago." Peters wanted to give out as little information as possible. He hoped he wouldn't be pressed for a lot of details.

"There's nothing new about trouble over at Rough Riders," said an elderly man sitting at the top of the stairs. "Happens all the time. You're in luck wantin' to talk to Morrison. He went in his apartment no more than ten minutes ago. Apartment 110. He lives right next to me."

"Thank you," replied Peters as he carefully made his way through the assemblage. He quickly reached Apartment 110 and knocked on the door. It slowly opened several inches. The chain latch was in place. Peters saw a pair of eyes glaring at him.

"What do you want?" The tone of the question expressed anxiousness and annoyance.

"My name is Tom Peters. I'm a private investigator, and I'm looking for Johnnie Morrison."

"Why?" Peters detected an element of fear in the query.

"I'm working for an attorney named Jack Randolph. Mr. Randolph is representing Carlos Delgado, who has been charged with aggravated battery on William Jones. I've been retained to help in the defense of Mr. Delgado's case." Before Peters could continue, Morrison interrupted.

"What does any of this have to do with me?" Morrison was becoming more and more irritated.

"If you could open the door, and let me speak to you face-to-face, I could explain everything to you and be done with my questions in five minutes."

Morrison closed the door, unlatched the chain, and opened it back up. "You've got three minutes. Step inside and ask your questions. I don't want anyone listening to us. There's a lot of nosey people around here."

Peters stepped inside and closed the door. Morrison did not invite him to sit down, so they stood in the hallway. Peters was relieved Morrison was listening and hoped he'd get some valuable information.

"I appreciate your time, Mr. Morrison. I'll be quick."

"Good."

"Mr. Delgado told me about how you were at Rough Riders Bar when he was attacked by Mr. Jones and knocked to the floor. He also told me you and someone else helped to pick him up."

"That's right."

"Do you know who the other person was that helped to pick up Mr. Delgado?"

Morrison shook his head. "I never saw him before or since then. I don't know who he was."

"Did you see Mr. Jones strike Mr. Delgado?"

"No, I didn't. I was minding my own business having some whiskey. The first I knew there was a problem was when I heard Delgado and the chair fall down on the floor."

"Then what happened?"

"Jones was standing over the dude, mocking him. And in a flash, the bartender came and threw his butt out. That was good to see."

"Why's that?"

"Because Jones is a no-good fool, and he's a bully. He thinks he still runs things like he did when he was in prison. But the truth is no one around here can stand him. I'm glad Delgado let him have it."

Peters knew he needed to be very careful with what he said to Morrison. "Mr. Delgado insists he didn't attack Mr. Jones, and I believe him."

"Whew. That's going to be hard to prove."

"We'll do it," replied Peters in a firm voice.

"Good luck."

"Mr. Delgado also told me you followed him out of the bar and told him where Jones lived. Was that because of your dislike of Mr. Jones?"

"Yeah, that's right." Suddenly, Morrison looked liked a deer caught in headlights. "Wait a minute here. I didn't know Delgado would attack Jones with a wrench as the paper said. I only thought he'd give him a black eye like what Jones did to him, so don't try to get me involved in this."

"You are involved with this, Mr. Morrison. I'm not saying you'll be arrested but, eventually either the Sheriff's office or the state attorney will find out who you are, and you'll be interviewed. The only reason you haven't been so far is no one in the bar knew who you were and you didn't tell Mr. Delgado your last name or exactly where you lived."

"So, how did you find out?"

"I've got my sources."

"It seems like you do." Morrison was exasperated.

"I already told you I believe Mr. Delgado is innocent. Is there any information you can give me to help show he is?"

"Like what?"

"Like someone who may have seen what went on at Jones apartment the night after he returned from the bar. You said people around here are nosey. I'm looking for someone who knows something about the attack but hasn't come forward."

Morrison hesitated and shook his head.

"Listen, Mr. Morrison. Any information which you can provide to help prove Mr. Delgado's innocence can only assist you as well. If Mr. Delgado never attacked Jones, then you've got absolutely nothing to worry about."

Morrison thought long and hard about Peters' comment. "You're right. There is someone around here who always seems to know what's going on."

"Who is it?"

"Leroy Collins. He lives in Jones' building. I think its Apartment 115."

"Thanks. I'll check it out."

"And when I say good luck, I really mean it."

As Peters continued his investigative work, Josh Wilbur arrived at Delgado's home. Josh was cleared by the court system to visit with Carlos. He knocked at the front door and waited, but not for long.

"Thanks for comin' to see me, Wilbur. It's better than watchin' the boob tube all night long."

Josh wanted to respond with a joke, but he quickly decided against it. He was warned by Robert Williams about Delgado's anxiety and negative state of mind.

"No problem, Carlos. Glad to be here. And I brought some chocolate chip cookies with me. I remember from our time together at the four-day prison ministry retreat at Newtown how much you like them."

Carlos motioned for Josh to follow him. They sat down on the couch in the living room. Carlos quickly opened the box of cookies and began to eat one. He offered the box to Josh, who happily accepted.

"These are great, Wilbur. Thanks for bringin' them. How about some ice cold milk to go with them?"

"Sounds great. Thanks."

Delgado hurried out to the kitchen and came back with two large glasses of milk. Josh couldn't help notice his pensive look as he sat down.

"What's wrong, Carlos?"

Delgado exhaled deeply as he responded. "I was thinkin' about what you said about our prison ministry retreat at Newtown. That's when I almost got into a fight with Jones while he was still in there. But you had the guts to step between us and stop anythin' before it got started. You saved me then. Now, I guess it's up to God to step in. I sure hope He does." Carlos bowed his head.

Josh was searching for the right words to respond. Before he did, Delgado continued. "Although I have to say, I recognize now what a stupid thing it was for me even to be in that bar, or to have been goin' there for as long as I did. Hindsight is great, huh?" Delgado folded his arms across his chest.

"We all make mistakes in life and regret them afterwards. I know I've sure made a lot."

Delgado couldn't help but smile. "Wilbur, you remind me of a choir boy. You're a little bit of a wise guy, but I can't imagine you ever doin' anything really bad. Certainly not like me, or most of the guys I've known in my life."

"That's not true. I'm fortunate I've never gone to jail."

"For what?" Carlos was incredulous.

"Drinking alcohol excessively and then driving. There's been more than a few times I've done that. Thank God nothing happened. I have not even thought about drinking and driving since what happened to John. Then I found out about Robert's mistake. I also heard from a number of men in prison about their unfortunate decisions about getting behind the wheel of a car after they had too much to drink or used drugs."

"Well, that's not a good thing, for sure, but you're still nowhere near my level of being a sinner."

"We're all sinners, Carlos. But thank the Lord, we have a merciful Savior who will always forgive us if we come to Him and earnestly ask to be forgiven."

"You sure don't look like him, but now you're starting to sound like Williams." Before he could go on, Delgado saw the hurt look on Josh's face. He knew he needed to fix that immediately.

"Wilbur, don't take everything I say so seriously. I'm only jokin'. Sometimes, I need to do that in order to relieve the pressure I'm feeling. I appreciate what Williams teaches me, and I respect him. And I respect you too. Don't forget it, no matter what comes out of my mouth. Okay?"

"Okay." Josh grinned at Carlos, who was greatly relieved.

"Now hand me some more of those cookies. They're another thing that helps to pick me up."

"Sure thing," responded Josh, as he passed the box to his smiling friend.

14

"I can't stand it. Where are they?"

"Calm down, Coral. It's only 11:40. Lourdes said she might be a few minutes late. They'll be here." Maria Rodgers smiled sweetly at her volunteer.

"I know they will. I don't know why I'm so nervous." Coral looked over anxiously when she heard the door open.

"Lourdes, Lydia, it's so good to see both of you." Coral ran around the counter and hugged Lourdes. The gesture was returned with a warm smile. Even Lydia loosened up and allowed Coral to hug her as well.

"Ladies, Coral and I are glad you're both here. Come on to the room where the ultrasound machine is so we can get started." The three women quickly followed Maria.

As they entered the room, Lourdes asked a question. "I know we talked a little bit on the phone about me having an ultrasound, but having never gone through this procedure, can you tell me what's going to happen?" Maria saw the look of concern on her face.

"It's really simple, Sweetheart. Before I came to work for Choose Life, I was an obstetrical nurse for twenty years, and before that I was a neonatal nurse for ten years. As part of my job, I became trained in administering ultrasounds. I've done hundreds of them, although the ultrasound test being done today is more limited than what an obstetrician's office would perform. What we'll do today is a trans-abdominal scan."

"What's that involve?" Lourdes bit her lip as she waited for the answer.

"We'll have you lie down on this table on your back with your abdomen exposed. Then Coral is going to rub some cool gel over your belly to improve the sound conduction. After that, I'll slide this transducer I'm showing you back and forth over your stomach to transmit sound waves. The computer will translate the resulting echoes into pictures onto the video monitor you're looking at. Then your baby will appear on the screen before your eyes."

"I won't feel any pain, will I?" Lourdes grimaced.

Maria gently reached for Lourdes hand. "You won't feel a thing. This is a noninvasive diagnostic test. It won't take long."

"How long will it take?" Lourdes exhaled and carefully searched Maria's eyes.

"Between fifteen and twenty minutes."

"Okay, let's do it."

"Before we get started, because you're around nineteen weeks along in your pregnancy, if the baby is in the correct position, there's a good chance I'll be able to tell the sex. If I can, do you want to know?"

Lourdes looked at her sister as she blurted out, "Yes."

As the test was administered, Lydia sat in a chair next to her sister and held her hand. Both of them were fascinated by the pictures being shown on the video monitor, and by Maria's explanation of what they were seeing.

"There's your baby!" shouted out Maria. "The tissue and bone show up in the light areas, and the amniotic fluid is in the dark areas. I am going to be able to record the baby's measurements and take some still pictures. We can see the baby's shape, position, and movement." Maria explained in detail about what they saw on the monitor.

"This is amazing," cried out Lourdes. Tears started to roll down her cheeks.

"It really is incredible," replied Lydia, who was also becoming emotional.

"And guess what, the baby's in a good position. I can tell the sex."

"Tell me," responded Lourdes with great fervor.

"It's a boy." Maria and Coral looked at each other. Both of them were also emotionally impacted by this wondrous moment.

"I can't believe it," said Lourdes to Lydia in a tone so soft it was barely audible. She tightly squeezed her sibling's hand.

"Neither can I. To see the baby move around inside of you is unreal. I never visualized anything like this. Wow!" Lourdes was stunned.

"This is a blessed time, ladies," declared Coral. "I'm glad I was here to be a part of it."

"So am I," replied Lourdes. She reached her arm out to hug Coral, who bent down, and kissed her on the cheek.

"And thank you, Maria, for everything you've done."

"You're welcome, Lourdes. We're almost done with the ultrasound. I'm going to be able to give you a picture of what you saw if you want. It will be a little grainy. Would you like to take a picture with you?"

"Absolutely!" Lourdes beamed.

The test was now completed. From all they had seen and heard, both Maria and Coral believed Lourdes had determined to have the baby. Maria knew it was time to hear from Lourdes. She gently approached the subject.

"So, is what went on helpful for you to make a decision about what to do with the baby?" Both Maria and Coral held their breath as they waited for the answer.

"Yes, it was." Lourdes glanced at Lydia, who nodded her approval.

"I'm going to have the baby, and give him up for adoption."

Coral immediately cried so hard she had a profound impact upon the other three women. All three joined in her tears of joy. Then each hugged one another. It was a moment of unbridled happiness, peace and union. God's hand in Lourdes' choice was unmistakable. A baby's life was spared, and the culture of death was rejected.

"Besides, with what went on here today, I have to say that listening to all three speakers last Sunday, especially Anthony, had a big impact on my deciding to have the baby."

"We saw you two out in the parking lot after the services talking to Anthony and hoped he would be a positive influence in your decision," admitted Coral.

"He was. He's such a nice guy, with a wonderful attitude about life. And he's really cute." Lourdes laughed.

"You can say that again, girl," answered Coral. "He's one handsome young man."

"It sounds like you've got a crush on Anthony almost as bad as Lourdes does," responded Lydia, with a giggle.

Coral waved her hand in the air. "I'm too old, and too happily married, to have a crush on Anthony, but he's sure fair game for you, Lourdes."

Lourdes blushed. "We'll see what happens. You never know."

A serious look came across Lourdes' face. She posed a question which was important to her. "When Anthony spoke at church, and then when he talked to Lydia and me, I could feel his pain over never knowing his mother. And John spoke about the open adoption, which he said was great for everyone. When I go through the adoption process, I want it to be an open adoption, with the right to see my baby. I don't want to interfere with his growing up and all the decisions that have to be made on his behalf, but I do want to keep in contact on a face-to-face basis. Do you think that's going to be a problem?"

"Not at all, Lourdes," answered Maria. "There are plenty of adoptive parents who will agree to an open adoption."

"Great. I have another question. Do you think I can have the adoptive parents agree the baby can be named Anthony? I want to do that as a tribute to him."

"I don't see that as a problem either." Maria smiled at Lourdes, which encouraged her all the more.

"Terrific. You previously told me about medical referrals, as well as getting assistance going through the adoption process. I really need help because I know nothing about any of this."

"Don't worry, Lourdes. We've got you covered. You and Lydia come into my office, and I'll get you started. And you, Coral Williams, better get going. You've got a prayer for life gathering to get to in Wellington, don't you?"

Coral looked at her watch. "My gosh, you're right. How time flies. I'll see you two ladies again real soon."

"Yes, you will," said Lourdes. "Thanks again for your help." This time it was Lourdes who initiated an embrace with Coral.

"You're welcome. I can't wait to share your joyous news with the people praying in Wellington."

After Coral left the Choose Life office and made her way to Wellington, she couldn't stop thinking about what had happened not only today but also previously regarding her contact with the Castillo sisters. It was as though someone kept whispering in her ear. What was the message she was receiving?

15

The next day Robert and Coral sat at their kitchen table eating dinner. Robert noticed how quiet Coral was. It was unlike her. He decided he needed to find out why.

"You're bein' awfully silent tonight, Sweetheart. Why?" Robert looked at his spouse with love and concern.

Coral took a deep breath and pondered what she would say. "I've got something on my heart we need to talk about. I'm trying to figure out the best way to tell you."

Robert took Coral's hand in his. "Baby, whatever you need to talk about, just let it out. I'll listen and help in any way I can."

"I know you will, Honey." Coral smiled and continued. "Ever since I met the Castillo sisters I've talked to you about how I feel God has been speaking to me about something special. At first, I couldn't figure it out. But yesterday after Lourdes had the ultrasound and decided to choose life for her baby by giving him up for adoption what God was trying to say started to become clearer. I've been thinking about this all last night and today. What I've got to tell you is not easy." Coral stopped and looked her husband directly in the eyes.

"Well, don't keep me in suspense. I want to hear about it." Robert's toothy grin surfaced.

Coral hesitated a few moments. Then she launched into an explanation of what was on her mind. "You're not going to believe this, but I think God is calling us to adopt Lourdes' baby boy."

"You're right; I don't believe it." Robert was flabbergasted. "What makes you think God is calling us to adopt this baby?" Robert had his hand on his forehead as he waited for the answer.

"All of the circumstances that have occurred since I first met the two ladies have led me to feel God wants us to adopt the child."

"What specifically are you talkin' about?" Robert exhaled deeply as he waited for the answer.

"The first thing is how Lourdes had her sister stop the car and took information from me about alternatives to abortion. That happened right after they came out of the clinic they went to for information about the abortion process."

"Yes, I recall you telling me about it. What else?"

"Then, Lourdes called me and then came to Choose Life's office with her sister to get more information about options to abortion. I felt Lourdes and I really started to bond."

"Is that it?"

"No. The next thing is when Lourdes came to First Baptist to hear the speakers talk about how adoption over abortion had been such a blessing in their lives. Then we saw Lourdes out in the parking lot speaking so excitedly with Anthony."

"I remember. How do those things lead you to believe God is calling us to adopt Lourdes' child?"

"There's more."

"I should have known." Robert lowered his head as he waited for the continued explanation.

"Yesterday, after Lourdes came in for an ultrasound, is when I believe I started to recognize what the Lord was putting on my heart about adoption. When I saw the picture of the precious infant on the video monitor and then heard from Lourdes about how she wanted to have the baby, and give him up for adoption, it hit me like a ton of bricks. Especially after I left the office and was riding to Wellington to pray with the group for an end to abortion." Robert could feel Coral's excitement, but he did not share in it.

"So you really believe adopting Lourdes' baby is something God wants us to do?" Robert folded his hands as he waited for the response.

"Yes, it is," answered Coral in a firm and convincing tone. "Now, tell me what you think?"

Robert bowed his head, and silently prayed. Then he looked up and spoke to his wife in a soft, matter-of-fact tone. "You won't like what I think."

"Well, I have to know. If there is going to be an adoption, we both need to agree to it. So what are your feelings?"

"Right now, I can't say I'm in favor of any adoption, but I know I need to go deep in prayer to the Lord about what you've brought up."

"Please tell me why you're not in favor of adoption." Coral looked as though she might start to cry. Robert felt awful about her reaction, but he knew he must be honest with his wife about his feelings.

"One of the main reasons is because of our age. I'm fifty-three, and you're forty-nine. We're not exactly youngsters to be raising a baby at this point in our lives."

"Robert, we're not old, and we're both in great health. There are more and more families who adopt children in their mid-life years. There's also a lot of families who have grown children come back to live with them, and they bring their own children as well. So, I don't see our age as a problem. What else is bothering you?"

"My past criminal record. I'm an ex-felon who served ten years in jail for killing a man by driving drunk. That may haunt us if we ever go through this adoption process." Robert looked forlorn.

"I can't believe that will be a major issue. You've been out of prison now for over four years. And you've become much more than a model citizen. In fact, in your last years in prison, you were a Godly example to many men who you brought into a closer relationship with Christ. And now, look at all the work you do for First Baptist. I have no doubt Pastor Gilbert and many others will attest to your fitness to be a father." Coral stopped and grabbed her husband's hand. Then she continued.

"Honey, there must be something else bothering you. Tell me what it is." She waited patiently while Robert struggled to respond.

"Before we got married, and up to this day, we've never talked about having kids. I knew about your inability to bear a child because of the hysterectomy you had. So, I assumed we never would have one – that it would just be you and me."

"Robert, I feel there's still something you're not sharing with me?" Coral looked deeply into her husband's eyes. He turned away and let out a mournful sigh.

"There is something else. After my boy was murdered, and all the pain I went through, I could never envision me wanting to have another child. I know it's selfish and not of the Lord, but it was the way I felt, and

at this moment, I still do. I'm not sure I can change."
Tears began to roll down Robert's cheeks. He wiped
them away.

Now it was Coral's turn to be stunned. Robert's
revelation was something they had never discussed nor
had she envisioned. She struggled with how to respond.

"Honey, I am so sorry. I guess I've just been
thinking of myself. I sure don't want to go forward with
an adoption if it causes you anguish. That wouldn't be
good for anyone."

"No, you're not thinkin' of yourself. It's me who is.
What I need to do is to go to the Lord in prayer. Give
me a few days to sort this out. Is that okay?" Robert's
gentle and caring response touched Coral greatly.

"Of course, it is. I don't want you to rush into any
decision, so take all the time you need."

"I won't need more than a few days. But there is
something else I'm wondering about."

"What's that?"

"How do you know Lourdes wants us to be the
parents? Are the terms she wants about an open
adoption going to work for us?"

"I can't answer those questions for certain because
I've never talked with her about it. I needed to speak
with you first, but I think she would be delighted to
have us as the parents. I don't feel there would be any
issues about the terms of the adoption."

"One last thing. Is there any conflict about you
adopting a baby with the Choose Life office involved
when you volunteer for them?"

"That's something else I'd need to look into, but I
don't see any problems."

"Fair enough. Give me a few days, and then we'll
talk about it again."

16

It was early Monday morning, and Carlos Delgado was already at work. For the past two years he worked for an air conditioning business in West Palm Beach owned by Steve Ramrell. John Taylor had introduced Carlos to Ramrell when they were all volunteers for a four-day prison ministry retreat at Newtown Correctional Institution. After Delgado lost his prior job with another air conditioning company as a result of false allegations of inventory theft by his employer, Ramrell offered him his current position. Carlos proved to be an outstanding employee, and Ramrell assigned him to some of the company's largest commercial accounts. But this morning, as Delgado was going over the day's assignment log, Ramrell approached him with two much smaller jobs to handle.

"Good morning, Carlos. Good to see you here bright and early on a Monday."

"No problem. I'm glad to be out of my house after bein' cooped up all weekend."

"Steve Jacobs called in sick today, and his back-up, Paul Pardon, has jury duty. Earlier this morning, I received calls from two of our residential customers whose a/c units went out yesterday. They're both in a hurry to get them repaired. Would you mind handling both? One is in Jupiter, and the other is in Boca Raton, so they will probably take up your whole day. I know the residential stuff is small potatoes compared to what you normally work on, but I can really use your help."

"Of course, I don't mind. After everything you've done for me over the last two years, especially with not firing me after I was charged with aggravated battery, it's the least I can do for you. But I have one request."

"Sure, what is it?"

"I'm supposed to meet with my lawyer at his office at four this afternoon. Assuming I get both jobs finished, would you mind if I didn't come back in here today so I can meet with him?"

"No problem. Knowing how good you are at what you do, I'm sure both homes will have their a/c back up and running, leaving you with plenty of time to get to your attorney's office." Ramrell hesitated for a few moments, and then posed a question. "If I'm not being too nosey, how is your defense going? Do you think your lawyer is doing a good job for you?"

"You're not nosey at all. I appreciate your concern. Sometimes I feel good about my case, other times, I'm scared, but I think Mr. Randolph has done a good job, especially with this private investigator he hired. I'm supposed to get an update today."

"Great. I hope it all goes well. I will keep you in my prayers for your defense to be successful."

"Thanks. I can use all the prayers I can get."

During the course of the day, Delgado's first call went well. He was in and out of the house in Jupiter within two hours. Now, he was at his second call in Boca Raton, and it was only noon. He anticipated no problem being at his attorney's office on time. As he knocked on the door of the home, he was greeted by a petite, frail-looking elderly woman. When she saw

Carlos standing there with his work uniform, her face lit up.

"Thank God, you're here. It's been so hot. My prayers have been answered."

Carlos smiled at her greeting. "I don't know if anyone has ever told me I'm the answer to their prayers, but it's good to hear."

"You are, son, you are. Now come in so you can get my air going again."

"I'll do my best."

"Of course, you will. By the way, my name's Anita. What's yours?" Her sweet disposition touched Carlos.

"Carlos, and it's nice to meet you."

"Likewise. Can I get you a bottle of water? I know how hot it is outside and in here."

"Not right now. Maybe later. I'll let you know. First, I want to get started on diagnosing what the problem is."

Two hours later, Carlos called out for Anita. She made her way over to him as fast as she could.

"I've got good news and bad news," declared Carlos.

"Well, give me the good news first, son."

"All the problems with the a/c unit cooling the house on the left side are fixed."

"Great. So, I guess the bad news is about the a/c on the bedrooms side."

"Yes. There is a bad breaker up in the crawl space on the side of the house where the bedrooms are. It's really not a big deal except for the fact that I don't have the replacement part in my truck. I'm goin' to have to get you one, but I don't think I have the time to do it today."

"Oh, my," said Anita in a voice so low Carlos barely heard her. "I guess I'll have another sleepless night. I hate leaving my bedroom windows open when I live here alone. Well, I'll have to make do until you can get back here. When do you think that will be?" Anita looked up at Delgado with her wide eyes.

Carlos initially thought about telling Anita to sleep on the couch on the side of the house where the a/c was fixed but, then he decided he shouldn't. She was too old and sweet, and he recognized she probably wouldn't sleep well other than in her bed. He struggled with what to do when a thought came to him.

"Let me call my office to see if they have the part in stock. If they do, maybe someone could drive down toward here, and I could meet them half way."

"That would be wonderful." The excitement on Anita's face again moved Delgado.

After determining the office had the part in stock, Carlos quickly left to meet one of the secretaries who took it with her to give to him. An hour and a half later, the breaker was replaced, and the a/c was again blowing cold air. He was glad he could help Anita today, but was apprehensive about being late for his meeting. Randolph was a very busy man, and Carlos desperately wanted to get the full scoop on what was happening with his case. He couldn't bear the thought of having the meeting postponed. Anita sensed Delgado's anxiety, and in her sweet, disarming way posed a question.

"I know something's wrong, son. Can I help you in some way?" The kind and genuine look of concern in her eyes led Carlos to confide in her in a way he didn't think was possible.

"The reason I seem so uptight is I'm on my way to my lawyer's office, and I'm runnin' late. Plus, I'm concerned about what he might say to me." The frown on Delgado's face caused Anita to throw out another question.

"You're not in trouble, are you?" Anita was genuinely concerned, and Carlos knew it.

"Yes, I am." He hesitated a few seconds and then blurted out, "I'm an ex-con. Been out for nearly three years with no problems, but a while ago, I was charged with aggravated battery on a man. I didn't do it, but if I'm found guilty by a jury, I'll go away for a long time." Carlos couldn't believe he just told this stranger about his troubles.

Anita wasted no time in responding. "I can tell from everything you said and did today to help me, you're a good man. If you say you're innocent, I believe you. I will pray for you every day the jury will find you not guilty. Don't give up on God. I've gone through a lot of troubles in my life, and sometimes I couldn't figure out where God was. But just when I thought I couldn't bear it anymore, He sent me people to help me through those tough times. So hang in there, son. I know everything is going to work out okay for you. Please let me know what happens with your case."

Anita reached out to shake Delgado's hand. He softly grasped it, while telling her how much he appreciated her prayers and encouragement. He thought she might be an angel sent to help him in his battles.

An hour later, Carlos sat in Randolph's office. He was thirty minutes late, but it didn't matter. Randolph had plenty of time available to speak with him. There were two major issues on Delgado's mind. He immediately addressed the first.

"What did the assistant state attorney say about your offer that I agree to probation for five years?" Carlos waited for the answer with great angst.

"He rejected it out of hand. The state's position is you've committed a felony of the second degree, and you're subject to a sentence of up to fifteen years. The fact you were previously convicted of aggravated battery and served five years in prison doesn't help as it relates to their position."

"Yeah," protested Carlos. "But I got out of prison almost three years ago and have been as clean as a whistle up until this problem. So why are they bringing my past up?"

"I understand your position, Carlos." The two of them had been through this discussion several times. Jack was exasperated with the repeat debate, but did his best to hide it from his client. "From the state's perspective, your past criminal record is relevant. In any event, the best offer the state will give, at least for now, is seven years." Randolph held his breath, for he knew what was coming. Delgado was about to explode.

"You've got to be kidding me!" Delgado screamed out. "That is such bull! I can't believe this!" Carlos got up from his seat and paced around the room. Randolph closely watched him. Part of Jack's assessment was how well Delgado would hold up in the courtroom before a jury under intense cross-examination.

"You can go tell the state attorney's office to eat dirt as far as I'm concerned. I will never agree to so much time in prison. This is goin' to drive me nuts!" Carlos slunk back down in his chair.

"I've already let them know there's no way you will ever voluntarily agree to doing that much time or anything close to it." Randolph studied Delgado's reaction.

"Good. Let's move on to what I hope is much better news. What's the deal with the private investigator you hired? Is there any positive news?" Delgado's arms were folded across his chest, which heaved up and down.

"As a matter of fact, there is. Tom was able to speak at length with a guy named Leroy Collins. It seems he's in the know about a lot of things that happen in the neighborhood around Jones' apartment building. There's some great information Tom got directly from Collins, as well as some other leads Collins gave him."

"Don't keep me in suspense," barked out Delgado. "Tell me everything Peters found out."

17

On Saturday at noon, the Castillo sisters arrived at Choose Life's building in Pahokee. They went into Maria Rodgers' office. Coral Williams locked the front door and joined them.

"Lourdes and Lydia, thanks for coming to see us," said Maria. "We've got a lot to talk about."

"There's nothing wrong, is there?" Lourdes nervously asked.

"Of course not, Sweetheart. We wanted to have a face-to-face discussion about possible parents for your baby." Maria smiled at the Castillo sisters.

"Wow, already!" exclaimed Lourdes. "That's awesome. Please tell us."

Maria looked over at Coral before replying. "I'm going to let Coral fill the two of you in on the details."

Coral had a lump in her throat and was shaking. Lourdes and Lydia both saw how emotional she already was. Neither could understand why.

"Ever since I met the two of you after you both came out of the abortion clinic and stopped to get information about options to abortion, I felt someone was speaking to me about Lourdes and her baby. Those feelings continued to become stronger and stronger as time went by, and we had more contact with each other. Last Saturday, it really hit home after we saw your precious baby boy and learned Lourdes decided to go forward with the pregnancy and have him adopted."

Coral was struggling to continue. "I've never had any children of my own, and I never will because of a hysterectomy I had years ago. But deep down, I always wanted to have a baby."

Lourdes and Lydia glanced at each other. They now suspected what Coral had to tell them. Both were eagerly awaiting Coral's next words.

"Let me do my best to cut to the chase. I believe God is calling my husband and me to adopt your baby." Tears rolled down Coral's cheeks. "I don't know what the two of you think, but that's why Maria asked you to come here today." Although Coral was greatly relieved to have gotten out her message, she now fought the fear of being rejected.

Lourdes sprang from her chair and wrapped her arms around Coral. She was now the one with tears streaming down her face. "You don't know how happy you've made me, Coral. I was hoping for my baby to have a mother like you. This is wonderful news!"

Lydia was on the same page as her sister. "I feel the same as Lourdes. The baby will be very fortunate to have you as his mother. Thank you so much." Lydia's face lit up. Neither Coral nor Maria had ever seen Lydia so happy.

Maria was quiet and very joyful to witness this blessed event, but the discussion about the adoption wasn't concluded yet.

"There's something else we need to discuss," said Coral in a somber tone. Both Coral and Lourdes sat back down.

"What is it?" asked Lourdes cautiously. "Is something wrong?"

"No, nothing's wrong," stammered Coral. "At least I hope not."

"What do you mean?" asked Lydia in a skeptical voice. The radiance she exuded only moments ago was gone.

"I need to talk to both of you about my husband. He knew we were meeting today and insisted we have this discussion."

"Doesn't he want to adopt the baby?" asked Lourdes in a solemn tone.

"No, that's not it at all. Robert, my husband, wants both of you to be fully aware of his background before any decisions are made by Lourdes to move forward with us adopting your son."

"Oh, boy," remarked Lydia. "What are we in for?"

"Hopefully nothing," answered Coral. "Here's the deal. Robert is an ex-felon who served ten years in state prison." Coral stopped to gauge the sisters' reaction.

"For what?" asked Lydia. She was shocked, as was Lourdes.

"Robert pled guilty to driving under the influence of alcohol, resulting in a car crash, which killed an elderly man. It is a part of his life that he deeply regrets." Coral began to become emotional again.

"Was there a reason why your husband was drunk and then chose to drive?" Lourdes wanted all the facts behind the crash. She was totally focused on Coral's explanation.

"Unfortunately, it was a time in Robert's life when some terrible things happened to him and his family. Robert and I have only known each other for three years and were married two years ago. It was about fifteen years ago he was happily married to another woman. He had a son who was a high school senior and was the pride of his life. One night, his boy came out of a school dance with some friends. A van came by with three people in it. They started firing shots at random. Robert's son was killed."

"How awful!" exclaimed Lourdes as she cupped her hands over her mouth.

"After the murder, Robert's life took a steady downhill turn. He ended up divorcing his wife, and became an alcoholic. Then he lost his job. He had no faith in God and nothing to live for. He was totally smashed when he caused the car wreck. He's admitted at that point in time he didn't even care he had taken a life. It was a good five years after he entered prison before he slowly began to turn his life around."

"How did he do that?" asked Lydia.

"He did it with the help of the prison chaplain, outside prison minister volunteers, and inmates who had already turned their lives over to Jesus. They were all a positive influence on him returning to be the man of faith he was raised to be. In fact, during his last several years in prison, he became a chaplain's assistant and brought many inmates to Christ. Since he's been out of prison, he's been a terrific influence on many people in this community. I'm sure the two of you could speak with Pastor Gilbert, who's in charge of the church where Anthony and the two others spoke, and find out from him the good Robert has done. I admire him and love him for all the wonderful things he's done, not only for me, but for many others as well."

"Let me interject my thoughts, ladies." Maria had been quiet throughout this discussion but knew she now needed to speak out. "I've known Robert for two years and have always been impressed by his kind and loving demeanor toward other people. I believe he will be a great father to Lourdes' baby, as will Coral be a wonderful mother. The two of you will have no worries with them as the boy's parents. I say that from my years of experience with adoptions. If I didn't believe it, I never would support the Williams as adoptive parents."

"I have no reason to doubt what you said, Maria," answered Lourdes, "And I respect Mr. Williams for the tough times he overcame. My thoughts haven't changed about having Mr. Williams and Coral as the parents." She smiled at Coral, who blew Lourdes a kiss in response.

"I agree with Lourdes," added Lydia. "I would like to meet Mr. Williams sometime soon, so we all can get to know one another better."

"That's a great idea, Lydia. I'll arrange it."

Suddenly, Lourdes let out a loud laugh. She shook her head from side to side, and put her hand over her stomach.

"What's so funny?" asked Lydia. She was puzzled by her sister's behavior.

"I know we haven't met Mr. Williams yet, but I remember seeing him both sitting and standing next to Coral at church. I can't believe how tall and big he is. He's like a giant compared to everyone else. I was thinking about him holding little Anthony after he's born. What a sight that will be."

Lourdes laughed again. This time she was joined by the other three women. After the merriment ended, Coral spoke.

"Robert and I want the two of you to know if you decide to go forward with us as the adoptive parents, we will pay for any medical bills your insurance company doesn't cover. You won't need to worry about any of those expenses."

"Thank you," said Lourdes. "We really need the help."

"And you won't need to worry about any legal fees for the court proceedings," added Maria. "Robert and Coral will have their own attorney, who will handle the paperwork and courtroom procedures, and they will be responsible for paying him. But, Lourdes should also have her own attorney to represent her. Your lawyer can answer any questions you have and guide you in the process. He would also review the legal documents to make sure everything is okay from Lourdes' perspective. I know several lawyers who have assisted birth mothers place their child for adoption, and they didn't charge a fee when the mother could not afford to pay. I'll give you their names and phone numbers for you to call. Hopefully, one of them will represent you without charging a fee."

"It sounds like everything is coming together." Lourdes was jubilant.

"There's something you ladies don't know about," remarked Lydia. "It seems Mr. Anthony Davis has taken quite a liking to my sister. He called Lourdes up and asked her out on a date."

"And what did you say, girl?" Coral sat with her arms folded across her chest as she waited for the answer.

"How could I say no to a guy that nice and cute?" Lourdes was gushing.

"I see good things coming out of this relationship." Coral was delighted.

"We'll see what happens," answered Lourdes. "I'm hoping for the best."

18

Three weeks later on a Sunday afternoon, Robert Williams was with Carlos at Delgado's home. The two of them sat in the living room.

"I'm sorry I haven't been here the past two weeks, Carlos, but I have to say Coral and I had a great time on our vacation. The mountains in Colorado were spectacular. It really is God's country." Robert did his best to open up today's discussion on a positive note. It wouldn't be easy to maintain an optimistic mood.

"Well, I'm glad you and your wife had a good time. I've never been out to Colorado so I don't know what it's like, and I'll probably never get out there, especially if I'm convicted. I can't tell you how tough it is on me while I wait for the trial to start. It's a good thing I had my attorney push for a trial date so I can get this disaster over with." Delgado hung his head.

"When's the trial start?"

"Four and a half months from now."

"That's pretty quick."

"Not quick enough as far as I'm concerned. With every day that goes by, it seems like I'm sinkin' deeper and deeper into a pit I can't get out of, and that's really scary. You know what the worst part is?"

"Tell me," replied Robert in his compassionate tone. He wanted to help Carlos in any way he could.

"It's the fact I could be sentenced up to fifteen years in prison if the jury convicts me. All that time for a crime I didn't commit. Unbelievable!" Carlos was rapidly falling into a tailspin.

"Has your lawyer been able to get any kind of a plea deal from the state attorney's office?"

Carlos sighed loudly and threw his arms up in the air. "Those guys won't come up with anything reasonable. Their best offer is that I plead out to seven years, which I am never goin' to do. We'll go to trial and hope for the best."

"Seven years is tough. Do you think your attorney has done a good job so far?"

"I don't have any complaints. He's getting stonewalled because I'm an ex-con who was previously convicted of aggravated battery. It doesn't matter to the state I've been out of prison with a lily-white record for three years until this charge." Delgado was seething.

"Has your legal team come up with any witnesses who might help your case?"

"There is some positive news there, but my lawyer has told me not to talk with anyone about it, so I better not."

"I understand." Robert hesitated and then carefully posed another question.

"Have you heard anythin' about how Jones is doing?"

"He's out of rehab and back in his apartment. Other than that, I don't know what's goin' on with the bum. And I don't care. I'll leave it up to my lawyer."

"How have you been doin' with your spiritual life lately?" Robert already knew the answer, but he had to ask.

"It's the pits. Taylor came over one Sunday to talk while you were away. And Wilbur came by the next week. They tried to help me, but it just didn't work. I'm not blaming them. It's me. I'm depressed all the time thinkin' about goin' back to prison, especially if it's fifteen years. If it happens, my life is over." Carlos threw his head against the back of the sofa and closed his eyes. Robert saw he was sinking into the abyss. He struggled for the right words to try to comfort Delgado.

"I've got a couple of suggestions for you. Do you have your Bible?"

"It's in my bedroom." Delgado was annoyed. He wasn't ready for more instruction, although he recognized Robert's efforts were well-intentioned.

"Would you go get it please? And bring back some of those sticky flags if you have any." Robert's caring demeanor helped to diffuse Carlos' despondency.

"Okay. Although I don't know what good it's goin' to do. If God wanted to help me, He would have done so by now."

Robert said nothing in response. He waited for Delgado to return. A couple of minutes later Carlos was back with his Bible and the sticky flags. He handed both to Robert.

"Listen Williams, I appreciate everything you're tryin' to do for me, but I am one big sinner. Always have been and always will be. God's not interested in me and is not about to help me."

Delgado's dialogue inspired Robert to open the Bible to The Acts of the Apostles. "I want to talk to you for a few minutes about one of the worst sinners in the Bible, until he turned his life over to Jesus. Once he did, he became one of Christ's greatest evangelists."

"Who are you talkin' about?"

"The great persecutor of Christians, first named Saul and then later called Paul. The book of Acts details his conversion." Robert thumbed through Acts looking for portions of it to share. He didn't want to be too lengthy nor did he want to read verbatim from Acts, for he thought Delgado was not in the proper frame of mind to listen to and absorb the Word. He decided to provide Delgado with a synopsis of Saul's conversion. Robert could have done so without opening the Bible, but he felt Delgado would be more receptive if he were looking through it when he spoke.

"One of Christ's disciples was named Stephen. He was one of seven men chosen to supervise distribution of food to the needy in the early church. Stephen was also a powerful speaker and was confronted in the temple by different groups who were antagonistic to the disciples. Many of those who heard him speak could not bear to have their evil motives exposed, so they dragged him outside of Jerusalem and stoned him to death. Saul was present and approved of his death.

"Afterwards, Saul went to the high priest and obtained letters to the synagogues in Damascus, so that if he found any followers of Christ, whether men or women, he might take them as prisoners to Jerusalem to be prosecuted. While he, along with others, was on the road to Damascus, a light from Heaven blinded him. He fell to the ground and heard a voice ask why he was persecuting Him. The voice was that of Jesus. He told Saul to get up, go into Damascus, and he would be told what to do. After Saul got up, he was sightless and had to be led by the hands of others into the city. After several days of blindness and not eating or drinking anything, a disciple named Ananias went to Saul. Ananias placed his hands on Saul and told Saul he was sent by Jesus so that Saul may see again and be filled with the Holy Spirit. Then Saul could see again.

He was baptized, ate some food, and regained his strength. After spending several days with the disciples in Damascus, Saul began to preach in the synagogues that Jesus is the Son of God.

"Paul, formerly called Saul, moved from being a violent persecutor of many Christians to being a superb evangelist for Christ. Perhaps, he is the greatest evangelist ever. My point is Paul's conversion shows us no man is too great a sinner to be redeemed by Jesus, including you. So stop believing the lies of Satan that God isn't interested in you and won't help you. All you need do is to go to Him in sincerity and ask for His assistance. You will always be heard."

Delgado held his head in his hands. His eyes were closed as he softly said, "Williams, you have a way of gettin' to me no one else does. I really missed you when you were gone."

"I'm not finished yet," answered Robert in a humble and soothing voice.

"Okay, let me have it." Delgado picked up his head and looked directly at his friend.

"There's one other portion of the Bible I want to talk with you about."

"What is it?"

"It's the First Letter of Peter. I'm goin' to put some sticky flags on some pages for you to read as I did on the pages we talked about with Saul's conversion. There's one sentence I want you to keep in your mind whenever you start to feel overwhelmed by your circumstances, whether it's the criminal trial or anything else you face. It's not long, so it won't be hard to do."

"What is it?"

"Cast all your anxiety on God because He cares for you. Remember, believe, and do that, and you will overcome whatever issues you may face."

"I hope you're right. I'll do my best."

"That's all I can ask. By the way, there's something I want to tell you about, and it's wonderful news!" Robert was joyful. His disposition raised Delgado's spirits.

"Don't keep me waitin'. Spill the beans."

"Coral and I are in the process of adoptin' a baby boy."

"Say what?" Delgado was overwhelmed.

"You heard me. We're about to become parents of a precious child."

"Ain't that something? How old is the little guy?"

"He hasn't been born yet." The puzzled look on Delgado's face caused Robert to explain quickly.

"There's an eighteen-year-old girl from Belle Glade who's pregnant. She's single, and the father wants nothin' to do with the child. The only family member she has is a twenty year old sister, who she lives with. The young lady doesn't feel she and her sister can raise the boy. She thought about an abortion, but thank the Lord, she decided to have the baby and give him up for adoption. It's a long story about how Coral and this woman met, but they really hit it off, and one thing led to another. So, Coral and I are goin' through the process of adoption."

"I think that's great, Williams. I don't want to be a spoilsport, but, let me ask you a question."

"Go ahead."

"Is there any issue about you bein' an ex-con, and serving ten years in prison?"

"I was worried about the same thing, but I've met with the birth mother and her sister, and we hit it off great. They didn't have any concerns. Coral and I have met with the lawyer, who will handle the adoption for us and he didn't think we would have any problems. So far, the process has all gone smoothly. Hopefully, with the Lord's help, it will stay that way."

"Glad to hear it. By the way, when will the big event take place?"

"Believe it or not, around the same time your trial takes place."

"You're kiddin'."

"No, sir."

"Well, I see the timing as a good sign. Let's hope I'm right."

19

Four and a half months later, Carlos Delgado sat in a courtroom on the tenth floor of the Palm Beach County Courthouse in West Palm Beach with Jack Randolph. Today was the first day of Delgado's trial. Although Carlos was relieved there had been no delays with the trial starting, he now began to feel the pressure of a jury possibly convicting him of aggravated battery and a substantial prison sentence being imposed, one which could be as high as fifteen years. He cringed at the thought. Delgado and Randolph were the only people present in the courtroom. It was Monday at 2:15 p.m. A jury was picked in the morning and early afternoon by the attorneys, and the Court adjourned the case until 2:30 for a lunch break. The trial was being presided over by Judge Loretta Brown, a former prosecutor, who worked in the State Attorney's office for twenty years before being appointed to the bench ten years ago. Although she was a small woman, her voice and demeanor more than compensated for her size. Judge Brown was totally no nonsense if a lawyer stepped out of line. Although Carlos was wary of her background as a criminal prosecutor, Randolph did his best to assure his client she was a fair and impartial judge with substantial courtroom experience. Delgado's response was to wait and see what happened.

There were six jurors chosen by the attorneys: Jose Frias, an airplane mechanic; Rose Gillespie, a retired real estate broker; Donna Bradley, an insurance agent; Oscar Reynolds, a truck driver; Jeff Bronson, a CPA; and Rosalina Cruz, a housewife. In addition, there was one alternate juror – Jeremy Brooks, a retired fireman. Although Brooks was the alternate juror and would not participate in the jury deliberation process unless another juror was unable to do so, he had not been told that by Judge Brown. Delgado and Randolph started a discussion about the jurors.

"Well, Randolph, I've got to hand it to you. I thought you did a great job pickin' the jury. I can see you've done it a lot of times."

"More than I care to count," responded Jack with a wry smile. "But what was really important today is we had a great panel to choose from. I'm feeling good about who our jurors are, and their backgrounds."

"I'm glad to hear it. The only thing that matters to me is they come back with a not guilty verdict. Unless they do, it don't matter a hoot to me who they are or what their backgrounds are." Delgado was somber as he spoke.

"I understand, Carlos." Before Randolph could continue, the rear door to the courtroom popped open. It was Assistant State Attorney Peter King, who was prosecuting the case for the State.

Delgado stared at King. Over the course of the case, Carlos had come to dislike King intensely. He was a big, muscular guy, along the lines of Randolph, whom Delgado respected, but Carlos viewed King as a "punk kid." King had practiced law for ten years and at thirty-five years old was Randolph's junior by twenty years in both age and legal experience. King was brash and outspoken and had played hardball in the plea deal negotiations. He adamantly refused to take a guilty plea of less than a seven-year sentence. Delgado saw King as a political power wannabe, desperately trying to work his way up the ladder to become the State Attorney. Carlos hoped Randolph's age and experience would work to his advantage. But King was no pushover. He was a formidable foe, having tried in his career as a prosecutor more than 100 jury trials some of which were very high profile with big stakes outcomes.

"Good afternoon, gentlemen," called out King in a supercilious tone. "Are the two of you ready for the fun and games to begin?" Although King was already getting under Delgado's skin, Randolph knew better than to bite on the bait being thrown out. Jack answered in a calm and cool manner.

"The fun and games will begin when the jury exonerates my client. Until then, it's full steam ahead." Randolph winked at King, who waved his hand contemptuously at Jack, as he sat down.

Before any further exchanges could ensue, Bailiff Kevin Harrison appeared from the door behind the bench. At the same time, Roxanne Miller, the court reporter, opened and walked through the rear door. She was closely followed by Joanne Murphy, the clerk from the Palm Beach County Circuit Court Clerk's office, who was assisting in the trial.

"I see we have everyone here," said Bailiff Harrison. "All the jurors are in the jury room. I'll get Judge Brown so we can get started." Harrison disappeared through the door behind the bench. Two minutes later he reappeared and instructed everyone to rise as Judge Brown entered the courtroom.

"Are the parties ready to proceed?" asked Brown.

"The State is ready," answered King.

"As is the defense, Your Honor," replied Randolph.

"Excellent. Bailiff Harrison, please bring in the jury."

As the bailiff brought the jury into the courtroom, Carlos took a deep breath. He stared intently at each one as they walked in. Thoughts of his first trial where he was convicted years ago of aggravated battery crept into his mind. He desperately hoped the result would not be repeated. Silently, he asked God for His help in being found innocent.

After the jury sat down, the Court addressed them. "Ladies and gentlemen, we are now ready to begin the case of The State of Florida versus Carlos Delgado. As I mentioned during jury selection, we anticipate this case will take three days to try. We will start with the opening statement of the State, followed by the opening statement of the defense." Judge Brown looked over at King.

"Please proceed, Mr. King."

"Yes, Your Honor," said King as he slowly approached the podium. A hint of a smile crossed his lips as he began the battle. He lived for times like these.

"Ladies and gentlemen of the jury, the State thanks you for your service on this case. Although you're taking time away from your jobs or families, all of you are performing a vital function in our legal system. We need fair and impartial jurors, as all of you are, to reach a decision as to the guilt or innocence of the Defendant, Carlos Delgado. In this case, the Defendant is charged with the crime of aggravated battery on another person by use of a deadly weapon. The deadly weapon was a wrench and it was used in a vicious attack to strike the victim, William Jones, across the back of the head three times. The attack was so severe that Mr. Jones spent several months in a hospital and then a rehabilitation center. You will hear evidence from a doctor who has treated Mr. Jones about the extent of his injuries and his permanent disabilities."

King closely watched the jury to gauge their reaction. He noticed the three female jurors seemed to be repulsed by his description of the attack, while their male counterparts were all stone-faced. No surprise there. King was determined to sway all the jurors to accept the State's version of the evidence.

"The evidence will also show Mr. Jones and the Defendant have a long and checkered history with each other. In fact, as part of their history, on the same night but prior to the attack, they got into an altercation at Rough Riders Bar in the north end of West Palm Beach. As a result of the fight, the Defendant went to Mr. Jones' apartment, where he sneaked up behind him and smashed him across the back of his head with a wrench. Mr. Jones was struck not once, not twice, but three times."

Delgado bit his lip as he listened to King's statement of what had occurred. He knew he was in for a tough fight to be exonerated. He deeply regretted his thirst for vengeance that propelled him to go to Jones' residence.

"You will also hear testimony from an eyewitness who saw the Defendant crouched over Mr. Jones with the wrench in his hand." The comment caused all the jurors to look at each other. Their reaction caused King to be delighted. On the other hand, both Randolph and Delgado managed to keep a stoic look. Jack had worked long and hard in preparing Carlos never to show any sign of panic or concern in front of the jury. So far, Randolph's instructions were working. But the case had just begun.

"I've given all of you some of the highlights of what the evidence will show. The State believes after you consider all of the evidence you will determine justice can only be done by finding the Defendant guilty of aggravated battery upon Mr. Jones. Thank you for your attention."

King nodded at the jury and returned to his chair. Randolph rose from his seat and confidently strolled to the podium. His years of experience in the courtroom masked the tension he felt.

"Ladies and gentlemen, I know each of you recall I asked you during jury selection if you were able to keep an open mind and listen to all the evidence before making a decision in this case. Not only the State's evidence, because they go first, but to wait for Mr. Delgado's evidence as well before reaching a verdict. You each told me you could."

All the jurors nodded in agreement. "Thank you," responded Randolph. "That's really important to do in this case because just like most things in life, there are two sides to every story. What you hear when we present Mr. Delgado's case will be vastly different from what the State will claim when it puts on evidence. For instance, Mr. King told you Mr. Jones and Mr. Delgado got into an altercation at Rough Riders Bar. The evidence will show Mr. Jones was the instigator of that fight, and he was thrown out of the bar because of it. But there's an even bigger and more important split between the parties as to what the evidence will reveal."

Randolph stopped for a few moments to make certain he had all the jurors' attention. They were all ears, so he continued. "You will hear from Mr. Delgado that he did go to Mr. Jones' apartment after the incident at the bar, and Mr. Delgado will admit he went there to pay Mr. Jones back for having sucker punched him at the bar. Mr. Delgado knows he shouldn't have gone to Jones' residence, but at the time he was infuriated over the unprovoked assault and battery on him by Mr. Jones. Mr. Delgado will testify in detail as to what happened at Mr. Jones' apartment and that he had no part in the attack which took place upon Mr. Jones. You will hear from other witnesses who will corroborate what Mr. Delgado tells you, so please listen to all the evidence before making a decision in this case. We respectfully submit if you do, you will come back with a verdict of not guilty in favor of Mr. Delgado. Thank you."

As Randolph went back to his chair, Judge Brown wasted no time in calling out instructions in a loud and clear voice. "Call your first witness, Mr. King."

King quickly sprung from his chair and announced, "The State calls John McCloud."

Bailiff Harrison scurried out of the courtroom in search of McCloud. He was back in a matter of seconds with the witness. As McCloud walked past the jury box, several of the jurors appeared astonished at the size of the man. McCloud approached the bench, was sworn in by the clerk, and took his seat on the witness stand.

Judge Brown nodded at King to proceed. He quickly complied.

"Please tell us your name and home address."

"John McCloud. I live at 55 Palmer Circle, Lake Park, Florida."

"Do you have a nickname you go by, Mr. McCloud?"

"Yes, people I know call me Big Jake. I guess the reason's obvious," he answered with a laugh. His laughter was echoed by the jury.

King saw Judge Brown intently watching him and decided not to respond as he initially planned. No sense risking the Court's ire this early in the proceedings over an inconsequential matter.

"Where do you work, Mr. McCloud?"

"At Rough Riders Bar in the north end of West Palm Beach."

"What do you do there?"

"I'm one of the bartenders and also one of the owners."

"How long have you worked as a bartender at Rough Riders?"

"Ten years, ever since I bought into the business."

"Were you working on the night of Saturday, December 8, 2012?"

"Yes. I'm always tending bar on Saturdays. I haven't missed a Saturday in five years."

"Do you know the Defendant, Carlos Delgado?" King turned around and pointed at Carlos.

"Yes, I know him."

"How do you know the Defendant?"

"He's one of my customers."

"How long has he been a customer for?"

McCloud scratched his head. "I can't give you an exact time frame. My best recollection is for two or three years."

"How often would Mr. Delgado come into the bar during those two or three years?"

"Normally, it would be on Saturday nights. Not every Saturday night, but maybe a couple of times a month."

"Do you also know a man named William Jones?"

"Yeah, I know him." Big Jake had a look of disgust.

"Is Mr. Jones a customer also?"

"Not any more. He was."

"Was Mr. Jones a customer on the night of Saturday, December 8, 2012?"

"Yes."

"Was the Defendant at the bar that evening as well?"

"Yes."

"Were they there at the same time?"

"Yes."

"How do you recall they were both at the bar at the same time on December 8, 2012?"

"Because they ended up getting in a fight, and I threw Jones out. I remember the date because it was my birthday."

"Did you see the fight?"

"Yes."

"What did you see?"

"I was at the other side of the bar. I didn't hear what was said between Delgado and Jones, but I saw Delgado with his back to Jones, and Jones spinning the stool Delgado sat on around. Then I saw Jones punch Delgado on the side of the face and knock him off the stool onto the floor." McCloud looked over at the jury panel and saw they were all intently listening to him. Some of the jurors were taking notes with the pads they had been given by Bailiff Harrison.

"What did you do when you saw Jones knock Delgado to the floor?"

"I ran over to Jones, picked him up by the back of his shirt collar and pushed him out of the bar. Someone held the door open for me, and when I got to the door I threw him outside. He fell to the ground, picked himself up, and ran away."

"Did you go back and talk with the Defendant?"

"Yes, I asked him how he was."

"What was his response?"

"He said he was okay."

"Did the Defendant say anything else?"

"He asked me if I knew where Jones lived."

"What did you tell the Defendant?"

"I asked him why he wanted to know."

"What did the Defendant say?"

"He told me he was going to pay Jones back for what he did and there was no way Jones was getting away with sucker punching him." Carlos saw some of the jurors watching him. He did his best to keep his poker face on.

"Did you tell the Defendant where Jones lived?"

"No."

"Why not?"

"Because I didn't know where Jones lived. I also told him even if I did know, I wouldn't tell him because it would only cause more trouble, and he should go home and take care of himself."

"What was the Defendant's response?"

"I can't remember his exact words, but it was something like he'd find out somehow and then Jones would pay the price."

"What happened next?"

"He left the bar without saying anything else. What happened after that, who knows?" Big Jake shrugged his shoulders.

"Thank you, Mr. McCloud. I have no further questions."

King sat down, as Randolph approached the podium for cross-examination of Big Jake.

"Mr. McCloud, you mentioned Mr. Jones is no longer a customer at your bar. Why not?"

"Because I had problems with him before then, with him shooting off his mouth. He's loud, and a troublemaker. I warned him several times about not causing issues with other customers." McCloud hesitated for a few moments as he pondered what he said. He quickly added, "But he had never hit anyone before. After he punched Delgado that was the last straw. He was never coming back in my bar again."

"Did you tell him that?"

"Before I threw him out I told him I had warned him before about not acting up, and what did he think he was doing getting into a fight in my bar. So I told him to get out and never come back, and then I threw him out." McCloud angrily shook his head.

"Did Jones say anything to you in response?"

"He didn't say a word. I think he was too scared to open his mouth." Everyone in the courtroom could relate to that sentiment. Big Jake was someone you didn't hassle.

"Did Mr. Delgado have a lot to drink at the bar before the fight started?"

"No, I think he was maybe on his second beer when Jones hit him. Delgado never has a lot to drink in my bar. Two or three beers are it."

"Did Mr. Delgado appear or act like he had been drinking before you served him his first beer?"

"No, he didn't."

"Can you recall how much Mr. Jones had to drink before the fight?"

McCloud shook his head. "No, I really can't."

"Did Jones appear like he might be drunk that night?"

"Not really. If he did, I wouldn't have been serving him." McCloud put his right hand on his head and moved it down his face. "In fact, I think I didn't serve him a drink that night. I seem to recall him walking in, seeing Delgado sitting at the bar, and going over to him."

"Did you hear anything said by Jones or Mr. Delgado?"

"Not a word. I was on the other side of the bar. I really wasn't paying a lot of attention to either of them until I saw Jones spin Delgado's stool around and sucker punch him."

"After you threw Jones out of the bar and you went to see how Mr. Delgado was, did he appear to be hurt?"

"He was groggy, that's for sure. And the side of his face was puffed out where he got hit. It also looked like he was going to get a black eye."

"After Mr. Delgado left the bar, you don't know where he went, do you?"

"No, sir. I have no idea."

"I have no further questions, Your Honor."

"Any re-direct, Mr. King?" asked Judge Brown.

"None, Judge."

"You're excused Mr. McCloud."

"Thank you."

After McCloud left, the Court recessed for fifteen minutes before the testimony continued. Carlos was relieved there were no surprises with McCloud's testimony. Now he waited for the next round.

20

"Call your next witness, Mr. King," instructed Judge Brown.

"The State calls John Morrison to the stand."

Morrison was quickly led into the courtroom by Bailiff Harrison, and sworn in by the clerk. As he took his seat in the "hot box" he was already beginning to sweat. He dreaded being here, but had no choice as King had subpoenaed him to testify. For him, the sooner his testimony was over, the better.

"State your name for the record." King's demeanor changed from how he had questioned McCloud. He was determined to cause Morrison a great deal of anxiety with his questions.

"John Morrison. Everybody I know calls me Johnnie."

"Where do you live?"

"122 McNear Street in West Palm Beach."

"What do you do for a living?"

"I'm a janitor for a private maintenance company."

"Do you know a man named William Jones?"

"Yeah."

"How?"

"He lives across the street from me. So I've seen him around."

"Do you know the Defendant in this case, Carlos Delgado?"

"The name doesn't ring a bell."

In an angry voice, King replied, "That's Mr. Delgado sitting right there," as he pointed to Carlos. "Do you know him, sir?"

"I can't say I know him."

King was becoming testier. In a booming voice, he hollered out, "Have you ever seen Mr. Delgado before today, Mr. Morrison?"

Judge Brown immediately responded, before Randolph could make an objection. "Lower your voice right now, Mr. King. I don't want you screaming at the witness. Is that understood?"

"Yes, Your Honor," replied King in a repentant tone which masked his true feelings. He felt he had begun to accomplish his objective of striking fear into Morrison.

"Mr. Morrison, before today have you ever seen the Defendant, Carlos Delgado?" King's voice was much lower.

"Yeah, I've seen him once before."

"Where?"

"At the Rough Riders Bar."

"When?"

"I think it was sometime last year. I can't give you an exact date." Morrison exhaled deeply as he waited for the next salvo.

"Was it sometime shortly before last Christmas?"

"That sounds about right."

"Was William Jones also in the bar the night you saw the Defendant at Rough Riders?"

"Yes."

"Do you know if Mr. Jones and the Defendant got into a fight that night?"

"Yes, they did."

"Did you see the fight?"

"I didn't see the actual fight."

"What did you see?"

"The first I knew there was an issue was when I heard Delgado and the chair fall down on the floor."

"How far away were you?"

"Delgado was sitting at one end of the bar. I was in the middle. Maybe about thirty feet away."

"What happened next?"

"The bartender, who was a really big guy, came running around the bar. He was hollering at Jones and then took him by the collar and pushed him out of the bar. While the bartender was kicking Jones out, I went over to Delgado and helped him get up. There was another guy who picked him up as well. I don't know his name."

"Then what happened?"

"The bartender came back in and started talking to Delgado. I went back to my barstool and sat down. I don't know what they were talking about."

"Did you see the Defendant leave the bar?"

"Yes."

"Did you follow him outside?"

Morrison lowered his head and hesitated in his response.

"Mr. Morrison, did you understand my question?" This time King's voice was subdued.

"Yes, I followed him out," blurted out Morrison.

"Why did you follow out the Defendant?"

"Because I wanted to talk to him."

"About what?" King worked hard to suppress his smile. He loved what was about to be revealed to the jury.

Morrison's body shook as he responded. "To tell him where Jones lived, in case he didn't know."

"Why did you want to tell him where Jones lived?"

Morrison hung his head and rubbed his hands over his face. He knew the jurors were closely watching him, but couldn't help his reaction. When he spoke, his voice quivered. "Delgado seemed like he wanted to get back at Jones. He was really angry and looked like a guy wanting to even the score. If he did, I was going to let him know where to find Jones."

"Why did you even care, Mr. Morrison?"

Once again, Morrison hesitated in his response. When it finally came, he answered in a low tone, "Because I can't stand Jones and wanted to see Delgado pay him back."

"Did you in fact go outside and tell the Defendant where Jones lived?"

"Yes."

"What did the Defendant say after you told him where Jones lived?"

"He said something like he'd go to Jones' apartment now, and if he was home, it would be too bad for him."

"Didn't you care that something bad might happen to Mr. Jones if the Defendant went to his apartment to confront him?" King was delighted. He did his best not to show it.

"Look," stammered Morrison, "I thought the worst that could happen was Delgado would return the punch. That's all. I never thought anything really bad would happen."

"But something really bad did happen to Mr. Jones, didn't it?"

"I guess so," muttered Morrison.

"I have no further questions of this witness, Judge."

"You may cross-examine, Mr. Randolph," replied the Court.

"Thank you, Your Honor," answered Randolph as he shot out of his chair.

"Mr. Morrison, after you heard Mr. Delgado and the stool he was sitting on fall to the floor, did you notice what Mr. Jones did?"

"Yes, he was standing over Delgado, mocking him. Jones was talking really loud then. I heard him say something like, 'I told you that you're nothing but a little baby. You just got what you deserved. Get up and I'll give it to you again'."

"You told Mr. King in your direct-examination that you couldn't stand Mr. Jones. Why is that?"

"Because Jones is a fool and a bully. He always hassles me with his superman attitude. He's got no friends, only enemies."

"In your answer to Mr. King's question about something really bad happening to Mr. Jones, you said you guess so. You don't know whether Mr. Delgado went to Mr. Jones' apartment and attacked him, do you?"

"No, I certainly don't know that," shot out Morrison in an excited voice. Then he added, "I sure hope Delgado didn't attack Jones."

King jumped out of his seat. "Your Honor, I move to strike Mr. Morrison's gratuitous statement that 'I sure hope Delgado didn't attack Jones' from the record. And I also move the Court to instruct the jury to disregard it."

"Your motions are granted, Mr. King. The statement is stricken from the record." Then, turning her attention to the jury, she stated, "The jury is instructed to disregard Mr. Morrison's statement that he hopes the Defendant didn't attack Mr. Jones." Judge Brown addressed Jack. "Do you have any further cross, Mr. Randolph?"

"No, Judge."

"Any re-direct, Mr. King?"

"No, Your Honor."

"You're excused, Mr. Morrison." As soon as those words came from the Court's mouth, Morrison made a mad dash out of the room.

"Who's your next witness, Mr. King?"

"Josh Wilbur, Your Honor."

Randolph stood and posed a request. "Judge Brown, may counsel approach the bench for a moment?"

"Yes."

Both attorneys quickly stood directly in front of Judge Brown. In a hushed tone, Randolph said, "Judge, I have a legal issue to take up with the Court about some testimony I expect Mr. King will elicit from Mr. Wilbur. May the jury be excused for a few minutes so we can discuss the matter?"

"Is this related to the Motion to Suppress Evidence I previously heard and ruled on?"

"Yes, it is."

"Okay, we'll excuse the jury." The Judge then spoke directly to the jurors. "Ladies and gentlemen, the Court has a legal matter to take up with counsel, so I'm going to have all of you head back to the jury room for a few minutes. We won't be long."

Bailiff Harrison led the jurors out of the courtroom. As he did, Delgado wondered what was going to happen now.

21

"Mr. Randolph, what is it you need to bring up outside the presence of the jury?" Judge Brown was annoyed. She didn't like disruptions in the flow of the trial. But from Randolph's perspective, this conference was important, so much so, he had no choice but to risk the Court's ire.

"When you heard the Motion to Suppress Evidence last month, one of the issues was how much the jury would be allowed to hear about Mr. Delgado's prior conviction for aggravated battery."

"Yes, I recall," responded Judge Brown, as she interrupted Randolph. "And my ruling was, and still is, as long as Mr. Delgado admits in his testimony he has been convicted of a felony one time, the jury will hear nothing further about the nature of the crime. But if the Defendant denies the conviction, Mr. King can impeach him by introducing into evidence a certified record of the conviction. Now what does that have to do with Mr. Wilbur's testimony?" The judge glared at Randolph as she waited for his reply.

"Based on the deposition Mr. King took from Mr. Wilbur, I anticipate Mr. King will ask questions of Mr. Wilbur relating to the altercation which Mr. Jones and Mr. Delgado had two years ago at Newtown Correctional Institution. This incident occurred while Mr. Jones was an inmate, and Mr. Delgado visited there for a four-day retreat as part of a prison ministry team. My specific concern is the jury is not allowed to hear from Mr. Wilbur, or even more importantly, from Mr. Jones or Mr. Delgado when they testify to any evidence regarding the nature of the crime Mr. Delgado was in prison for. I know Your Honor has denied our motion the jury not be allowed to hear any evidence about Mr. Delgado being at Newtown, but the specific nature of what is to be told the jury is what I'm concerned about."

"What's your response, Mr. King?"

King smiled as he answered. "First, Your Honor, all of this is nothing but a rehash of Mr. Randolph's Motion to Suppress Evidence, which you've denied. Secondly, the only inquiries about Mr. Delgado being at Newtown I will ask Mr. Wilbur, Mr. Jones, or the Defendant have to do with the history of bad blood between Mr. Jones and the Defendant. I won't ask any questions to anyone about the nature of the crime Mr. Delgado was convicted of or even how long he was at Newtown. I simply want the jury to know of the long and checkered relationship these two men have, just as I mentioned to them in my opening statement. I believe that information being given to the jury is totally consistent with your prior ruling." King stopped to gauge the Court's reaction.

"You're correct, Mr. King. That's what I want to see happen here. As long as no one crosses the line, and that includes any statements made by any witnesses, we won't have any problems. Has your concern been satisfactorily addressed Mr. Randolph?"

"Yes, Your Honor. Thank you."

"Good. Now, let's get the jury back in here, and Mr. Wilbur on the stand."

Five minutes later, the trial resumed. Josh Wilbur sat in the witness stand. He had been sworn in and was waiting for the questions to begin. He was nervous. Although he had been in court many times as an attorney, this was the first time he was a witness in front of a jury. Adding to his anxiety was the fact King subpoenaed him to testify on behalf of the State against his friend. Josh would answer all questions truthfully, for he was under oath, but he was also determined not to hurt Delgado's case. His legal training would be an invaluable resource to attempt to achieve his goal.

"Tell us your name, please, and where you reside?" King looked at Josh with resolve. He knew of the friendship between the two men and that Josh was reluctant to say anything harmful about Delgado.

"Josh Wilbur, and I live at 58 Rosemont Place, Palm Beach Gardens, Florida."

"What do you do, Mr. Wilbur?"

"I'm a trial attorney and work on civil litigation cases."

"How long have you been a trial attorney?"

"For six years."

"Where do you work?"

"In Palm Beach, at the law firm of Taylor, Archibald, and Hughes."

"How long have you worked with that firm?"

"Ever since I graduated from law school. It's been almost six and a half years."

The preliminaries were over. Now, it was time for King to move to the heart of the matter. He folded his arms across his chest and posed his question.

"Do you know the Defendant, Carlos Delgado?"

"Yes, I know Mr. Delgado."

"How do you know the Defendant?"

"I first met him at a prison ministry team meeting. We were both new members on the team."

"How long ago was that?"

"A little over two years ago."

"What was the prison ministry team meeting about?"

"We were preparing to go into Newtown Correctional Institution in Belle Glade for a four day retreat with some of the inmates. As part of our preparation, the ministry team met once each week for ten weeks."

"Did the prison ministry team go into Newtown?"

"Yes."

"Did the Defendant and you go?"

"Yes."

"Did the Defendant give a talk to the inmates as a part of that retreat?"

"Yes, he did."

"Where at the prison was the talk given?"

"In a large room adjacent to the chapel."

"During the talk, did the Defendant ever mention he was an ex-inmate at Newtown?"

"Yes, he did." King glanced at the jury. He saw in their reactions his point had been made.

"After the Defendant's presentation, was there a break taken?"

"Yes, there was."

"Was the break taken outside the room, on the grounds of the prison?"

"Yes."

"Did you go outside during the break?"

"Yes."

"Did you see the Defendant outside during the break?"

"Yes, I saw Mr. Delgado."

"What was the Defendant doing?"

Josh carefully pondered his answer. He knew King was trying to lead him down a road where he didn't want to go.

"Could you be more specific, please?"

"Sure," fired back King in a patronizing manner. "Was the Defendant by himself, or was he with someone?"

"He was with someone."

"Did you know the person who the Defendant was with?"

"Not at the time."

"Have you come to know who the Defendant was with?"

"Yes."

"Who was it?"

"William Jones." Josh looked over at the jury. He noticed several of them were taking notes.

"What were you doing when the Defendant was with Mr. Jones?"

"I was speaking with an inmate."

"How long did you speak with that inmate?"

"Not long."

"Why?"

Josh hesitated for a few moments, and then quickly answered. "Because I could hear Mr. Delgado and Mr. Jones speaking loudly to each other. It appeared they both were agitated, so I excused myself from the conversation I was having and went over to Mr. Delgado and Mr. Jones."

"Then what happened?"

"I could hear Mr. Delgado question Mr. Jones as to why he called him a hypocrite. Mr. Delgado told him he had done his best to turn his life around since he left prison, and he hoped Mr. Jones would do the same."

"Did Mr. Jones say anything?"

Randolph jumped from his chair. "I object to the hearsay, Your Honor!"

"Sustained. Rephrase your question, Mr. King." Judge Brown strummed her fingers on the bench.

King quickly responded. "Did Mr. Jones appear to accept Mr. Delgado's statement that he hoped Mr. Jones would turn his life around?"

"No, he did not. He became more angry and agitated. I was afraid they would get into a fistfight."

"So what did you do?"

"I stepped between them and asked them to calm down. I told them no good would come out of any altercation and that Mr. Delgado would get thrown out and potentially be arrested. I also told Mr. Jones he would face a disciplinary hearing and possible further prison time."

"What happened next?"

"They both backed off and walked away from each other."

"So there was no fistfight?"

"No, there was not."

"Did Mr. Delgado ever tell you Mr. Jones and he had a bad relationship with each other while they were both in Newtown as inmates?"

"Yes, it was sometime that weekend after the altercation between them."

"No further questions, Your Honor."

"Do you have any cross, Mr. Randolph?"

"Just a few questions, Your Honor." The Court nodded at Randolph to proceed.

"Mr. Wilbur, when Mr. Delgado gave his talk to the inmates, was it well-received?"

"Yes, it was very well-received. I can vividly remember when he finished, there was a lot of loud applause and many happy smiles. Although Mr. Jones may not have been impressed, the rest of the inmates sure acted like they were."

"When Mr. Delgado finished his talk, did he appear to be in a good mood?"

"Absolutely. When he walked by my table to go sit down, he had a huge grin on his face. Everything had gone very well."

"Until the encounter outside with Mr. Jones?"

"Yes." Josh sighed.

"You mentioned Mr. Delgado told you he had a bad relationship with Mr. Jones while they were both at Newtown. Did Mr. Delgado ever say why?"

"Yes. Mr. Delgado said Mr. Jones was always looking for trouble, and he would continually harass Mr. Delgado for no reason."

"Nothing further, Judge Brown."

"Any re-direct, Mr. King?"

"No, Your Honor."

"You're excused, Mr. Wilbur."

"Thank you, Judge." As Josh walked out, his eyes locked with Delgado's. They briefly smiled at each other, although Josh felt his friend's anxiety.

Judge Brown looked at her watch and then addressed King. "Who is your next witness, Mr. King?"

"William Jones."

"I know he will be a lengthy witness. Instead of starting his testimony now, we'll stop for the day. Ladies and gentlemen of the jury, please remember my instructions that none of you are to talk with anyone about this case. Please be back here at 9:00 a.m. tomorrow. Court is adjourned."

22

"How do you think the first day of the trial went?" inquired Robert Williams in a concerned voice. Robert and Carlos sat at the kitchen table in Delgado's house. Carlos delayed his answer until he could finish one of the chocolate chip cookies Robert brought.

"My lawyer told me not to talk about the testimony with anyone while the case was goin' on. I can't say anything about who said what, but I can say I'm happy with the job Randolph's doin' for me. So far we haven't run into any delays. If it stays that way, the trial should be over in two days." Carlos put his hands behind his head and looked at the ceiling. "I hope it's over for good. This whole thing has got me uptight. I hardly slept last night. Maybe, it'll be better tonight."

"I'm glad you're happy with Mr. Randolph. John's got nothin' but good things to say about him. And before I forget, I will try to be at the trial Wednesday afternoon. If I can make it, I'll stay until the verdict. I hope that's okay with you."

"It sure is. I can use all the support I can get. Thanks." Delgado's voice trailed off as he spoke.

Suddenly, Robert's eyes lit up as he thought of what he wanted to share. "There's some good news I'd like to tell you." He waited for Delgado's reaction.

"Go ahead. I can use good news. What is it?"

"It won't be long now before the baby boy we're adoptin' will make his way into the world. The birth mom has already started with some labor pains, and the doctor thinks it could be any time now." Robert's smile lit up the room. Carlos was positively affected by his reaction.

"That's great. Come to think of it, I remember you told me a while back the baby might be born around the time of my trial. I also recall tellin' you I saw that as a good sign. Maybe something good is comin' for both of us." Carlos rubbed his hands together and grinned at the thought. Robert laughed, and for a few precious moments, all the cares of the world evaporated. But reality quickly set back in as Delgado pondered a thought that came across his mind.

"There hasn't been any problems in the adoption with your past felony conviction or with anything else?"

"Not so far. There was a complete background check done on me and Coral as well. In the paperwork we filled out, there's been full disclosure about my conviction and about how I've changed my life since then. A home-study professional named Catherine Walker did a preliminary home study on us, and we passed with flyin' colors. We still have to go to court and have the judge approve the adoption. My lawyer says he doesn't think there will be any problems. The last thing to be done will be a final home study after we get the baby." Robert stopped and pondered what else he wanted to say.

"I was concerned about a possible conflict with Coral as the adoptive mother when she volunteered with the Choose Life office involved in the adoption. Coral vetted the situation with the Program Administrator for Choose Life. She didn't believe there was an issue either, but she called the lawyer who represents the birth mother to make sure he didn't see any problems. The bottom line is the attorney did his due diligence and determined the birth mom freely and voluntarily entered into the adoption with no pressure or influence put on her by Coral, the Program Administrator or anyone else with the Choose Life office. So, with God's help, we'll get through it all."

Robert stopped and looked Carlos straight in the eyes. "And with God's help, so will you."

"Thanks, Williams. I'll give it my best shot to trust in God."

23

"Tell us your name and address, please." It was 9:15 a.m. on Tuesday. King just began to question his first witness of the day.

"My name is William Jones. I live at 115 McNear Street, Apartment 103, in West Palm Beach." All the jury intently watched Jones. They knew from the trial yesterday he was a key witness. He appeared to be a formidable one as well, despite the cane he walked into the courtroom with. He stood 6'3" and weighed 230 pounds. With his size, bald head, and a number of tattoos on his neck and forearms, Jones could easily intimidate many people.

"How long have you lived there?"

"It's been almost a year."

"Where did you live before then?"

"I was in prison at Newtown Correctional Institution in Belle Glade." Jones' voice was deep and raspy. There was not a hint of an apology with regard to his incarceration.

"How long were you at Newtown?"

"Ten years." Jones was nonchalant with his answer.

"While you were at Newtown did you know the Defendant in this case, Carlos Delgado?"

"Yeah, I did."

"Do you see the Defendant here in the courtroom today?"

"He's sitting right here." Jones pointed at Carlos. Delgado remained stone-faced, as did Randolph.

"Your Honor, may the record reflect Mr. Jones has pointed at and identified the Defendant?"

"The record will so reflect," answered Judge Brown.

"How did you know the Defendant at Newtown?"

Jones snickered. "How else would I know him? He was an inmate." Another scoff emerged from Jones.

"How would you describe your relationship with the Defendant while you were at Newtown?"

Jones arched his eyebrows in quizzical fashion. "What's that mean?"

"Did the two of you get along with each other?" King hoped the question would now make sense to the witness. He wasn't disappointed.

"Are you kidding me, man? We couldn't stand each other." Jones showed his disgust as he looked straight at Delgado. There was no visible response from Carlos.

"Why couldn't the two of you stand each other?"

Jones shook his head from side-to-side. "How much time you got? I could go on for hours."

King was irritated with Jones' comment, but did his best to get Jones on track. "We don't have hours for you to tell us why the Defendant and you couldn't stand each other. Would you please tell us some of the main reasons?"

Jones folded his arms across his chest, and then rubbed his right hand up and down his neck. "To start with, I'm black and Delgado is Puerto Rican. I was one of the top dogs with the black brothers I stuck with. Delgado hung a lot with other Puerto Ricans, and most of the inmates in those two groups didn't like each other. That's one of the reasons but not the main one."

"What's the main one?"

"Delgado thought he was a real tough guy. He was always bragging about being a martial arts expert. He'd go around the yard when there wasn't any guards watching doing all these stupid karate moves like we were supposed to be afraid of him, but I sure wasn't scared of him. He was a punk. Still is." Jones again looked squarely at Carlos. This time Carlos momentarily bit his lip, but then put his game face back on. Delgado knew the jurors were eyeing him.

"Did you and the Defendant ever get into a fight while the two of you were at Newtown?"

"We came close a lot of times, but then some guard always came around, and we'd back off. Neither of us wanted to be put in the hole. But there was one time when no guard was present, and I let him have it for mouthing off to me."

"Explain what happened please."

"Delgado was putting on his antics with his karate moves. I told him to quit before I stopped him. He started insulting me, telling me I couldn't stop him from doing anything. He told me if I tried, he'd smoke me. So I let him have it."

"How did you do that?"

"I threw a punch at him, and knocked him over." Jones grinned at the memory.

"Then what happened?"

"He got up and tackled me like he was some kind of linebacker. But there wasn't much there. I jumped back up and was ready to deliver another hit on him. Fortunately for him, a guard came around the corner then. We scattered, and nothing else happened."

"After the Defendant was released from Newtown, did you ever see him again at the prison?"

"Yeah, I think it was around a couple of years ago."

"How did you happen to see the Defendant then?"

"He was some kind of part of a Christian ministry team that came into Newtown for a retreat. I don't know why they let someone like him come in with them, but he did."

"Did you go to the retreat?"

"Sure. Why not? I didn't have anything better to do. And I always heard from inmates who had gone before about how good the food they brought in was. There sure ain't any good food the prison feeds you." Jones looked over at the jury and smiled. The gesture wasn't returned.

"So you saw the Defendant during the retreat?"

"Unfortunately, not only saw him, but had to listen to him as well. He was giving some talk to the inmates who went. It wasn't much that's for sure." Jones chuckled.

"Do you remember what the talk was about?"

"It had to do with him being so happy since he got out of prison. He made a big deal about how God was now watching over him because he had turned his life around. I didn't buy into any of it. It was all for show, and the inmates sitting at the table with me thought the same thing." Jones appeared disgusted.

"After the talk ended, was there a break taken outside on the prison grounds?"

"Yes."

"Did you see the Defendant then?"

"Yeah, I did. He was standing by himself. I guess nobody wanted anything to do with him. Anyway, I went up to him to tell him what I thought about what he said."

"What did you tell him?"

"I told him he was a hypocrite and he should never have come into the prison with the ministry team. I also told him a fool like him was never going to change."

"What was the Defendant's response?"

"He gave me some bull about trying his best to turn his life around since he got out. Then he had the nerve to tell me he hoped I would do the same." Jones was now angry as he recalled the conversation.

"What did you say to the Defendant after he told you that?"

"I told him not to worry about me – he needed to take care of himself. I said to him all his talking was nothing but a big act because he always liked being the center of attention. And all he was trying to get was attention."

"What happened next?"

"We were ready to get it on with each other, but some skinny, white guy from the ministry team stepped between us and warned us about the trouble we'd both be in if we got into a fight."

"So what happened?"

"We backed off and went our separate ways. After that, I didn't go near Delgado for the rest of the weekend. I was glad when he left."

"I'm going to change topics now, Mr. Jones."

"Okay."

"Earlier in your testimony you told us you've been out of prison for about a year."

"That's right."

"Were you able to get a job after you got out?"

"Yeah. My brother owns a trucking company. He hired me to work in his warehouse, loading and unloading trucks. After I got my driver's license back, I was able to get a commercial license to drive trucks for him. I started out with short hauls, and, after I was doing it for awhile, I started driving cross country." Jones stopped and put his head in his hands. Then he looked over at Judge Brown and addressed her. "Judge, before I get asked any more questions, can we take a break? I'm feeling light-headed right now."

"Yes, we can take a recess, Mr. Jones. Court will be adjourned for fifteen minutes."

After the jury left, Jones wobbled from the witness stand with his cane. He refused any help as he left the courtroom and took a seat on a bench outside the room. He held his head in his hands and would not speak with anyone.

Fifteen minutes later, Jones was back on the stand. The Judge and jury were seated, and King stood at the podium, ready to resume his questioning.

"Are you feeling okay to continue, Mr. Jones?" asked Judge Brown.

"Yeah, let's do it." Jones shook his head from side-to-side.

"Did there come a time after you were released from prison you came into contact with the Defendant?" King waited to see how Jones would respond to his inquiry. He hoped Jones would be able to carry on in an effective manner.

"Yeah, unfortunately." Jones grimaced at the thought. "It was on a Saturday night, sometime last December. I can't give you an exact date."

"Where did you see the Defendant?"

"At a bar near my apartment called Rough Riders."

"Do you recall what time it was?"

"Sometime after eleven p.m. I remember getting home from a long haul, taking a shower, and leaving around eleven to go have a few drinks."

"What happened when you got to the bar?"

"After I walked in, I looked around to see if anyone I knew was there. I spotted Delgado sitting on a stool at the bar. I couldn't believe it!" Jones' temper began to flare. "I walked over to where he was and tapped him on the shoulder."

"Why?"

"Because I still had unfinished business with him from the last time I saw him at Newtown."

"What happened after you tapped him on the shoulder?"

"I reminded him I was about to pop him out in the yard before the little choir boy minister stepped between us. I told Delgado he was lucky because he would have gotten the beat down he deserved."

"What was the Defendant's response?"

"He told me to leave him alone and get away from him. Then he turned his back on me." Jones was livid.

"What did you do?"

"I spun around his chair and took him by the collar. I told him he deserved what he was about to get. Then I popped him."

"What happened then?"

"He fell off the chair onto the floor. I told him to get up and fight like a man, but he stayed there like the baby he is. The next thing I know I'm attacked from behind by the bartender who pushed me out of the bar."

"What did you do?"

"I left and went home. I didn't want to be in that place if they were going to protect Delgado."

"Did you go straight home?"

"No, I made a stop at a convenience store that was open late to pick up some cigarettes and beer."

"How long were you in there?"

"There was a long line, and only one clerk was working. Maybe ten to fifteen minutes."

"And then you went home?"

"Yes."

"What did you do when you arrived at your apartment?"

"I went in, turned on the kitchen light, and put the beer in the freezer and the cigarettes on the counter. Then I went into the living room and turned on the TV. I came back to get the cigarettes, and headed back to the living room to watch some shows. Then all of a sudden it happened." Jones became frenetic.

"What happened?"

"I felt these hits across the back of my head. It was like my head was on fire. The pain was unbearable. Then everything went blank. When I woke up, I was in the hospital." Jones shivered as he recalled the trauma he experienced.

"How long were you in the hospital?"

"Three weeks."

"Did you have to have an operation when you were in the hospital?"

"Yeah. They had to repair my skull because it was fractured. I don't remember what the name of the operation was."

"Your surgeon will testify about that," stated King as he looked at the jury. "After you were discharged from the hospital, did you go home?"

"No, I was at a rehab place for almost three months."

"What problems did you experience that you were sent to a rehabilitation center?"

"A lot. Terrible headaches, dizziness, I couldn't sleep well. I felt tired all the time, and sometimes when I tried walking, I'd fall over. I also had problems with my vision being blurred."

"Have those issues stopped since you were discharged from the rehabilitation center?"

"No, they haven't. They're not as bad, but I still have them. That's why I'm walking with this cane."

"Have you been able to return to your job?"

"Not yet. I'm on disability. The doctor's not sure when I can return to work."

"The night you were attacked, did you have a tool box in your apartment?"

"Yes."

"Were there wrenches in your tool box?"

"Yeah, there were a lot of wrenches."

"I have no further questions of Mr. Jones, Judge."

"Before we start cross-examination, let's take a ten-minute recess," replied the Judge.

24

As Randolph stood at the podium to begin his cross, Carlos hoped his lawyer would discredit Jones. Randolph wanted nothing more. He was aggressive from the get-go.

"You testified on direct-exam when Mr. Delgado and you got into a fistfight at Newtown it was you who threw the first punch, correct?"

"Yeah, that's right."

"You also testified when you saw Mr. Delgado at Rough Riders Bar, it was you again who threw a punch at Mr. Delgado, right?"

"You got it." Jones smiled. It wouldn't last long.

"And you hit Mr. Delgado those two times because in your opinion he had disrespected you and deserved a beat down, correct?"

"It wasn't my opinion," snarled Jones. "It was a fact."

"Everything you've ever said to Mr. Delgado is a fact, while anything Mr. Delgado ever said to you is disrespectful, isn't it, Mr. Jones?"

King jumped from his seat. "Objection, Judge. Mr. Randolph is arguing with the witness."

"Overruled," replied the Court. "Answer the question, Mr. Jones."

Jones was irritated. "The truth's the truth. Delgado's a bum. Nothing that comes out of his mouth is true, and he's always out to agitate someone or to show off. That's the feeling of a lot of guys who knew him in prison."

"And that includes the inmates at your table when Mr. Delgado spoke at the prison ministry retreat, correct?"

"All the inmates at the table agreed he was nothing but a hypocrite. None of them bought into his routine."

"Did you notice any inmates at the retreat who seemed to appreciate Mr. Delgado's talk?"

"Not really."

"Josh Wilbur testified in this case yesterday. He's the prison minister you called the skinny white guy who stepped between you and Mr. Delgado before a fist-fight broke out."

"Okay. So what?"

"Mr. Wilbur told the jury Mr. Delgado's talk was well-received by the inmates. He said there was a lot of loud applause, many happy smiles, and the inmates acted like they were impressed. Was what Mr. Wilbur told the jury wrong, Mr. Jones?"

"Yeah, I think so. I didn't see or hear any of that."

Randolph looked over at the jury to see if his point about Jones lack of veracity had been made. Jurors Jose Frias and Jeff Bronson nodded at him. That was a good sign for Randolph.

"Let's switch gears for a few minutes and talk about the night you saw Mr. Delgado at Rough Riders Bar."

"Go ahead."

"When you walked in and saw Mr. Delgado you went straight over to him to confront him about your unfinished business from Newtown, right?"

"That's right. I needed to set the record straight."

"So you tapped Mr. Delgado on the shoulder, and when he turned around, you let him have it verbally, correct?"

"Right again."

"And in response, Mr. Delgado told you to leave him alone and get away from him. Then he turned his back on you, is that fair to say?"

"That's what happened."

"And then you spun around the stool Mr. Delgado sat on and sucker punched him, didn't you?"

"No, that's wrong. First, I spun around his stool and then grabbed him by the collar. And then I told him he deserved what he was about to get. Then I punched him. So it was no sucker punch. He had plenty of time to defend himself. He was too scared. Nothing new there."

"Yesterday, John McCloud, the bartender at Rough Riders whose nickname is Big Jake testified to the jury about you hitting Mr. Delgado."

"Oh, yeah. What did he have to say?"

"Mr. McCloud told the jury he saw you spin the bar stool around and sucker punch Mr. Delgado. Was Mr. McCloud wrong too, just as Mr. Wilbur was?"

"There was no sucker punch. McCloud's wrong too." Jones was indignant.

Randolph looked over at the jury again. Both Frias and Bronson nodded at him again. This time they were joined by juror Donna Bradley. Another good sign for Randolph.

"Mr. McCloud also said after he saw you sucker punch Mr. Delgado, he came running over to you and asked what you were doing getting into a fight in his bar. Then he stated he warned you before about making trouble, picked you up by your collar, pushed you out the door, and told you never to come back. He also testified someone else held the door open and he threw you out with such force you fell down, got up, and ran away. Do you agree with Mr. McCloud's testimony?"

"No, I don't," answered Jones in a troubled voice.

"What don't you agree with?"

"I don't remember him saying anything to me about prior trouble or never to come back. He attacked me from behind and pushed me out the bar. I don't remember falling down or running away. I left because if they wanted to protect Delgado, I didn't want to be there."

"Didn't Mr. McCloud disrespect you, Mr. Jones, by attacking you from behind, throwing you out of the bar, and protecting Mr. Delgado?"

Jones hesitated before he gave his answer. "Yeah, he did."

"Then why didn't you put him in his place like you did with Mr. Delgado?"

Jones shook his head. "Look, man, I ain't no fool. You saw the size of the guy. I wasn't about to take him on. Besides, if he wanted Delgado there, I didn't want to be."

"So after you were thrown out of the bar, you went home. But first you stopped at a convenience store to get some beer and cigarettes, right?"

"Yeah."

"And because there was a long line with one clerk, you were in there about ten to fifteen minutes?"

"That sounds right."

"As I understand your testimony on direct when you arrived at your apartment, you went in, turned on the kitchen light, and put the beer in the freezer and the cigarettes on the counter."

"Yes."

"Then you went into the living room and turned on the TV."

"That's right."

"After that, you came back to get the cigarettes, and headed back to the living room to watch some shows."

"Correct."

"And then all of a sudden you felt these hits across the back of your head. It was like your head was on fire. The pain was unbearable. Then everything went blank, and when you woke up, you were in the hospital."

"That's what happened."

"When you first got home, did you unlock your door with your apartment key, or was the door unlocked?"

"From what I recall, when I left I was in a hurry to get to Rough Riders for a couple of drinks. I had gotten back from a long haul, and really needed them. So, I took off as fast as I could, and shut the door, but I didn't lock it."

"Weren't you concerned about leaving the door unlocked?"

"Back then, not really. I didn't have any problems with people trying to get into my apartment, and neither did anyone else in the building. Now, it's a different story. I go nowhere without first locking my door, and when I get back, I lock it as soon as I get in."

"After you got in the apartment on the night of the attack, did you lock the door?"

"I don't really remember. Again, I wasn't all that worried about it back then."

"Do you recall whether you fully closed the door after you went in?"

"You know, it's possible I didn't. I was carrying a case of beer, and from what I remember, I sort of pushed it with my shoulder after I walked in. It may not have shut all the way."

"Describe for us the way your apartment is arranged when you walk in the front door."

"When you open the door, the kitchen is on the right side. On the left is a wall that goes on for maybe fifteen feet. Beyond that, on the left is the door to my bedroom and on the right is my bathroom. The living room is in the back of the apartment."

"Where were you in the apartment when you were attacked?"

"I was beyond the area where the bedroom and bathroom are, at the beginning part of the living room."

"Based on what you've described about the layout of your residence, it seems as though the person who hit you was in the apartment before you got there and either came from the bedroom or bathroom area. Or that individual came from outside the front door into your apartment and hit you as you were walking into the living room."

"I'd say yes to that. I don't know how else it could have happened."

"And I want to verify you never saw the person who hit you, is that correct?"

"Yeah, that's correct. I never saw who it was."

"You mentioned having a toolbox in your apartment, with wrenches in it. Where was the toolbox located on the night of the attack?"

"I brought it in earlier that night when I returned from my cross country haul and left it on the kitchen counter, a few feet inside of the front door."

"The Sheriff's Department has shown you the wrench used to hit you, correct?"

"Correct."

"And that wrench came from your toolbox, didn't it?"

"That's right." Jones shook his head in disgust.

"The night of the attack did you have any money on you?"

"No, I spent it all on the beer and cigarettes."

"Did you have any cash you left in the apartment?"

"I think there was around a hundred dollars in my bedroom. I really don't remember exactly how much."

"Was the money taken from your apartment the night of the attack?"

"I told the Sheriff's Deputy who talked to me while I was in the hospital about the money. They came and looked for it, but didn't find any, so it must have been taken the night I was hit."

"My cross is concluded, Your Honor."

"Thank you, Mr. Randolph. Any re-direct, Mr. King?"

"No, Judge."

"You're excused, sir." Jones got up and left without saying a word. He slowly lumbered out, and looked at no one. The same was not true of the jury. All of them were closely focused on Jones as he exited the courtroom. Carlos was greatly relieved Jones was gone, but he was flustered thinking about the jury possibly being sympathetic to him.

Bailiff Harrison approached the bench and handed Judge Brown a note from her judicial assistant. After reading it, the Judge said, "Counsel and members of the jury, I have an emergency matter I need to take care of now. I won't be too long. Let's take a thirty-minute adjournment." Judge Brown hustled out of her chair and quickly disappeared through the door behind the bench.

25

"Please state your name and address for the record." King smiled at the witness.

"My name is Latoya Johnson. I live at 115 McNear Street, Apartment 107, West Palm Beach, Florida."

"How long have you lived there, Ms. Johnson?"

"It will be three years next month."

"What do you do for a living?"

"I'm an elementary school teacher at West Palm Beach Elementary School. I teach third grade."

"Are you married?"

"No, I'm single."

"Do you know a man named William Jones?"

"Yes."

"How do you know Mr. Jones?"

"He lives in the same apartment building as me, in Apartment 103."

"How long have you known Mr. Jones?"

"Ever since he moved in. I think it's been around a year."

"Are you aware of Mr. Jones being attacked in his apartment on the evening of Saturday, December 8, 2012?"

"Yes, I am."

"How are you aware of that?"

"I'm the one who called the police about it."

"Please explain to us what you know about the attack on Mr. Jones." Johnson had all the jurors' undivided attention as she began her answer.

"I went out that night with some friends to see a movie. I got back to the apartment building around 11:45 p.m. My apartment is two doors down from Mr. Jones. As I walked past Mr. Jones' door, I noticed it was open. There was a light on in the kitchen. When I looked inside, I couldn't believe what I saw." Johnson became emotional and struggled to continue. Her feelings, although sincere and heartfelt, were nothing compared to what Carlos experienced. He was petrified.

"Take your time, Ms. Johnson. When you're ready, tell us what you saw," responded King in a soft voice.

"Mr. Jones was down on the floor on his stomach, and there was a man crouched over him with a wrench in his hand." Johnson trembled and looked down at the floor.

"What happened then?" King was delighted with the way the witness's testimony was unfolding.

"I screamed as loud as I could. And when I did, the man dropped the wrench and ran out of the apartment. On his way out, he bumped into me and almost knocked me over." King saw the jury absorbing every word of Johnson's testimony.

"Did he speak to you, or did you speak to him?"

"No."

"Did you get a good look at the man who you saw crouched over Mr. Jones and then run from the apartment and bump into you?"

"I sure did."

"Do you see that man in the courtroom today?"

Carlos took a deep breath. He struggled mightily to control his emotions, but managed to keep his best game face on. Randolph fared better. He had been through moments like these many times in his career.

"Yes, he's in the courtroom. That's him sitting at the table over there, in the brown shirt with the brown sports coat." All the jurors intently focused their attention on Delgado. Although he knew this moment was coming, now that it arrived, he was devastated. He didn't know how Randolph would overcome Johnson's testimony. Thoughts of returning to prison invaded his mind. He was sinking ever deeper into an abyss from which a return seemed impossible.

"Judge Brown, I move the Court to have the record reflect Ms. Johnson has identified the Defendant in response to my question."

"The record will so reflect, Mr. King."

"Thank you, Your Honor." King turned his attention back to the witness.

"Ms. Johnson, what happened after the Defendant bumped into you?"

"He sprinted out of the building within seconds, but I don't know where he went."

"What did you do after the Defendant left?"

"Right after the Defendant ran out, two other tenants came out of their apartments and walked over to me. They wanted to know what was going on, so I told them what I had seen, and we all went into Mr. Jones' apartment together. He appeared to be unconscious, and I immediately called the police on my cell. They were there within minutes. Then the paramedics came and took Mr. Jones to the hospital."

"That's all my questions," Judge Brown.

"You may cross examine, Mr. Randolph."

Randolph stepped to the podium deep in thought. He knew he needed to be short and sweet with his cross. The last thing he wanted to do was alienate the jury, especially when Carlos would take the stand and admit to what Johnson testified about. Still there were a few key points to be made.

"Ms. Johnson when you first came into the hallway of the apartment building, it was around 11:45 p.m., correct?"

"Yes."

"And you were by yourself, right?"

"That's right."

"When you looked into Mr. Jones apartment, you never saw Mr. Delgado hit Mr. Jones with the wrench did you?"

"No, I did not."

"So there's no way for you to know who hit Mr. Jones with the wrench, is there?"

"No, there's not."

"For all you know, someone else could have come into the apartment before Mr. Delgado and struck Mr. Jones with the wrench?"

"I have no way of knowing whether that's true or not."

"Before the night of December 8, 2012, you had never seen Mr. Delgado had you?"

"No, I had not."

"So when Mr. Delgado bumped into you, you didn't know who he was, correct?"

"That's correct, I didn't know him."

"Thank you Ms. Johnson. I have no further questions."

"Any re-direct, Mr. King?"

"No, Judge."

"Thank you for coming, Ms. Johnson. You're excused."

As she exited the courtroom, Randolph and Delgado quietly discussed Johnson's testimony and their strategy.

26

"Who's your next witness, Mr. King?"

"Deputy Sheriff Anthony Maxwell, Your Honor."

Bailiff Harrison was out the door in a flash and quickly returned with the witness. After Deputy Maxwell was sworn in, King began his questions.

"Please tell us your name and address."

"My name is Anthony Maxwell, and I live at 5305 Mango Court, Loxahatchee, Florida."

"What's your occupation, sir?"

"I'm a Deputy Sheriff with the Palm Beach County Sheriff's Office."

"How long have you been a Deputy Sheriff?"

"Ten years."

"Please explain to us what your job responsibilities have involved for the past ten years."

"For the first five years, I was assigned to duty in a patrol car. The area I covered was in western Palm Beach County. Five years ago, I became a crime scene investigator and have worked in that capacity ever since."

"What is it you do as a crime scene investigator?"

"When a violent crime takes place, involving either death or serious bodily injury, I'm one of a number of investigators who may be called to the scene to undertake an inspection of what occurred, to examine, obtain, and preserve evidence and to work on the case until an arrest is made."

"Is there normally a lead investigator for each case involving a violent crime?"

"Yes."

"Let me focus your attention on the evening of Saturday, December 8, 2012. On that night did you investigate a crime scene at an apartment building located at 115 McNear Street, in West Palm Beach?"

Maxwell momentarily looked at a file he had brought to court with him and then responded quickly. "Yes, I did, but the call didn't come in until almost midnight. So by the time the other officers and I arrived it was shortly after midnight on the morning of December 9, 2012."

"Were you the lead investigator?"

"Yes, I was."

"Were you the first officer to arrive at the scene?"

"No, when I arrived three deputies were already there."

"Please explain to us what you saw and what you did after you arrived at the crime scene."

His nerves frayed, Carlos held his breath as he waited for the answer. Maxwell, however, was as calm and collected as could be. His dozens of court appearances over the years made testifying nothing to be anxious about.

Maxwell responded in a deep voice which went hand-in-hand with his muscular physique and outgoing personality. "After I arrived, I went to Apartment 103 and saw the victim on his stomach down on the floor. He was unconscious, but none of the other officers moved him. Instead, they called the paramedics who came a few minutes after me. Before the paramedics got there, I spoke with the other officers about a wrench lying on the floor a few feet from the victim. No one touched the wrench, and a fingerprint expert from the Sheriff's office was called to the scene to make an investigation about fingerprints on the wrench and elsewhere in the apartment. The other officers briefed me on what they learned from a witness who saw a man run from the apartment. Then the paramedics arrived and transported the victim to the hospital."

"Did you learn the name of the victim?"

"Yes, his name is William Jones."

"What else happened that night as part of your investigation?"

"I interviewed the female witness who saw the man run from the apartment. Maxwell looked at the file he brought with him. "Her name is Latoya Johnson. I also took statements from two men who came out of their apartments after they heard Ms. Johnson scream. Neither one of them saw anything."

"Did the fingerprint expert from the Sheriff's Office come to the scene that evening?"

"Yes, he arrived just as the victim was being taken out of the apartment by the paramedics to the hospital."

"What is his name?"

"Roger Flanagan."

"What did Mr. Flanagan do after he arrived?"

"When he came in, I immediately showed him where the wrench was lying on the floor."

"Did you touch it?"

"No, and neither did any of the other officers who came to the apartment. And I verified with Ms. Johnson and the two other male residents I spoke with none of them touched the wrench either."

"What did Mr. Flanagan do with the wrench?"

"After he put on a pair of gloves, he picked the wrench up and put it into an evidence bag. When he left the apartment that night, he took the wrench with him to the lab to collect fingerprints and other evidence from the wrench."

"What else did Mr. Flanagan do that evening?"

"He dusted the apartment for fingerprints."

"What other actions were taken in the apartment that night?"

"The other officers and I made a thorough search of the apartment looking for any clues which might exist to help us determine who the perpetrator was."

"Was anything found?"

"No."

"Where there any pictures taken at the crime scene?"

"Yes, one of the deputies took a number of pictures, including some of Mr. Jones lying on his stomach on the floor."

"Did you bring some of those pictures with you today?"

"Yes, I did."

"May I approach the witness, Your Honor, to see the pictures?"

"Yes."

After King reviewed a number of the pictures, he selected two of them showing Jones lying on the floor with the wrench next to him. The pictures were admitted into evidence without objection by Randolph. King then asked for and received the Court's permission to show the pictures to the jury. Delgado closely scrutinized each juror's reaction as the photographs were passed among them. He wasn't happy with what he saw.

King continued with his interrogation. "Did you talk with Mr. Jones about the attack?"

"Yes, but it wasn't until several days after the assault took place."

"Why so long?"

"I first tried speaking with him on Sunday morning, but he was still unconscious. When I went back on Monday he had regained consciousness, but his doctor told me he was in critical care and unable to be interviewed for at least a couple of more days. So I waited until Wednesday and went back. I was able to speak with him, but he was groggy, and I didn't stay long. A week later I did complete a full interview with him."

"Was there anything you learned from Mr. Jones that was helpful to you in your investigation?"

"The main thing of interest was he got into an altercation earlier in the evening with the Defendant at Rough Riders Bar, but by then we already knew it."

"How did you know?"

"The Defendant came with his attorney to the Sheriff's Department and turned himself in on the Monday after the attack."

Carlos looked over at the jury and saw they were all fixated on him. He wanted to crawl into a hole.

"Who did the Defendant surrender to at the Sheriff's Office?"

"Me."

"How did that come about?"

"Mr. Randolph, the Defendant's attorney, called our office and advised he wanted to come in with his client regarding the attack on William Jones. I was called immediately to meet with them as I was the lead investigator on the case."

"Did you meet with them?"

"Yes."

"What happened?"

"Mr. Randolph did quite a bit of the talking, but he let the Defendant tell me his version of the events, and he allowed the Defendant to answer all my questions."

"What did you find out as a result of the meeting?"

"The Defendant claimed he was minding his own business sitting at the bar at Rough Riders when Mr. Jones approached him in a hostile manner, verbally chastised him, and then sucker punched him. The Defendant also told us Mr. Jones was thrown out by the bartender. After that, according to the Defendant, he left the bar and was told by a person he knew only as Johnnie where Mr. Jones lived. The Defendant admitted he went to Mr. Jones apartment to pay him back for the sucker punch." Maxwell looked at his file before he continued. "The Defendant also claimed once he got to the apartment, he saw the door partially open and went in. Once inside, he turned on a light switch in the kitchen because it was dark and saw Mr. Jones on the floor lying on his stomach. The Defendant also asserted he approached Mr. Jones to see if he was okay and noticed a wrench lying on the floor next to him."

As Maxwell continued on, Delgado felt his head spin. He saw the jury was captivated by the testimony and began to become convinced there was no way he would walk out from the courtroom a free man. His mind suddenly went back to Robert Williams' advice that Carlos cast all his anxiety upon God because He cares for you. Delgado felt nowhere else to turn and tried his best to give up his concerns to the Lord. He momentarily closed his eyes as Maxwell's rendition of what Delgado told him concluded. He was grateful the topic was finished, but there still were many more moments of fire to face in the courtroom.

"After the meeting with the Defendant and his attorney was concluded, what happened next?"

"I consulted with my superiors and also with your office, and it was determined charges of aggravated battery upon Mr. Jones would be filed against the Defendant."

"I have no further questions of Deputy Maxwell, Your Honor." King slowly walked back to his chair. He was very pleased how the testimony developed.

"You may cross-examine, Mr. Randolph," responded Judge Brown.

As Jack took his place at the podium, he noticed all the jurors watching him. He smiled and then began his cross. There weren't many points he wanted or needed to make with Maxwell.

"Deputy Maxwell, you never interviewed any witnesses who saw Mr. Delgado strike Mr. Jones, did you?"

"No, sir, I did not."

"When you interviewed Mr. Jones in the hospital, he told you he left around a hundred dollars in cash in the bedroom in his apartment before he went to Rough Riders Bar on the night of the attack, correct?"

"Yes, that's correct."

"Did you or the other deputies search Mr. Jones' bedroom the night of the incident?"

"Yes, we did."

"Did you find any cash in there?"

"No, we did not."

"After Mr. Jones told you about having some cash in his apartment, what did you do?"

"I returned to the apartment to search his bedroom again to make sure there wasn't any money in there."

"Did you find any money?"

"No, I did not."

"What conclusion did you come to after you returned to the apartment and found no money?"

"That whatever cash Mr. Jones had in his bedroom was taken by someone on the night of the attack."

"Do you know who that someone is?"

"No."

Carlos felt a surge of adrenaline rush through his body. He hoped the jury would use this testimony for his benefit.

"In your testimony on direct-examination, I believe you stated Mr. Delgado came with me to the Sheriff's Office on the Monday after the attack and turned himself in."

"Yes, I did."

"But Mr. Delgado didn't really come to turn himself in. Didn't Mr. Delgado come with me to tell the Sheriff's Department what he knew about the attack?"

"Objection, Your Honor. Counsel is arguing with the witness," hollered out King.

"Overruled. And keep your voice down, Mr. King. I've warned you about speaking so loudly once already," scolded Judge Brown.

"Yes, Judge," King meekly replied.

"Please answer the question, Deputy Maxwell," instructed the Judge.

"I'd have to say your statement is more correct than how I phrased it on direct."

"Thank you, Deputy Maxwell," responded Randolph. "And it's fair to say during the course of the meeting among Mr. Delgado, you, and me, Mr. Delgado fully cooperated with you, isn't it?"

"Yes, that would be fair to say. The Defendant told me his version of the events and answered all of my questions."

"I have no further questions, Judge Brown."

"Any re-direct, Mr. King?"

"No, Your Honor."

"You're excused, Deputy Maxwell. Ladies and gentlemen of the jury, we'll take a lunch break now. Please be back in one hour."

Neither Delgado nor Randolph wanted anything to eat. They went inside a conference room next to the courtroom to discuss the morning's events. King, on the other hand, hustled over to a Clematis Street eatery to enjoy a pizza with some colleagues from his office. He couldn't wait to share the details of how the trial was progressing. From his perspective, it was a slam dunk.

27

"Please tell us your name and where you live." King grinned at his witness.

"My name's Roger Flanagan. I live at 555 South Sycamore Street in Boca Raton, Florida."

"Where do you work, sir?"

"I work at the Palm Beach County Sheriff's Office on Gun Club Road in West Palm Beach."

"What's your job?"

"I am a forensic fingerprint specialist."

"What is a forensic fingerprint specialist?"

"A forensic fingerprint specialist is a person who uses his education, knowledge, and experience to analyze fingerprint, and in some cases, footprint clues left at crime scenes."

"What is your educational background?"

"I received a Bachelor of Science degree in 1998 from the University of Maryland. My major was investigative forensics."

"What does the term forensic science mean?"

"Forensic science is sometimes referred to as medical jurisprudence. It's any aspect of science as it relates to the law. In the context of what I do, it's the application of scientific method to solving mysteries." Flanagan looked over at the jury and smiled. His testimony had already begun to captivate the jurors.

"After you received your degree in 1998, where did you go to work?"

"At the Palm Beach County Sheriff's Department. I've been there for fifteen years."

"Have you had the same job as a forensic fingerprint specialist for the past fifteen years?"

"Yes, I have."

"As part of your job, do you investigate crime scenes?"

"That's what I do." Flanagan smiled again and then quickly added, "Of course, there's a lot of follow-up work done in our crime lab as well as testifying as an expert witness in court."

"Are you able to give us an approximate number of crime scenes you have investigated over the course of your fifteen-year career?"

Flanagan stopped and thought about the answer. He was doing the math in his head. "An approximate number is in excess of two thousand."

"Have you testified before in court as an expert witness?"

"Yes, many times."

"About how many times? An estimate is fine."

Flanagan again pondered the answer. He put his hand on his chin, and then replied, "I'd estimate my expert testimony as being in excess of three hundred times."

Carlos watched the jury. They appeared to be spellbound by Flanagan's testimony. The thought made him sick to his stomach. "Your Honor," called out King. "I tender Mr. Flanagan as an expert witness in the area of forensic fingerprint analysis."

"Mr. Randolph, do you have any questions of the witness as to his background?"

"No, I don't, Judge, and we stipulate that the witness is qualified as an expert."

"The Court accepts Mr. Flanagan as an expert witness in forensic fingerprint analysis. You may proceed, Mr. King."

"Mr. Flanagan were you called out to an apartment building located at 115 McNear Street in West Palm Beach in the early morning hours of Sunday, December 9, 2012, to investigate a crime?"

Flanagan thumbed through the file he brought with him. "According to my notes, I arrived at that location at 12:15 a.m. on December 9, 2012, and went to Apartment 103."

"What did you see when you arrived?"

"There were four deputies in the apartment. The paramedics were also there and were getting ready to move a man who was lying on his stomach on the floor onto a stretcher to transport him to the hospital. Deputy Anthony Maxwell saw me come in and called for me to come over to where he was standing. He pointed to a wrench lying on the floor next to the victim."

"What did you do then?"

Flanagan again glanced at the notes in his file. "I asked Deputy Maxwell whether any of the deputies or paramedics touched the wrench and received a negative answer. Then I put on a pair of plastic gloves and took out an evidence bag I had with me. I picked up the wrench, placed it in the evidence bag, marked the bag by date and location, initialed it, and took the bag to my car so I could take it back to our lab for fingerprint testing. I locked my car and went back inside the apartment."

"Then what did you do?"

"I dusted the apartment for fingerprints."

"Please explain to us how the process works."

"I dusted objects such as door handles on the inside and outside doors, dressers in the bedroom, and other areas a perpetrator might have touched. I dusted those areas by applying a fine powder or dust to locate fingerprints. The dust clings to the oils left behind by ridges on the edge of human fingerprints. I then lifted the print off the objects by applying a piece of adhesive tape, thereby lifting off the dust in the pattern of the fingerprint and pressing this into place on fingerprint cards. Then I put the fingerprint cards into an evidence bag."

"What did you do next?"

"I went back to our office and gave the wrench and the fingerprint cards from the apartment to our evidence clerk to be locked up. On Monday afternoon, I got the evidence bags from the clerk. Then I lifted fingerprints from the wrench, and did a lab analysis on both the wrench and fingerprint cards by using computer software and microscopic imaging. Subsequently, I loaded the fingerprints into our state and national databases."

"Was there anything else you did as part of your investigation?"

"I'm trying to remember. Let me look at my file." Flanagan quickly perused his notes. "Now I recall. It was Monday afternoon when Mr. Delgado came to the Sheriff's Office with his lawyer to meet with Deputy Maxwell. Shortly after the meeting concluded, it was determined that charges for the attack would be brought against Mr. Delgado. When he was booked, his fingerprints were taken, and I was able to compare them to the fingerprints I found on the wrench and on objects at the apartment."

"What did the comparison show?"

"Mr. Delgado's fingerprints were on both the wrench and the outside door handle. And they were also on a kitchen light switch."

Carlos gulped. He knew this moment was coming, but now that it arrived, the reality of it struck with double the force of the blow delivered by Jones at Rough Riders. How would he survive such seemingly damning testimony?

"Were you subsequently able to match up the Defendant's fingerprints with the wrench, door handle, and light switch in some other way?"

"Yes."

"How?"

"As an ex-convict, the Defendant's fingerprints showed up in our state database. That served to additionally confirm the Defendant's fingerprints were on the wrench, outside door handle, and light switch."

"Speaking of the wrench you lifted fingerprints from, did you bring it with you today?"

"Yes, I have it here in the evidence bag I used to store it in the night of the attack."

"What size wrench is it?"

"It's a good-sized one. It's open ended on both sides. One side is 15/16 inches and the other side is 1 inch."

"Since the night you put the wrench in the evidence bag, when the wrench was not in your possession, where was it?"

"Locked up in the evidence locker at the Sheriff's Office."

"Did anyone other than you and the evidence clerk have access to the wrench?"

"The only time it was accessed by anyone other than me for investigative purposes was when Mr. Randolph and you came to take my deposition at the Sheriff's office."

"Did either Mr. Randolph or I take the wrench out of the evidence bag and touch it?"

"No, sir. The wrench was in the bag at all times during the deposition."

"Your Honor, I move the wrench into evidence as the State's Exhibit number 3."

"Any objections, Mr. Randolph?"

"None, Judge."

"The wrench is admitted into evidence as the State's Exhibit number 3 without objection."

"I have no further questions, Your Honor." King was gleeful as he sat down.

Delgado was the polar opposite of King. He desperately hoped for his lawyer to bring out the proverbial smoking gun.

"Mr. Flanagan, you have no way of knowing if Mr. Delgado struck Mr. Jones with the wrench, do you?" Randolph's voice was elevated, but not to such a degree that Judge Brown would intervene.

"Well, I know that his fingerprints were on the wrench, the outside door handle, and the light switch."

"I realize that, sir," answered Randolph in an irritated voice, "But there were also other fingerprints on the wrench, the outside door handle, and the light switch weren't there?"

"Yes, that's right."

Randolph looked over at the jury, as did Delgado. They both saw all of them paying close attention to the cross.

"Let's talk about the outside door handle, first."

"Okay." Flanagan was nonchalant. He had been through this trial process far too many times to become unnerved.

"Besides Mr. Delgado's fingerprints, you also found Mr. Jones' fingerprints on the outside door handle, correct?"

"Correct."

"But there were also four other fingerprints on the door handle that you could not and still cannot identify, correct?"

"Yes, that's also correct."

"And you aren't able to tell us when any of those fingerprints were put on the door handle, are you?"

"No, I can't."

"With regard to the wrench, besides Mr. Delgado's fingerprints, you also found Mr. Jones fingerprints on the wrench, right?"

"Yes, that's right."

"And you also found two other sets of fingerprints on the wrench that you cannot identify, can you?"

"No, I can't."

"And once again, you are unable to tell us when any of those fingerprints were put on the wrench, is that fair to say?"

"Yes, that's fair to say."

"Regarding the light switch, you found Mr. Delgado's fingerprints on there, correct?"

"Yes."

"Besides Mr. Delgado's fingerprints, you also found Mr. Jones fingerprints on the light switch, correct?"

"Correct."

"But there were also three other fingerprints on the light switch that you could not and still cannot identify, correct?"

"Yes, that's also correct."

"And you aren't able to tell us when any of those fingerprints were put on the light switch, are you?"

"No, I can't.

"Did you find Mr. Delgado's finger prints anywhere else in the apartment?"

"No."

"And that includes Mr. Jones bedroom, right?"

"Yes."

"But you did find two other sets of fingerprints on the handle to the top drawer of Mr. Jones dresser, didn't you?"

"Yes, I did."

"One of those set of fingerprints is Mr. Jones, correct?"

"Yes."

"And you cannot identify the other set of fingerprints on the top drawer of the dresser, can you?"

"No, I can't."

"But you do know the set of fingerprints on the top drawer of the dresser matches up to fingerprints on the outside door handle, on the light switch, and on the wrench, right?"

"Yes, that's right."

"So the same person, whom you are unable to identify, touched the outside door handle, the wrench, the light switch, and the top dresser drawer in Mr. Jones apartment, correct?"

"That is correct."

"I have no further questions of this witness, Your Honor."

At last, Carlos felt a glimmer of hope. It was now King's turn to sweat. He considered asking some questions on re-direct, but quickly decided against it. Judge Brown dismissed the witness.

28

"How many more witnesses do you have, Mr. King?" Judge Brown squinted as she posed the question.

"One more, Judge. Dr. John Spencer."

"Is he outside now?"

"Yes, Your Honor."

"Please get the witness, Bailiff Harrison," instructed the Court.

A minute later, Spencer was sworn in by the court clerk. As he sat down, he looked at Judge Brown and smiled. The gesture was returned in a similar fashion. Spencer previously testified in Brown's courtroom on many occasions. She was always impressed with his scholarly knowledge and ability to communicate complicated medical evidence in a simple way to the jury.

"Please tell us your name and where you live?" King seemed almost in a festive mood. He couldn't wait for the jury to hear Spencer's testimony.

"My name is Dr. John Spencer, and I live at 2388 Old Dominion Road, Delray Beach, Florida."

"Where do you work, Dr. Spencer?"

"I am a neurosurgeon on staff at St. John's Hospital in West Palm Beach. I also have my own private practice as a neurologist. My office is in Delray Beach."

"Please explain to us what neurology is."

"Neurology is the branch of medicine concerned with the study and treatment of disorders of the nervous system."

"You mentioned you were both a neurologist and a neurosurgeon. What's the difference between the two?"

"Neurologists treat disorders affecting the brain, spinal cord, and nerves. Examples would be headache, movement, and seizure disorders. Neurologists do not perform surgery. They refer patients to a neurosurgeon. A neurosurgeon is a physician who specializes in the diagnosis and treatment of disorders of the central and peripheral nervous system. Neurosurgeons perform surgery as part of the treatment of a patient."

"Is there a difference in the educational requirements between the two fields?"

"Yes, both fields require four years of pre-med and then four years of medical school. After graduation from medical school, neurologists have a one-year internship in medicine or surgery, followed by three years of specialty training in a neurology residency program. Neurosurgeons, after graduation from medical school, have a one-year internship in general surgery, and then between five to seven years in a neurosurgery residency program."

"Please explain to us what your educational background is."

Randolph slowly rose from his chair to address the Court. "Judge Brown, in the interest of time, the Defendant stipulates Dr. Spencer is an expert in the fields of neurology and neurosurgery."

"I appreciate the Defendant's stipulation," answered King, "but we have plenty of time, and the jury is entitled to know Dr. Spencer's qualifications to testify in this case."

"You're correct, Mr. King," responded the Court. "I'll accept the Defendant's stipulation to Dr. Spencer being an expert witness, and I'll allow you to continue on with questions about Dr. Spencer's qualifications."

"Thank you, Judge." King turned his attention back to the witness. "Please tell us about your educational background."

"I received my Bachelor of Science degree from Harvard University in 1970. I then went to Harvard Medical School and received my M. D. in 1974. After graduation, I participated in a one-year residency in surgery at Johns Hopkins Hospital, followed by three years of specialty training at the same institution in a neurology residency program."

"What was your class rank while at Harvard undergrad and then medical school?"

"I was number three in undergrad school and number two in my medical class."

"After you completed your three years of specialty training in neurology, what did you do next?"

"I went to work for a neurology practice in Baltimore, Maryland, and worked with them in private practice for five years."

"Then what did you do?"

"I decided to also become a neurosurgeon. I went back to Johns Hopkins and completed a five-year neurosurgery residency program."

"What did you do next?"

"In 1988, I came to work for St. John's Hospital here in West Palm Beach as a neurosurgeon. I've been there ever since. I have also maintained my own private practice in neurology since 1990."

"Can you give us an estimate as to how many surgeries you have performed in your career as a neurosurgeon?"

Spencer answered without blinking an eye. "In excess of twenty-five hundred."

Carlos saw how impressed the jury appeared to be with Spencer's qualifications, and Spencer's easy-going and down-to-earth personality helped form a bond with them. Even Delgado couldn't help but be fascinated by this physician.

"Have you testified before in court as an expert witness in the field of neurosurgery or neurology?"

"Yes, I have."

"Are you able to estimate how many times?"

"Yes. In excess of two hundred times."

"I want to change topics now."

"Sure."

"Do you have a patient named William Jones?"

"Yes."

"Did you bring your file for Mr. Jones with you?"

"Yes." Spencer picked up a thick medical file and waved it at King.

"Did you perform surgery on Mr. Jones?"

"Yes, I did. It was at St. John's Hospital."

"When was the surgery?"

Spencer looked in his file. "Surgery was performed on Mr. Jones beginning at 5:15 a.m. on Sunday, December 9, 2012."

"Why was the surgery performed?"

"Mr. Jones had suffered a traumatic brain injury as a result of being hit on the back of his head by a hard instrument."

"Did you know what kind of an instrument it was?"

"Not at the time surgery was performed. Later on, I found out from the police a wrench was used to cause the brain trauma."

"Could you tell from your examination of Mr. Jones and the surgery you performed how many times he was hit on the back of the head?"

Spencer thumbed through his file. "Yes, he was struck on the back of the head with a great deal of force three times."

"You said Mr. Jones suffered a traumatic brain injury. Was there a degree of severity of the brain injury you would categorize it as?"

"Yes. Brain injuries can be categorized as mild, moderate, severe, or catastrophic. In Mr. Jones case, he suffered a moderate brain injury."

"Please explain to us what a moderate brain injury is."

"A moderate brain injury occurs when a person has been unconscious for up to twenty–four hours. Mr. Jones was unconscious from when he arrived and was still unconscious when the anesthesia was started. Based on the information we received from the police, Mr. Jones was attacked around 11:45 p.m. So there was already over a five-hour period of unconsciousness before the surgery was started."

"How was it determined surgery was needed for Mr. Jones?"

"A screening neurological exam was performed which showed signs of increased intracranial pressure. Also, a CT scan of the brain was done. We determined the patient's skull was fractured and surgery was necessary."

"Please explain to us what the surgery involved?"

"After anesthesia was administered, the patient's head was shaved and a scalp incision made in the area in the back of his head where the damage was most extensive. The scalp was then retracted from the bone of the skull. A craniotomy was performed next as a piece of skull was cut off and put aside. The exposed dural membrane was carefully cut. We found bits of bone embedded in the brain tissue. These fragments were removed, and the hemorrhaging was stopped. The dura was then carefully sutured back over the brain. Because there was extensive skull damage, the skull flap we removed was not put back. Instead, a hardened plastic plate was placed over the brain to protect it from further injury."

Carlos watched the jury as the details of the surgery was revealed. Several of them had grimaced as Spencer described the operation. Delgado felt like vomiting as he thought about the jurors being sympathetic for Jones and convicting him.

"After the surgery was completed, how long did Mr. Jones remain in the hospital?"

Spencer looked at his file and immediately answered. "Three weeks."

"Did he go home then?"

"No, he was unable to properly care for himself. He was suffering from terrible headaches, and fatigue due to a lack of sleep. He would sometimes fall over when he walked, and he also experienced problems with his vision being blurred, so he was sent to a rehabilitation center for further treatment."

"How long did he stay at the rehabilitation center?"

"I believe he was there for about three months. Let me check my file." Spencer thumbed through his notes. "Yes, that's correct. It was just short of three months."

"Are you still treating Mr. Jones?"

"Yes, I am."

"Is he able to return to work?"

"Not at the present time. He's still experiencing headaches, dizziness, fatigue, and blurred vision. I've prescribed different medications for him to take, and they are helping; but he's not ready or able to resume his job yet. I can't tell you right now as to when he might be able to go back. We'll just have to wait and see how everything develops. When a person such as Mr. Jones suffers a traumatic brain injury, the results sometimes follow him for the rest of his life."

"I have no further questions for Dr. Spencer, Judge Brown."

"Do you have any cross, Mr. Randolph?"

Randolph quickly came to a decision. There wasn't much he could get from Spencer that would be helpful to his case. In fact, asking more questions might do more harm than good. Except for one inquiry. "I have one question for the witness," answered Jack as he stood up and remained at counsel table. "Dr. Spencer, there's no way for you to know who attacked Mr. Jones, is there?"

"No. There's no way for me to know."

"Thank you, sir." Randolph sat back down.

"You're excused, Dr. Spencer." After he left the courtroom, Judge Brown continued. "Do you have any further evidence, Mr. King?"

"No, Your Honor. The State rests."

"Do you have any motions, Mr. Randolph?"

"Not at this time, Judge."

"Both counsel please approach the bench."

As the Judge and two attorneys spoke quietly to each other, Delgado's mind raced. He couldn't understand what was happening and imagined no good would come out of this conference no one else could hear, other than the court reporter, who was diligently recording everything being said.

"Ladies and gentlemen of the jury, we're going to break early for the day," announced the Court. "I need to conclude the emergency matter from earlier today. Counsel for both parties confirmed with me we will have no problems in finishing the trial tomorrow. Court stands adjourned." Brown quickly left the courtroom.

It would be a long and sleepless night for Delgado, but before he went home, he would go again to Randolph's office to prepare for his trial testimony one last time. Any chance of success depended greatly upon how Carlos testified, particularly under the fire of cross King would bring.

29

"Slow down, Lydia! I want to make it safely to the hospital with the baby." Lourdes touched her stomach as she experienced another contraction. It was Tuesday at 11:00 p.m., and the Castillo sisters were headed to Palms Way Hospital in western Palm Beach County. Before Lydia could respond, Lourdes changed her mind. "No, never mind. Speed it up. I don't want to give birth in this car. You sure wouldn't know what to do."

Lourdes was becoming feistier as the labor pains increased in duration and intensity. Although her sibling was giving Lydia a hard time, she didn't want to respond in kind. Lydia bit her lip and spoke calmly. "Take it easy, honey. We're only ten minutes away. Everything is going to be fine." Lydia smiled and looked over at Lourdes. The gesture was not returned.

"That's what you say, but you're not the one having this baby. I am. And right now, I'm really scared." Lourdes was on the verge of tears.

Lydia searched for the right words to try to comfort Lourdes. After a few moments, she responded by telling her sister, "I know you're scared, but you've got a great doctor who's delivered thousands of babies. I'll be in the room with you, and so will Coral, just as you asked."

Lydia's cell phone rang. "Speaking of Coral, this is her calling." Lydia quickly answered and was off the phone in thirty seconds.

"What's going on?" asked Lourdes in a distressed tone. "She's still coming, isn't she?"

"Of course, she's coming. Mr. Williams is driving. They're only about five minutes behind us, so chill out, sis." Lydia winked and grinned at Lourdes. Instead of taking her sister's advice, Lourdes immediately fired off another question.

"Mr. Williams is not going to be in the room, is he? Not that I don't like him, but I don't think he should be there when the baby's born."

The question, accompanied by the serious look on her sister's face, caused Lydia to shake her head and laugh.

"What's so funny?" demanded Lourdes. She became more and more irritated.

"Your question made me laugh. Of course, Mr. Williams won't be in the birthing room. The only man who will be there is Dr. Sheppard. Mr. Williams will be waiting outside until after the baby is born."

"Good."

An hour later, Lourdes was in the hospital birthing room. Lydia, Coral and Dorothy Arcuri, the nurse assisting Dr. Sheppard, were in the room with Lourdes. Dr. Sheppard left to check on another patient. Before going, he predicted it wouldn't be much longer before the baby was delivered. Robert Williams was in a waiting area down the hall from the birthing room. He was alone in the room and intently read his Bible when he felt a hand touch his shoulder. He looked up as he heard a voice speak.

"It's good to see you here, Mr. Williams."

"Anthony Davis," replied Robert in a surprised tone. "What are you doing here so late at night?"

"Lourdes called me a few hours ago to tell me Lydia was bringing her to the hospital to have the baby. I told her I'd call after I woke up to see if the baby was born, but I wasn't able to go to sleep, so I decided to come here and wait. After all, the baby is being named Anthony." The young man beamed with delight.

"Well, I'm glad you're here. I can use some company. This waitin' around is not easy." Suddenly, a different thought came into Robert's mind. "Did you ask your parents if it was okay for you to come here now?"

"Yes, sir. I know better than to go out late at night without clearing it with them."

"Good man." Robert decided to change the subject. "Coral's told me you and Lourdes are datin'. I think that's great."

"She's a wonderful lady. We really hit it off, and I hope it stays that way."

For the next twenty minutes, Robert and Anthony discussed a variety of subjects as they waited for word on the baby's delivery. While they were talking, Coral appeared.

"Anthony, I'm glad you're here. Now Robert has someone to pray with him for Lourdes and the baby. Dr. Sheppard's in the room. The baby will be here any minute. I've got to get back." Coral raced out of the room.

Robert and Anthony took each other's hands. Robert began to pray for the health and safety of Lourdes and the baby. When he was finished, Anthony added his prayers. Just after Anthony finished his petitions to the Lord, Coral returned. She jumped into Robert's arms. Tears of joy flowed down her face.

"We have a beautiful baby boy! God is so good! It's time for the two of you to come and meet him."

Robert and Anthony quickly followed Coral to the birthing room. Coral already told the Castillo sisters Anthony was here. When the three of them entered the room, they saw Lourdes holding the infant. It was a scene of intense joy and thanksgiving. A baby was spared from abortion, and a new life was now in the world. God's hand in the birth of this child was unmistakable.

Lourdes gave baby Anthony to Coral to hold. Robert and Anthony stood on each side of her, while Lydia held Lourdes' hand. Dr. Sheppard already left to check on another patient, while the nurse momentarily stood in the corner watching with delight everyone's reactions.

"What a beautiful child! I can see his mother's face in him. Thanks for what you have done for us, Lourdes! And thank you too, Lydia." Robert stopped speaking and wiped away the tears running down his face. The entire room was overcome with emotion by the appearance of this precious child of God. Nurse Arcuri gently took the baby from Coral to record his weight and length.

"I can't wait to hear how big this boy is. He looks like he's going to make a great athlete." Anthony anxiously waited for the news.

Nurse Arcuri smiled as she announced the results. "He's sure large enough to be a football player. He weighs 9 pounds, 6 ounces and is twenty inches long."

"That's one big boy!" exclaimed Robert. "I can't wait to teach him how to throw a football."

30

As Carlos Delgado slowly walked to the witness stand, he silently prayed for the strength to persevere against the tremendous pressure and fear he was experiencing. He tried his best to cast all his anxieties upon God, but giving up his worries was far from easy. He felt the glare of the jurors as he took his oath and sat down in the "hot seat." Jack Randolph stood at the podium and unobtrusively nodded at him in an effort to encourage his client. Whether the gesture worked remained to be seen.

"Tell us your name please, sir."

"Carlos Delgado," he answered in a tepid voice. Carlos knew he needed to do much better to respond in a firm and sincere manner.

"And where do you live, Mr. Delgado?"

"759 Mary Street, West Palm Beach, Florida." This time the reply was more forceful and self-assured. Randolph nonchalantly nodded at Delgado again to confirm he was now on the right track.

"How long have you lived there, Mr. Delgado?"

"About a year and a half."

"Do you own the home?"

"Yes, I do."

"Are you married?"

"No, I've never been married."

"Where do you work, Mr. Delgado?"

"I work for Ramrell Air Conditioning Company in West Palm Beach."

"How long have you worked there?"

"It's been a little over two years."

"What are your job responsibilities?"

"I'm a service technician. Mostly for the bigger commercial accounts. Sometimes I work on residential a/c units, if the boss needs me to help out with a home."

"Do you like your job?"

"Yeah, it's great. And so is Mr. Ramrell."

"Have you done well working at the company?"

"I think so, and so does my boss. He's given me a bunch of raises and bonuses since I've been there." Carlos looked at the jury as he answered. They were all stoic. He knew he needed to work harder to try to get them to like him, and more importantly, to believe him.

"When were you born?"

"January 2, 1970."

"Where did you grow up?"

"In the Fort Lauderdale area."

"Did you have any brothers or sisters?"

"No. I'm an only child."

"Are your Mom and Dad still alive?"

Delgado looked down at the floor and then at Randolph. "No, they're both dead."

"What do you enjoy doing in your spare time?"

King quickly stood up. "Your Honor, the question is irrelevant and immaterial. I object."

Randolph fired back without hesitation. "Judge Brown, I'm trying to elicit some background information about Mr. Delgado the jury is entitled to hear. I don't have much more in this area."

"I'll give you some leeway, Counselor. Proceed."

"Thanks, Judge." Turning his attention to his client, Randolph asked, "Do you remember the question?"

"Yes. What I enjoy doin' in my spare time is to exercise, either runnin' or workin' out on a weight machine in my garage. On Sundays, a friend of mine in charge of a Bible class in the morning at a church in Pahokee comes to my home in the afternoon to study the Bible together. I find the time with him goin' over the Bible encouragin'." Carlos looked over at the jury. One of the female jurors seemed impressed. Her reaction bolstered him, at least for the time being.

"I want to change topics now." Carlos looked at Randolph with wide eyes. He knew they were about to get into the crux of the case.

"Do you know a man named William Jones?"

"Yes, I do."

"How do you know Mr. Jones?"

Delgado swallowed hard and looked at the jury. He was determined to do his best to convince the jurors of his innocence. "I met him when I was in prison at Newtown Correctional Institution."

"Had you been convicted of a felony?"

"Yes."

"How many times have you been convicted of a felony?"

"Once."

"And how many times have you been in a prison or jail?"

"Only the one time."

"How long has it been since you were released from Newtown Correctional Institution?"

"It's been a little over three years."

"You heard Mr. Jones testify in this case about his contact with you at Newtown, didn't you?"

"I sure did." Carlos appeared appalled.

"Do you agree with what he said?"

"I don't agree with most of it."

"Okay. I'm going to ask you some questions about Mr. Jones' statements and see what you agree and disagree with."

"Fire away." Carlos sat on the edge of his seat in anticipation of the questions. The jury saw he was eager to tell his side of the story, and they couldn't wait to hear it.

"Mr. Jones told the jury the two of you couldn't stand each other while you were both in Newtown. Do you agree?"

Delgado hesitated and pondered his answer. Then he quietly said, "Yeah, I agree. Neither of us liked the other from the first time we laid eyes on each other."

"One of the reasons Mr. Jones mentioned is he is black and you're Puerto Rican, and most of the inmates in those two groups didn't like each other. Is that correct?"

This time Carlos wasted no time in responding. "That's dead wrong. While I was at Newtown, I was friends with a lot of the black guys. Jones was one of the few exceptions."

"What was the reason, from your perspective, as to why Mr. Jones and you couldn't stand each other?"

"Jones was always shootin' off his mouth about how tough he was, and if you didn't do what he said, he'd threaten to lower the boom. He didn't scare me, and I never took any of his bull, so there was always a tension between us."

"What about Mr. Jones testimony you were the one who thought he was a tough guy and always bragged about being a martial arts expert? That you'd go around the yard when no guards were watching and try to intimidate inmates with your karate moves? Do you agree?"

"Absolutely not. That never happened." Carlos looked straight at the jury as he answered.

"Mr. Jones also testified one time when no guard was present, he let you have it for mouthing off to him. Do you recall the testimony?"

"I sure do," replied Carlos in a disgusted manner.

"Do you agree?"

"No way. It was nothing like he said."

"What did happen?"

"The only thing Jones said that's right was there were no guards around. He came up from behind me and shoved me so hard I fell to the ground. Then he started bad mouthin' me, so I got up and tackled him, and was on top of him. I was ready to let him have it when one of the inmates hollered out a guard was around the corner. So I jumped up and split. Jones ran off in the opposite direction. And that was the end of the fight."

"Mr. Jones also talked about how after you were released from Newtown you went back there as part of a Christian prison ministry team. How did you become a part of the team?"

"A guy I knew in prison who was released before me became a prison minister. After I got out, he talked to me about becoming a member of the team, and I accepted. So when the group went into Newtown for a four-day retreat, I went with them."

"And did you speak at the retreat?"

"Yes."

"What was the reason you spoke?"

Carlos again directly eyed the jurors as he spoke. He became more confident as his testimony continued. "The leader of the team asked me to talk about my life outside after I was released. I said okay."

"What was the message you wanted to give the inmates?"

"That I tried to turn my life around since being let out of prison. I talked about how the men on the prison team and some other friends were gettin' me into a relationship with God. I wanted to show the inmates I was doin' better than before on the outside, and they could too when they got out." When Carlos looked over at the jurors, several of the women smiled at his statement. Their reaction boosted his spirits.

"Do you believe your message was well received?"

"It seemed like it to me. There was a lot of applause, and when I returned to my seat, several of the inmates slapped me on the back."

"Was there a break after you talked?"

"Yes, most of the inmates and team members went outside to get some fresh air. I was one of them."

"You heard Mr. Jones' testimony about how you and he got into a confrontation while you were outside?"

"Yeah, I sure did." Delgado shook his head as he recalled the incident.

"Tell us what happened?"

"I finished talking to one of the inmates I knew and walked back toward the building where the retreat took place. I saw Jones coming toward me with a disgusted look on his face. When he gets up to me, he starts in about what a hypocrite I was. He wanted to know how a prison ministry team would let a bum like me come into prison with them. It was one insult after another. I couldn't stand it anymore and let him know what I thought."

"What did you tell him?"

"That I hoped he would turn his life around like I was tryin' to do. I told him he really needed to find God in his life, or else when he got out, he'd be right back in prison again."

"What was Mr. Jones reaction?"

"He became hostile, and started back up with more insults. We were about to get into a fist-fight when Josh Wilbur stepped between us and calmed us down. Fortunately, we walked away from each other, and that was the end of the conflict. Or so I thought." Carlos let loose with a sigh of utter exasperation.

"Are you talking now about the night at Rough Riders Bar?"

"Yes, I am."

"Was that the first time you had any contact with Mr. Jones since the incident at Newtown?"

"Yes, it was. I wish it never happened."

Carlos hung his head. Randolph quickly decided it was time to ask the Court for a break.

"Judge Brown, we're about to change topics. May we have a short recess before we continue?"

"Good idea, Mr. Randolph. Court will be adjourned for ten minutes."

Delgado was relieved. He needed a few minutes to refocus his thoughts and calm down before the barrage of questions started again.

31

"Mr. Delgado, are you familiar with a bar in West Palm Beach named Rough Riders?"

"Yes, I am, Mr. Randolph."

"How?"

"It's only a short distance from my house, maybe about a mile. Sometimes on Saturday nights, I'd walk there to have some beer."

"How long have you been a customer at Rough Riders?"

"Since I bought my house about a year and a half ago."

"Did you go to Rough Riders every Saturday night?"

"No. I'd say maybe every other week."

"Do you recall being at Rough Riders on the evening of Saturday, December 8, 2012?"

"I sure do." Carlos began to tremble, but then he stopped. Now was not the time to show any fear to the jurors.

"What time did you arrive at Rough Riders on December 8, 2012?"

"It was around eleven at night."

"What happened when you arrived?"

"I looked around to see if there was anyone I knew. I didn't recognize any of the people in there, so I went to the bar and ordered a brew from the bartender, Big Jake."

"Did Big Jake and you have a conversation?"

"Just some small talk. Then he moved down the bar to wait on other customers."

"What happened next?"

"There was no one I knew, so I sat by myself. I guess because I didn't have any one to talk to I drank the first beer pretty quick. I got another beer from Big Jake and started to drink it. All of a sudden, I felt someone push me real hard on my shoulder. When I turned around and saw it was Jones, I couldn't believe it. Before I could say a word, Jones lit into me with his bad mouth. The insults wouldn't stop comin'."

"What did he say to you?"

"He started goin' on about the last time he saw me at Newtown and what a hypocrite I was. That I didn't deserve to be on any prison ministry team and how I was lucky the 'skinny, choir boy minister,' as Jones called him, stepped between us, or I would have gotten a good beat down. And I would have deserved it." Carlos stopped and shook his head. Painful memories of that night were again resurfacing.

"What did you say to Mr. Jones?"

"I told him I was there to have a couple of beers and not to get into any arguments. I asked him to please leave me alone and let me enjoy my beer. Then I turned back around and couldn't see him."

"What happened next?"

"All of a sudden, he spun my stool around and immediately hit me on the side of the face. I never saw the punch comin'. It was hard enough I fell off the stool onto the floor. Then he stood right over me calling me names. I was shook up from the punch so I can't tell you exactly what he said." Carlos was agitated, and his face became beet red. Randolph knew he quickly needed to calm his client down.

"Take your time, Mr. Delgado. I know this is hard for you to talk about."

King thought briefly about objecting to Randolph's statement but decided against it.

Carlos picked up on Randolph's cue and looked over at the jury. He calmly continued. "The next thing I remember was Big Jake grabbin' Jones and tossin' him out of the bar. I was still on the floor, and two guys helped me to my feet."

"How did you feel when you got up?"

"Awful. I couldn't see straight, and I felt shaky. I could feel the side of my face was puffed up, and it really hurt."

"Did you talk to anyone about what happened?"

"Only to Big Jake."

"What did you talk about?"

"He wanted to know how I was, and I told him I was okay. I think he said something else to me about Jones, but I can't really remember what it was." Carlos stopped and took a deep breath before going on. "I do remember askin' him where Jones lived."

"Why did you ask him that, Mr. Delgado?" Randolph hoped the answer would come out as well as in their trial preparation sessions.

"Because I was very angry at Jones for sucker punching me for no reason. I wanted to pay him back for what he did to me. I realize now how stupid it was for me to want revenge, but at the time I was really hurt and not thinkin' right."

"Did Big Jake tell you where Mr. Jones lived?"

"No, he didn't know where Jones lived. So I left the bar."

"Did you come to find out where Mr. Jones lived?"

"Yes."

"How?"

"One of the guys who picked me up off the floor followed me out and told me where he lived."

"Was that John Morrison who testified here in court?"

"Yes, although at the time he only told me his first name."

"Why did Mr. Morrison tell you where Mr. Jones lived?"

"Because he said he couldn't stand Jones and wanted me to put him in his place."

"Did you go to Mr. Jones' home?"

"Yes." Carlos looked over and saw all the jurors were busy taking notes. He hoped it was a good sign.

"Where did Mr. Jones live?"

"It was about a half mile away from the bar in the opposite direction of my house."

"Do you remember the address?"

"Yeah, it was 115 McNear Street, Apartment 103."

"How long was it before you got there?"

"It took awhile because I was walking slowly trying to dust off the cobwebs. Maybe twenty to thirty minutes."

"What did you do when you got there?"

"I walked up the steps to the front door. It was unlocked so I went in. I looked for Apartment 103. There was a number on the door so I stopped in front of it. I saw the door was open a few inches. I pushed the door open and went inside." Carlos looked directly at his lawyer as he answered.

"Tell the jury what happened when you went inside Mr. Jones' apartment, Mr. Delgado."

Carlos took the signal from Randolph and immediately directed his attention to the jury. Although he quivered inside, he was determined to do his best to answer the question. He knew this was do-or-die time.

"After I went in, I saw someone down on the floor. It was dark, and I couldn't tell who it was. So I looked around for a light switch and turned it on. Then I saw it was Jones. He was on his stomach and the back of his head was bloody. I went over to him to see what was wrong and tried shakin' him to wake him up. But he wouldn't wake up. Then I saw a wrench on the ground and picked it up."

"Tell the jury why you picked up the wrench."

Carlos kept his focus on the jurors as he calmly continued. "At the time, I didn't even think about whether I should pick it up or not. I just did it. I couldn't figure out what happened to Jones or why the wrench was next to him, so I picked it up."

"Tell the jury what happened next."

"Right after I picked the wrench up, I heard a scream from the doorway. I never closed the door after I went in, and when I looked back, I saw this woman. And she just kept screamin'. I panicked, threw the wrench down, and ran out of the apartment. On the way out, I bumped into her, and just kept goin'. I never stopped runnin' until I got home."

"Did you attack Mr. Jones with the wrench, Mr. Delgado?" All eyes in the courtroom were on Carlos as he prepared to answer.

"No, absolutely not," Delgado emphatically cried out. "Jones was already down on the floor when I walked in. I never hit him with a wrench or anything else."

"What did you do after you got home when you ran from Mr. Jones' apartment?"

"I put ice on my face where it was hurtin' and also on my eye because I had a black eye. Then I tried sleepin', but I couldn't get much rest. I was really shook up from bein' hit by Jones. Then seein' him on the floor and hearin' the woman's screams really got to me." Carlos shook as he answered.

"What happened on Sunday?"

"On Sunday during the day and at night, I kept thinkin' I needed to see a lawyer and tell him what happened. First thing Monday morning, I went to John Taylor's law office. Taylor's a friend of mine, and I wanted to talk to him and get his legal advice. Taylor ended up referring me to you, and then Taylor and me went to your office on Monday morning."

"After you came to my office, I agreed to represent you?"

"Yes."

"And then you and I went to the Sheriff's Office to tell them what happened?"

"Yes."

"Did you cooperate with the Sheriff's Department in their investigation?"

"Yes, I did. I told them what happened, and answered all the questions I was asked."

"You didn't have anything to hide, did you, Mr. Delgado?"

"No, I did not."

"Judge Brown, I have no further questions of Mr. Delgado."

"Okay. Let's take a fifteen-minute break."

As Carlos left the stand, his eyes locked with King. The prosecutor had a sly grin on his face. He couldn't wait to get Delgado back on the stand. Carlos, on the other hand, wanted only for this nightmare to conclude.

32

As Delgado sat at the witness stand waiting for King to begin his cross, he felt his heart race. He knew this was the most important part of his testimony, and King would do everything possible to discredit him. Suddenly, the rear courtroom door opened and a giant of a man came in. Judge Brown, the jury, and Carlos all noticed him. He was hard to miss. It was Robert Williams. Delgado immediately felt a surge of adrenaline. He was ready for battle now that his friend was here. Robert quietly took a seat in the third row of the spectator area, as King began cross-examination.

"Mr. Delgado, you mentioned on direct you were convicted of a felony one time, correct?"

"Yes."

"As a result of the felony, you were sentenced to prison at Newtown Correctional Institution, right?"

"Right."

"And while you were serving prison time at Newtown, you met Mr. Jones, didn't you?"

"Yes."

"And you agree, don't you, from the first time you met Mr. Jones, the two of you couldn't stand each other."

"I agree."

"According to you, Mr. Jones was always shooting his mouth off and trying to scare the other inmates, including you, right?"

"It's not just according to me. It's a fact."

"Well, isn't it also a fact, Mr. Delgado, you went around the prison trying to be a tough guy and intimidate the other inmates?"

"Not like Jones, but to a lesser degree I did. I was in prison and had to take care of myself. That's what I needed to do. Not to start a fight, but to let others know I was up to the challenge if they tried takin' me on."

Robert grimaced as he thought back to his years at Newtown. As big as he was, and even though a significant portion of the prison population tried to turn away from the lifestyle and crimes that caused their incarceration, there were always men who would never reform and were dangerous to other inmates. In those instances, the survival of the fittest mode rang true.

"And you weren't shy about letting other inmates know you were a martial arts expert were you, Mr. Delgado?"

"Yeah, that's right."

"I understand from your testimony on direct you admit Mr. Jones and you got into a physical altercation while the two of you were at Newtown. I know you dispute his version of what happened, but you do admit the two of you hit each other, correct?"

"Yes, I admit it."

"The fight caused both of you to dislike the other even more, didn't it?"

"I won't disagree with that."

King smiled. He felt Delgado's cross was proceeding as he planned.

"After you were released from prison, the next time you saw Mr. Jones was when you came back to

Newtown almost a couple of years later as part of a prison ministry team, correct?"

"Correct."

"And while you were there, you and Mr. Jones got into a verbal confrontation during a break while the two of you were outside the building where the retreat took place?"

"Yes, we did."

"And if weren't for one of the prison ministers stepping between the two of you, and urging both of you to calm down, a fistfight would have taken place between Mr. Jones and you, right?"

"Yes."

"That confrontation helped stir the pot for the two of you disliking each other even more, didn't it?"

"No question about it."

"After that incident, the next time you saw Mr. Jones was at Rough Riders Bar on the evening of December 8, 2012, correct?"

"That's right."

"It was around 11:00 p.m. you got to the bar, wasn't it?"

"Yes."

"And when you walked in, you didn't see anyone you knew, so you went and sat down by yourself at the bar?"

"Yes."

"And then you ordered a beer, drank it down pretty quickly, and bought a second beer."

"I did."

"Then Mr. Jones comes from behind you, pushes you really hard on the shoulder, and then starts to verbally abuse you, correct?"

"Yeah."

"In response, you ask him to please leave you alone so you could enjoy your beer. Then you turn around so your back is facing Mr. Jones, and that's when Mr. Jones spins your chair around and viciously sucker punches you on the side of your face, which knocks you to the floor. Is all that correct?"

"Yes, it is."

"Then, when you were on the floor, Mr. Jones stood over you, hurling insults at you, until the bartender, Big Jake, came and threw Mr. Jones out of the bar. Did I get that right?"

"Yes, all of that is right."

"There were two other customers who helped you get off the floor, correct?"

"Correct."

"Then Big Jake came over to see how you're doing, and you asked him if he knew where Jones lives?"

"Yes, I did."

"In response to your question, Big Jake asked you why you wanted to know, and you told him that you were going to pay Jones back for what he did; there was no way Jones was getting away with sucker punching you. That's all true, isn't it, Mr. Delgado?" King's voice was getting louder as he bore down on Delgado. All the jurors intently listened for the response.

Carlos bit his lip and softly answered, "Yes, it's all true." His tone was in sharp contrast to King's.

"And it's also true, isn't it, Mr. Delgado, you were extremely angry with Mr. Jones for what he did to you?" King couldn't wait for the answer.

Carlos hung his head and forced out his response. His remorse was evident as he quietly replied, "Yes, I was."

Robert closed his eyes and silently prayed for Carlos to overcome the terrible situation he faced because of his temper and quest for revenge. Moving back in time to correct the mistake was impossible, but going forward in life with a new attitude, and being lifted up by a close relationship with Jesus Christ was a goal Robert prayed for Delgado to achieve.

"It's true, isn't it, Big Jake didn't tell you where Mr. Jones lived for two reasons? First, he didn't know where he lived. Second, Big Jake told you even if he knew where Mr. Jones lived; he wouldn't tell you because it would only cause more trouble, and instead, you should go home and take care of yourself."

"Yes, that's true." Carlos looked down at the floor. He had a hard time maintaining eye contact with the jury.

"So you left the bar, and on the way out, you told Big Jake somehow you'd find out where Jones lived, and then he'd pay the price, didn't you?"

"Yes, I did."

"You wanted revenge on Mr. Jones, didn't you?"

"That's true. I was stupid, but I was really hurt and not thinkin' straight."

"You found out where Mr. Jones lived because John Morrison, one of the guys who picked you up off the floor, went outside, and told you where he lived, correct?"

"Correct."

"And then you went to Mr. Jones' apartment to get your revenge, didn't you?" Although King increased the volume of his voice again, he was careful not to scream at Delgado. He didn't want Randolph or the Court to become involved and interfere with his cross.

"I can't deny I went there looking for revenge, but I never got it because when I arrived at Jones' apartment, he was down on the floor. I never hit him." This time

Life's Choices

Carlos looked straight at the jury. All of them were deeply absorbed in his testimony.

"When you arrived at Mr. Jones' apartment, the door was slightly open. You pushed the door open and went inside, right?"

"Right."

"At this point, you're still looking for your revenge on Mr. Jones, aren't you?"

"Yes." Delgado managed to eyeball the jurors despite his anxiety.

"Then you go in and see someone on the floor, but because it's dark, you can't tell who it is. So you turned on a light switch and saw it was Mr. Jones. Is that all correct so far?"

"Yes, it is."

"Mr. Jones was on his stomach, and you noticed the back of his head was bloody. You tried shaking him to wake him up, but he wouldn't wake up. Is that fair to say?"

"Yeah."

"Then, Mr. Delgado, you see a wrench on the ground next to Mr. Jones, and you decide to pick it up?"

"Yes." Carlos managed to keep his poker face on despite the tremendous pressure he felt.

"You don't really have a reason why you picked up the wrench do you?" King couldn't wait for the reply.

"I don't know what to tell you, Mr. King," stammered Carlos. "It was a reaction. I couldn't figure out what happened to Jones, or why the wrench was next to him, so I picked it up."

"And after you picked up the wrench, you heard a scream from the doorway, looked back, and saw a woman watching you. She kept screaming, so you threw the wrench down and ran out of the apartment.

As you're running away, you bumped into her and kept going. And you never stopped running until you got home. Is all of that correct, Mr. Delgado?"

"Yes, it is," responded Delgado in a firm tone, as he looked straight at the jury.

"In response to your attorney's questions on direct-exam, you stated you and your lawyer went to the Sheriff's Department to tell them what happened, correct?"

"Yes."

"You also said, in reply to Mr. Randolph's questions you told the Sheriff's Office what happened and answered all the questions you were asked because you didn't have anything to hide is that right?"

"Yes, that's right."

"If you didn't have anything to hide, sir, then why did you throw the wrench down and run out of Mr. Jones' apartment when Ms. Johnson saw you and started screaming?" King looked straight at the jury as he posed the question.

Delgado rubbed his hand across his face and looked over at the jury. "I panicked. The lady kept screaming and it scared the daylights out of me. Looking back at it now, I know I should never have run away, but I was still hurtin' from Jones hit, and not thinkin' clearly. It seemed like the only thing to do. I wish I hadn't, but I can't change what happened. It wasn't me who hit Jones. I never touched him."

"I have no more questions of the Defendant, Your Honor," King announced as he returned to his seat.

"Any re-direct, Mr. Randolph?"

"No, Judge." Randolph decided Delgado's testimony had gone well, and there was no reason to expose him to more questions.

"Court will be in recess for twenty minutes," stated Judge Brown as she hurried off the bench and out the door behind her.

33

Outside the courtroom, Robert Williams approached Delgado and firmly shook his hand. "I thought you did a good job with the state attorney's cross. I'm sorry I couldn't be here sooner, but I was up late last night." The smile on Robert's face caused Carlos to suspect the reason.

"Don't tell me the baby was born!" Now it was Delgado's turn to beam.

"Yes, he was. Little Anthony came into the world at 1:30 this morning." The look of joy on Robert's face made Delgado momentarily forget his courtroom trial. It was a time of much needed peace and appreciation, no matter how short.

"Is he a big kid?" Carlos couldn't wait for the answer.

"Oh, yeah. I see a linebacker position in the boy's future." Robert let out a deep belly laugh and was soon joined by Carlos.

"Is everything okay with the baby and the mother?"

"It's all good. The baby's healthy, and the birth mom delivered with no problems. God is good! All the time! He had an awesome plan for us we can now rejoice in."

Robert's comment stirred Carlos. He hoped God's plan for him would end in a similarly joyful manner.

"Where is the baby now?"

"He's at the hospital with his birth mom, her sister, and Coral. Later today, the hospital will release him to our attorney who's handlin' the adoption. Our lawyer has already made the necessary arrangements for us to get temporary custody of Anthony while we wait for the final adoption hearin' to take place."

"When's that?"

"I don't have an exact date, but sometime soon."

"Hopefully, everything will go as smoothly for you as it has so far."

"The outcome is in God's hands. I've put my trust in Him, so I'm not worried about it." Robert took a deep breath and then added, "And I hope you've put your trust in God as well, my friend."

"I'm tryin', Williams. I'm sure tryin'."

"Good. By the way, I ran into John Taylor and Josh Wilbur in the elevator. They've been involved in a trial that's supposed to end today. If it does, they will be here later."

"I hope they make it. I can use all the support I can get, especially while the jury decides the case."

Ten minutes later, Randolph's next witness was ready to testify. As Delgado looked at him, Carlos thought he looked unkempt. Carlos closed his eyes. He hoped the witness' appearance wouldn't affect the jury's belief in his testimony.

"Please tell us your name and where you live, sir?"

"My name's Leroy Collins. I live at 115 McNear Street, West Palm Beach."

"Is there an apartment number you live in?"

"Yeah, there is. Why do you need to know?" Collins was irritated at the intrusion to his privacy.

Before Randolph could respond, Judge Brown jumped in. "We want to know, Mr. Collins, because you're a witness in this case, and the names of all the witnesses and their full addresses are needed so we will have a record of who testified in this proceeding and where they reside. Please answer the question now, sir."

Collins glared at Brown. He was annoyed and briefly thought about refusing to answer the question, but as he looked around, he saw Bailiff Harrison closely watching him. He wanted no trouble from someone wearing a Sheriff's badge so he answered the question hurriedly. "Apartment 113 is where I live."

"Thank you, sir," answered Randolph. "How long have you lived in Apartment 113?"

Collins seemed to take an eternity as he mulled the answer in his mind. Carlos squirmed in his seat. Collins' testimony was not getting off to a good start. Finally, Collins replied, "A little over six years."

"Are you employed, Mr. Collins?"

"What business is that of yours? I thought I was here to tell you what I saw the night Jones was attacked; just like I told the guy you sent to see me."

"Mr. Collins," growled Judge Brown. "I've warned you once before about answering questions, and I'm not going to warn you again. Unless one of the attorneys' objects to the question you're asked, and I tell you not to answer the question, then you are to answer the question to the best of your ability. Have you got that, sir?" The Judge scowled at Collins as she waited for him to respond.

"Yeah, I got it," answered Collins in an annoyed manner. He immediately turned his attention to Randolph. "To answer your question, no, I'm not employed. I've been retired for five years, ever since I turned sixty-five."

"What type of work did you do before you retired?"

"I was a carpenter for forty years. I worked for myself."

"Do you live in your apartment by yourself?"

"Yes."

"Do you know a man named William Jones?"

"Yes."

"How do you know Mr. Jones?"

"He lives in the same apartment building as me. In Apartment 103."

"Do you know how long Mr. Jones has lived there?"

"I can't give you an exact date. Probably around a couple of years or so."

"How well do you know Mr. Jones?"

"Not well. I just see him coming and going. Once in awhile, he'll say something to me, or I'll say something to him." Collins shrugged his shoulders. "That's about it."

"Do you know if Mr. Jones was attacked while in his apartment on the night of Saturday, December 8, 2012?"

"I found out about it after it happened."

"When did you find out about it?"

"I think it was the next day. There were a bunch of tenants outside talking about Jones. That's how I found out."

"Were you at your apartment on the night of Saturday, December 8, 2012?"

"I'm always home at night. I've got no family. And I'm too old to be going out at nighttime."

"Did you come out of your apartment at all on Saturday night, December 8, 2012?"

"I came out to put the garbage from my apartment in the trash chute. Same as I do every Saturday night."

"Do you remember what time it was?"

"It was around 11:30, which is when I always go to bed."

"When you came out of your apartment to take your garbage out, did you notice anyone or anything in the hallway?"

"Yeah, there was a guy down at the other end of the hallway. He was bent over picking up some money or something. It looked like money. That's what I think it was. When he heard me come out of my apartment, he turned around and stood up straight. He was looking at me. And then, all of a sudden, he bends back down to pick up the rest of the money or whatever was on the floor, takes off, and goes out the building front door."

Carlos was totally focused on the jury to try to gauge their reaction. Although all the jurors paid close attention to Collins testimony, Delgado couldn't tell what impact, if any, it made.

"Did you know who this man was?"

"No, I had never seen him before."

"Could you tell what race he was?"

"Yeah, he was a black man. Tall and heavyset."

"Could you tell how old this man was?"

"He looked pretty young. Maybe late twenties or early thirties.

"How far away were you from him?"

"Not too far; maybe fifty to sixty feet."

Randolph pointed over at Carlos. "Is Mr. Delgado, who's sitting in here at counsel table, the man you saw?"

"No way. He doesn't look anything like him."

"When you saw this person pick up the money, what apartment was he near?"

"Just after Apartment 103, closer to Apartment 101."

"Did you go outside the building to take your garbage out?"

"No, there's a trash chute inside the building, just after Apartment 101. I just throw it in there."

"Did you ever see the man who picked up the money again?"

"No, I didn't."

"What did you do after you threw your garbage out?"

"I went back to my apartment and went straight to bed."

"Thank you, Mr. Collins. I have no further questions."

"Your witness, Mr. King."

"Thank you, Your Honor." King was determined not to let Collins' testimony provide a defense for Delgado. He immediately launched into his cross with fervor.

"Mr. Collins, you mentioned in response to one of Mr. Randolph's questions about Mr. Randolph sending a guy to see you. Who were you talking about?"

Collins shook his head. "I can't remember his name. He said he was a private investigator and worked on the case for the guy being charged for attacking Jones. He said the Defendant's lawyer had sent him to talk to me about what I knew. What else do you want to know?" Collins wanted out of the courtroom as soon as possible.

"Did the private investigator say anything about trying to find a reason why the Defendant should be found not guilty?"

"I don't remember him saying anything like that, but he sure was fishing for any help I might be able to give him. I told him what I saw, just like I talked about now."

"How in the world do you remember it was around 11:30 on the night of December 8, 2012, you saw the tall, heavyset black man in the hallway?" King skeptically looked at the witness, then the jury.

"Because the next day was when everyone was talking about Jones being attacked, and I always take my garbage out at 11:30 after the news is over, and then go to bed. That's how I remember," Collins insisted. He was determined to fight fire with fire and not take any guff from this lawyer.

"You testified on direct the guy you saw down at the other end of the hallway was bent over picking up some money or something. It looked like money, but you're not sure it was money, are you?"

"Like I already said, it looked like money. I think it was, but I can't be certain. But if it wasn't money, then I don't know why he was in such a hurry to pick the rest of it up and get out of there."

"When you walked past Apartment 103 to throw out your garbage, did you notice if the door to the apartment was open at all"?

"No, I didn't. I don't even remember looking at the door."

"Did you see anything on the floor when you walked past Apartments 103 or 101?"

"I do recall looking down at the floor to see if the guy left anything on it after he took off, but there was nothing there."

"After you went back into your apartment, what did you do?"

"I went in my bedroom, laid down on the bed, and went to sleep."

"After you fell asleep, were you woken up by any noise out in the hallway?"

"No, I was dead to the world. When you hit seventy, and it's late at night, and you go to bed, it's hard for something to wake you up. At least, for me it is."

"So you didn't hear any one screaming out in the hallway?"

"No, I didn't."

"So you slept straight through the night without waking up?"

"That's right."

"You mentioned in response to one of Mr. Randolph's questions the next day you found out about the attack on Jones because the tenants were talking about it."

"Yes, I did."

"Do you recall seeing the police at the apartment building interviewing tenants to see if they saw anything or knew about the assault on Mr. Jones?"

"Yes, and they talked to me when I was outside."

"What did you tell them?"

"Nothing. I didn't have anything to tell them."

"Did you tell them about the man you saw in the hallway picking something up from the floor, and then running off when he saw you?"

"No."

"Why not?"

"I didn't think it was important to what they were checking out. At least, not at the time I didn't."

"What do you mean at least not at the time you didn't?"

"Because at the time I never put together the guy I saw might have come from Jones apartment with the money, and maybe he was the one who attacked him."

"When did you put that together?"

"When the other lawyer's private investigator came and talked to me. He mentioned about how money was missing from Jones apartment the night of the attack. Then it occurred to me maybe the guy I saw had something to do with it."

"Did the private investigator suggest to you it was money on the floor you saw being picked up?"

"No, he didn't."

"Mr. Collins, you have no way of knowing whether or not the man you saw in the hallway had anything to do with the attack on Mr. Jones, do you?"

"No, I don't."

King looked over at the jury as he said, "Thank you, Mr. Collins. I have no further questions for this witness, Judge Brown."

"Any re-direct, Mr. Randolph?"

"No, Your Honor."

"You're excused, Mr. Collins."

A huge smile spread across Collins' face as he hustled from the courtroom. As he left, Carlos was deep in thought about the jury's perception of what they heard.

34

As the next witness sat in the witness seat waiting for Randolph to begin his questions, Delgado compared his appearance to Collins. This guy was impeccably dressed in a blue suit. Carlos hoped his testimony would come out as good as he looked.

"Please state your name and address." Randolph fiddled with his notepad as he waited for the answer.

"My name is Clyde Hawkins, and I reside at 115 McNear Street in Apartment 315." The response was delivered in a smooth and polished tone.

"How long have you lived there, Mr. Hawkins?"

"Next month will be three years."

"Does anyone live in the apartment with you?"

"No, I live alone."

"What do you do for a living, sir?"

"I'm a salesman for a pharmaceutical company. I go to hospitals and doctors' offices and sell my company's products."

"How long have you been engaged in that line of work?"

"Just over ten years."

"Do you know a man named William Jones who lives in your apartment building?"

"Yes, I know who Mr. Jones is. I don't know him very well, but I'm familiar with him."

"Are you aware Mr. Jones was attacked in his apartment on Saturday evening, December 8, 2012?"

"Yes, sir."

"How do you know about it?"

"On Sunday, the day after the assault, the tenants were all talking about it. And the Sheriff's Department was at the building to interview people to see if they knew anything about the crime."

"Did you speak with any of the deputies?"

"Yes, I did."

"What did you tell them?"

"I told them about a guy I saw running out of the building when I was coming in. He looked flustered and stuffed something in his pocket when he came by me."

"Were you able to tell what he stuffed in his pocket?"

"No, I could not. He was moving too fast."

"What did the man you saw look like?"

"Well, I didn't get a good look at him, but I can tell you he was a black man. He was tall, taller than me, and I'm 6'2". And he had a large frame. That's about all I can tell you about his appearance."

"Had you ever seen this man before?"

"No, I have no idea who he was."

Randolph walked over to where Delgado sat and put his hands on his shoulders. "The gentleman in front of me is Carlos Delgado. Are you able to tell us if Mr. Delgado is the man you saw running away from the building?"

Hawkins looked intently at Delgado. "Mr. Delgado is definitely not the man I saw. He looks nothing like him."

"Thank you, Mr. Hawkins," responded Randolph as he looked at the jury and moved back to the podium.

"Where were you coming from when you saw the person you've told us about?"

"My girlfriend and I had gone out to dinner. I had taken her home and was coming back to my apartment."

"What time was it when you saw the man running away from the building?"

"It was around 11:30. I know because I looked at the clock in my car when I got out of it."

"Did you tell the Sheriff's Deputies everything you just told us?"

"Yes, I did."

"Why did you tell them what you saw?"

"After I found out about the attack on Mr. Jones, it occurred to me the man I saw might have something to do with it. So, I told them what I saw."

"After you came into the building that evening, did you go straight to your apartment?"

"Yes, I took the stairs and went to my apartment and jumped into bed pretty quickly. It had been a long day, and I was tired."

"After you got into bed, did you hear any noise or commotion coming from the first floor?"

"No, sir, I did not. That's two floors below me and the building is well insulated. And as I said, it was a tiring day, so I was sound asleep."

"Thank you for your time, Mr. Hawkins. I have nothing further."

"Any cross, Mr. King?"

"Just a couple of questions, Judge." King turned his attention to the witness and asked, "You don't have any knowledge as to what the man you saw running stuffed into his pocket, correct?"

"You are correct."

"And you don't know whether or not the man you've described is the person responsible for attacking Mr. Jones, do you?"

"No, I do not."

"That's all I have of the witness."

"You're excused, Mr. Hawkins."

"Thank you, Judge." Hawkins left the stand and courtroom in as relaxed a manner as he entered.

"Do you have any more evidence to put on, Mr. Randolph?"

"No, Your Honor. The defense rests."

"Do you have any rebuttal, Mr. King?"

"No, I do not, Judge Brown."

"Then we'll proceed to closing arguments. Before we do, let's take a twenty-minute break." Judge Brown looked at her watch and then addressed the jury. "Ladies and gentlemen, by the time closing arguments are concluded, we'll run into our lunch hour, so what I'd like to do is have lunch brought into the jury room for you. There's a great sandwich shop across the street, and Bailiff Harrison will provide a menu for you to choose something when you first go into the jury room after the closing. I hope that's okay with everyone."

All the jurors nodded in agreement. "Great," responded Judge Brown. "Court will be in recess for twenty minutes."

After the Court and jury exited, Carlos told Randolph he would leave him alone so he could concentrate on his closing. Jack nodded in appreciation. As Carlos got up from his chair, he saw Robert Williams was still in the courtroom.

"Let's go outside and talk, Williams." Robert got up and followed Delgado. As the two of them were leaving, the courtroom door opened. John Taylor and

Josh Wilbur had arrived to support their friend. Carlos silently thanked God for bringing these three men into his life. Their support was a source of inspiration and encouragement, which were exactly what Carlos needed.

35

Delgado, Williams, Taylor, and Wilbur walked to the end of the hallway. There was no one else around. After a few moments of uneasy silence, Carlos broke the ice. "I really appreciate all you guys bein' here for the closing arguments. Williams already told me he can stay until the jury returns a verdict. What about you other two?"

Both John and Josh felt Delgado's distress. John wasted no time in responding, "Yes, we can stay. Our trial is over, so we're here to help you in any way we can."

Carlos nodded in gratitude. Then he decided to change the subject. "Well, don't keep me guessin'. Did you win?"

"We don't know yet," answered John. "It was a non-jury trial, and the judge didn't rule at the end of the case. It will probably be a couple of weeks before we hear from the court."

Carlos shook his head in disbelief. "Man, that's tough, waitin' so long to hear. It's sure a good thing I don't have that to go through. I can't wait to get this trial over with." Delgado dropped his head and let out an exasperated sigh. Then he grumbled, "Of course, if the jury finds me guilty, the fun and games will have just started." The despondent look on his face caused Robert to reply immediately.

"Let's say a prayer for the Lord to see you through this difficult time." Robert looked over at Josh and quietly asked, "Would you mind offerin' up a prayer for Carlos?"

Josh was surprised he was asked to say the prayer, but knew he couldn't refuse. With his entire trial lawyer's fortitude, he bowed his head and began a petition on his friend's behalf. "Dear God, we humbly come before You and ask You to watch over, guide, and protect Carlos during this time while he waits for the jury's decision. We ask You, Lord, no matter what the verdict is, You continue to sustain, comfort and care for our friend and Your son for all the days of his life. Please let him know You are always with him, and with You at his side, he has nothing to fear. Help him not to be terrified or discouraged, but to be strong and courageous. Please help him to remember You have blessed him with friends here on Earth who will always support him. In Jesus' name we pray. Amen."

"Amen," responded the other men.

"I hope the prayer was okay, Carlos."

"It was more than okay, Wilbur. It was what I needed. Thank you."

Suddenly, Randolph appeared outside the courtroom door and waved at the group to return to the courtroom. As they walked back, Carlos softly said, "I'm countin' on the prayer to get me through whatever happens today."

"Are you ready to begin your closing argument, Mr. King?"

"Yes, I am, Judge Brown."

"Please proceed."

As King strolled to the podium, visions of a guilty verdict flooded his mind, but he knew he had to be at the top of his game for the victory to occur. He took a deep breath and then nonchalantly began what he hoped would be an argument resulting in another win, bringing him a step closer to the State Attorney's position.

"Ladies and gentlemen of the jury, on behalf of the State of Florida, I want to thank you for your time and attention on this case. A criminal case with a charge of aggravated battery is not an easy trial to sit through, particularly when you heard about and saw what happened to Mr. Jones as a result of the attack upon him. In this case, I respectfully submit to you the evidence has shown, beyond a reasonable doubt, the Defendant, Carlos Delgado, is guilty of the crime of aggravated battery upon Mr. Jones." As he spoke, King turned around and pointed at Delgado. The gesture and words caused Carlos to cringe inside, but he managed to keep his best game face on.

"At the end of closing arguments, the Court will instruct you as to what constitutes aggravated battery under the law of Florida. The Court will tell you a person commits aggravated battery when he strikes another person causing great bodily harm, permanent disability, or permanent disfigurement or uses a deadly weapon in striking the other person. The task before you is to determine whether the Defendant struck Mr. Jones across the back of the head with the wrench inside the evidence bag I'm holding. You'll have this wrench in the jury room to consider in your deliberations." King showed the clear plastic bag containing the wrench to the jury and then continued.

"I submit to you the evidence has clearly shown Mr. Jones suffered great bodily harm and a permanent disability when he was struck viciously across the back of the head with the wrench. Not just once or twice, but three times. You saw Mr. Jones walk with a cane and heard him testify about spending three weeks in the hospital after his operation and then three months in a rehab center. You also heard Mr. Jones talk about how he still has terrible headaches, dizziness, can't sleep well, and has problems with his vision. Because of those problems, he has been unable to return to work.

"And it isn't just Mr. Jones' testimony you can rely on. You also heard Dr. John Spencer testify about how Mr. Jones suffered a traumatic brain injury as a result of the attack. Dr. Spencer told you in detail about the craniotomy he performed and confirmed Mr. Jones was in rehab for three months. Dr. Spencer also testified he was still treating Mr. Jones for headaches, dizziness, fatigue, and blurred vision. Moreover, Dr. Spencer said Mr. Jones wasn't able to return to work and couldn't tell us when he might be able to go back. In fact, the doctor said, and I quote, 'We'll just have to wait and see how everything develops. When a person such as Mr. Jones suffers a traumatic brain injury, the results sometimes follow him for the rest of his life.'"

King took a deep breath before continuing. He was on a roll and didn't want to lose momentum. Carlos noticed how the jury was totally absorbed in King's closing. He hoped Randolph would draw the same attention.

"Even, if for some reason, you don't believe Mr. Jones suffered great bodily harm or permanent disability, I nonetheless submit to you the wrench that was used to strike Mr. Jones three times is a deadly weapon. Look at the size of this thing." King again showed the wrench to the jury. "And as I told you, this wrench will be back in the jury room for you to examine. When you do, I believe you will determine, as I suggest, it is a deadly weapon.

"Once you find, as I believe you will, Mr. Jones suffered great bodily harm or a permanent disability or the wrench was a deadly weapon, then the only question remaining is whether or not the Defendant attacked Mr. Jones with the wrench. I submit to each of you the evidence is indisputably clear the Defendant was the perpetrator of this heinous crime." King began to work himself into a lather. His voice grew louder as he insisted, "The Defendant had motive to commit the crime, opportunity to commit the crime, and, in fact, did commit the crime. Let's start out in analyzing the evidence by reviewing the testimony of Mr. Jones and the Defendant about each other.

"Mr. Jones stated the two of them couldn't stand one another. The Defendant admitted the same thing. Mr. Jones gave his reasons why, as did the Defendant. It's irrelevant as to who's right and who's wrong as to why they felt like they did because there is no dispute there was very bad blood between the two of them. You heard each one's testimony regarding the fight they got into while both were inmates at Newtown Correctional Institution. You also heard the testimony of each of them about their verbal altercation at Newtown, when the Defendant returned as part of a prison ministry group. Once again, it's irrelevant as to whose side you believe because the evidence is clear these two guys hated each other. Those feelings continued right up to the time they met at Rough Riders Bar on the evening of December 8, 2012.

"Then, what happens at Rough Riders on that fateful night? Mr. Jones confronts the Defendant and ends up knocking him off his bar stool onto the floor. You heard

Mr. Jones deny he sucker punched the Defendant, and you heard both the Defendant and the bartender, Big Jake McCloud testify Mr. Jones did sucker punch the Defendant. Let's assume Mr. Jones was the aggressor and sucker punched the Defendant. Mr. Jones was wrong. The Defendant could have gone to the Sheriff's Department and filed a complaint against him, but the Defendant didn't. Instead, the Defendant wanted to get revenge against Mr. Jones. You heard the Defendant admit in his testimony how angry he was and how he went to Mr. Jones apartment to get his revenge after John Morrison, one of the customers who picked the Defendant off the floor, told the Defendant where Mr. Jones lived. What the Defendant should have done was to go home as Big Jake McCloud told him to do. He should never have gone to Mr. Jones' apartment to get revenge. Vigilante justice is not allowed under our laws. The Defendant was not free to take the law into his own hands. He should have let the Sheriff's Office handle any beef he had against Mr. Jones."

King continued on at a fevered pitch. Randolph sat stone-faced, as did Delgado, despite the fact both were feeling the heat being applied by King. Carlos desperately hoped his lawyer would be able to counter the Assistant State Attorney's arguments.

"When it comes down to whether the Defendant battered Mr. Jones, this is not a case of Mr. Jones' testimony against the Defendant. Mr. Jones doesn't know who hit him. He was attacked from behind and never saw the person. But we have a witness who saw the Defendant standing over Mr. Jones in his apartment with a wrench in his hand. Latoya Johnson told you how she saw the Defendant with the wrench in his hand, standing over Mr. Jones. The Defendant left the front door open after he went into Mr. Jones' apartment, and when Ms. Johnson saw what was going on, she started to scream. Ms. Johnson also told you when she screamed as loud as she could, the Defendant dropped the wrench, ran out of the apartment, bumped into her, and almost knocked her over."

King momentarily stopped and looked from juror to juror. He wanted to make certain the point he was about to make resonated with the jury. "It's not only Ms. Johnson's testimony about the Defendant holding the wrench in his hand as he stood over Mr. Jones. The Defendant himself admitted he had the wrench in his hand and was standing over Mr. Jones when Ms. Johnson saw him. Now, the Defendant doesn't admit he hit Mr. Jones with the wrench. Instead, he wants you to believe when he saw Mr. Jones on the floor on his stomach, he tried shaking him to wake him up, but couldn't. Then, according to the Defendant, he saw the wrench on the floor next to Mr. Jones, and decided to pick it up. Please recall when I asked the Defendant if he had a reason why he picked up the wrench, all he could say in response was he didn't know what to tell me. He said it was a reaction. He couldn't figure out what happened to Mr. Jones, or why the wrench was next to him, so he picked it up."

King rolled his eyes and shook his head from side-to-side. "I submit to you the Defendant's answer is total nonsense. There would have been no reason for him to pick up a wrench lying on the floor. He didn't pick it up. He used it to attack Mr. Jones in order to get his revenge. And when the Defendant testified he went to the Sheriff's office on Monday after the attack because he didn't have anything to hide, how does that make any sense? If the Defendant didn't have anything to hide, why did he throw the wrench down and run out of Mr. Jones' apartment after Ms. Johnson saw him and started to scream? His answer to me, when I asked him the question, was her screams made him panic. He admitted he should never have run away, but said he wasn't thinking clearly, and running away seemed like the only thing to do. Ladies and gentlemen, I submit to you: The reason the Defendant ran away was because he was caught in the act of committing a violent crime against Mr. Jones. His quest for vengeance got the better of him, and he unlawfully battered Mr. Jones. The only reason he went to the Sheriff's Department was because he knew eventually the altercation between Jones and him would come to light, and the woman who he heard screaming would identify him as the man in the apartment with the wrench in his hand.

"Based on the evidence you heard in the case, I respectfully submit to you there is no reasonable doubt the Defendant is guilty of the crime of aggravated battery against Mr. Jones. Therefore, the State asks you to return a verdict finding the Defendant guilty."

King nodded at the jury, picked up his notes from the podium, and slowly returned to his chair. Delgado's heart raced, and all eyes in the courtroom were focused on Randolph as he rose to give his version of the evidence.

36

Randolph placed his note pad on the podium and then moved to the side of it. His eyes moved from juror to juror as he began to speak. "I want to thank you, ladies and gentlemen of the jury on behalf of Mr. Delgado for the time and the attention you have given this case over the past three days. As Mr. King told you, seeing and hearing about the effect of the assault on Mr. Jones certainly was not easy, but both Mr. Delgado and I saw what close consideration you gave to all the witnesses' testimonies, and we appreciate your diligence. Mr. Delgado has been charged with a serious crime of aggravated battery by the State, and it was important for you to have carefully heard and weighed all the evidence in order to arrive at a verdict in the case. As Judge Brown will instruct you after the closing arguments are finished, the State has the burden of proving beyond a reasonable doubt Mr. Delgado committed the crime of aggravated battery upon Mr. Jones. One of the things Judge Brown will tell you is after carefully considering, comparing, and weighing all the evidence, there is not an abiding conviction of guilt, or, if, having a conviction, it is one which is not stable but one which wavers and vacillates, then the charge is not proved beyond every reasonable doubt, and you must find Mr. Delgado not guilty because the doubt is reasonable. I submit to each of you the evidence has shown the State has failed to meet its burden of demonstrating beyond a reasonable doubt Mr. Delgado is guilty of the crime of aggravated battery. Let's take a look at what the evidence in the case has shown."

Randolph moved back to the podium and glanced at his note pad. Then he looked over at Carlos, pointed at him, and began an impassioned plea. "You heard evidence from both Mr. Jones and Mr. Delgado regarding how they knew each other while both were inmates at Newtown Correctional Institution. Both of them told you they couldn't stand the other. There's no question there is an acrimonious relationship existing between these two men. But was the relationship so bad it would cause Mr. Delgado to sneak up behind Mr. Jones in his apartment and viciously strike Mr. Jones three times with a wrench on the back of his head? Was there any evidence Mr. Delgado was capable of committing such a brutal and cowardly act?"

Now it was Randolph's turn to increase the volume and intensity of his argument. He lived for times like these. "There certainly was no evidence Mr. Delgado could or would perform such a dastardly deed. In fact, consider how Mr. Delgado joined a prison ministry team after being released from Newtown. Then he went with those men into prison to speak with the inmates about how he was doing his best to turn his life around. Mr. Wilbur told you Mr. Delgado's message was inspirational to the inmates, and they greatly appreciated it. Except Mr. Jones, who sought Mr. Delgado out and nearly caused a physical altercation between the two men.

"Please also recall Mr. Delgado's testimony about how well he had done since being released from prison. He had bought his own home. He worked for an air conditioning company in West Palm Beach, where he was doing great at his job and was rewarded financially by his employer. He told you he studied the Bible on Sunday afternoons with a friend who was the leader of a Bible study class at a church in Pahokee. With all the positive and encouraging things Mr. Delgado was accomplishing in his life, do you believe he was capable of savagely attacking Mr. Jones as the State wants you to believe?"

Randolph momentarily stopped to gauge whether he had the jury's attention. He was satisfied he did and continued. "And what about the night of December 8, 2012, when Mr. Delgado was sitting at Rough Riders Bar, minding his own business, having a beer, and is accosted by Mr. Jones for no reason? You heard from Mr. Delgado how he tried to avoid a confrontation and asked Mr. Jones to please leave him alone. What was Jones response? He spun Mr. Delgado's bar stool around and sucker punched him with such force Mr. Delgado fell off the bar stool. It wasn't only Mr. Delgado who told you that. Big Jake McCloud confirmed how he saw Mr. Jones sucker punch Mr. Delgado. Then Big Jake threw Jones out of the bar.

"After Mr. Jones struck Mr. Delgado for no reason, Mr. Delgado was understandably angry. Anyone would have been. Unfortunately, because his anger got the better of him, Mr. Delgado made a mistake and went to Mr. Jones' apartment to pay him back. He should never have gone there, but does that mean Mr. Delgado committed the vicious crime the State alleges he did? Absolutely not!" Randolph worked himself up to a fevered pitch.

"There's not one witness who testified Mr. Delgado struck Mr. Jones. You heard Mr. Delgado deny he hit

Jones, and Mr. Jones can't tell you who attacked him. Even Latoya Johnson said she never saw Mr. Delgado strike Mr. Jones with the wrench, and there was no way for her to know who did. Now, Mr. Delgado made two other mistakes when he went to the apartment. He should never have picked up the wrench from the floor, and he should not have run away when Ms. Johnson started to scream at the top of her lungs. He panicked, and fear overcame him. Once again, does that prove Mr. Delgado battered Mr. Jones? No way! Consider this too: If Mr. Delgado had gone into Mr. Jones' apartment with the intention of viciously attacking and beating him unconscious, then why did he leave the door open so someone who came by could see what was going on? If that was his game plan, he would have closed the door after he went in so no one could see what was happening.

"Please also recall the testimony of Mr. Jones, who admitted when he left his apartment to go to Rough Riders Bar on December 8, 2012, he did not lock the front door. It's critical to combine that evidence with what Roger Flanagan, the forensic fingerprint expert, told us. Mr. Flanagan said besides Mr. Delgado's fingerprints being found on the wrench, the outside door handle and the light switch, there were also other fingerprints on all three. On the door handle, there were four fingerprints he could not identify. On the wrench, there were two other sets of fingerprints he could not identify. On the light switch, there were three other sets of fingerprints he could not identify. Mr. Flanagan also told us he did not find Mr. Delgado's fingerprints on the handle to the top dresser of Mr. Jones' which was in his bedroom. He did find two other sets of fingerprints on the handle to the dresser. One of them belonged to Mr. Jones, but he couldn't identify the other set of fingerprints."

Randolph moved from behind the podium and stood directly in front of the jury. He wanted to make certain he drove home the next point he would make. "The most important thing Mr. Flanagan told us was a set of fingerprints on the top drawer of the dresser matched up to fingerprints on the outside door handle, on the light switch, and on the wrench. The evidence from the State's own witness clearly and undisputedly shows the same person, who Mr. Flanagan was unable to identify, touched the door handle, the wrench, the light switch, and the top dresser drawer." Randolph folded his arms across his chest and looked directly at the jurors before he continued.

"The testimony of Mr. Flanagan needs to be considered in conjunction with what Deputy Maxwell told us. He testified when he interviewed Mr. Jones in the hospital; Jones told him he left around a hundred dollars in cash in his bedroom before he went out to Rough Riders. Deputy Maxwell also told us the deputies searched Mr. Jones bedroom the night of the attack and did not find any cash. Then, after interviewing Mr. Jones, Deputy Maxwell returned to the apartment to search his bedroom again to make sure there wasn't any money in there. He didn't find any. When I asked him what conclusion he reached after he returned to the apartment and found no money, the Deputy told us whatever cash Mr. Jones had in his apartment was taken by someone he couldn't identify on the night of the assault."

Randolph moved back to the podium and smiled at the jury. King sat emotionless, as did Carlos. "But that's not the end of the story," said Randolph. "We still have the testimony of Mr. Collins and Mr. Hawkins to consider. Mr. Collins, who lives down the hallway from Mr. Jones in Apartment 113, said on the night of December 8, 2012 he came out of his apartment at 11:30 to put his garbage in the trash chute. When he did, he saw a guy at the other end of the hallway near Mr. Jones apartment bent over picking up what Mr. Collins testified looked like money. When this guy, whom Collins doesn't know, sees Collins, he stands up straight and looks at Collins. Then, all of a sudden, the guy bends down to get the rest of the money, takes off, and goes out the front door of the building. Mr. Collins described the man he saw as a young black man, who was tall and heavyset. He also told us Mr. Delgado was not the man he saw in the hallway."

Randolph stopped to turn around and look at Carlos and then turned back to the jury. "In addition to Mr. Collins' testimony, Mr. Hawkins came into the courtroom and spoke to us. Mr. Hawkins lives in Apartment 315 of the apartment building. He told us on the evening of December 8, 2012, he returned home from dinner with his girlfriend around 11:30. When he was coming into the building, he saw a man run out. The guy looked flustered and stuffed something in his pocket when he came by Mr. Hawkins. Mr. Hawkins also testified the man he saw was black and was tall with a large frame. It was also Mr. Hawkins' testimony Mr. Delgado was not the man whom he had seen running out of the building. The next day Mr. Hawkins reported what he saw to the Sheriff's Department because it occurred to him the man might have something to do with the attack on Mr. Jones."

Randolph again moved away from the podium and stood in front of the jury box. He looked directly at the people who held his client's fate in their hands as he said, "I respectfully submit to all of you the State has failed to prove beyond a reasonable doubt Mr. Delgado committed the crime of aggravated battery against Mr. Jones. The fingerprint analysis by Mr. Flanagan, coupled with the statement by Deputy Maxwell about money being missing from Mr. Jones apartment the night of the attack, shows someone other than Mr. Delgado committed the crime. Why would Mr. Delgado steal any money from Mr. Jones? And how could he have, when his fingerprints were never found on Mr. Jones' dresser in his bedroom? Someone other than Mr. Delgado stole the money and attacked Mr. Jones. Both Mr. Collins and Mr. Hawkins saw the other person, and told you what they witnessed. Mr. Delgado is innocent of the State's charges, and we ask you find him not guilty." Randolph nodded at the jury and returned to his chair.

"Do you have any rebuttal, Mr. King?"

"Just briefly, Your Honor."

This time it was King's turn to stand in front of the jury box. He relished the opportunity of having the last words to the jury and wanted to make the most of it. He started out in a low spoken tone. "The State strongly contests and disagrees with the Defendant's assertion we failed to prove beyond a reasonable doubt the Defendant is guilty of aggravated battery upon Mr. Jones. To the contrary, the evidence has clearly shown the crime was committed by the Defendant." Gradually, the volume of King's voice increased. "Out of anger and rage over being struck by Mr. Jones, the Defendant savagely struck the victim three times across the back of the head with a deadly weapon, causing Mr. Jones great bodily harm and permanent disability." King's body began to shake as he continued.

"The fact other fingerprints, which can't be identified, were found in the apartment proves nothing. The fact money was missing from the apartment proves nothing. Mr. Delgado could easily have taken the money and not left any fingerprints. No one ever said the money was inside a drawer. It could have been out in the open on top of the dresser or somewhere else where the money could be picked up, and a fingerprint not left." King expertly eyed all the jurors to gauge their attention.

"Mr. Collins' testimony was he couldn't be certain what the man out in the hallway was picking up was money. And he also said the next day, when the police were at the apartment building interviewing tenants, he never told them anything he saw because he didn't think it was important regarding what they were checking out. The reason was he never put together the guy he saw might have come from Mr. Jones' apartment with the money, and he possibly was the one who attacked him. In fact, Mr. Collins told us he never put the thought together until Mr. Randolph's private investigator came and talked to him. Mr. Collins admitted he had no way of knowing whether or not the man he saw in the hallway had anything to do with the attack on Mr. Jones." King looked skeptically at the jury.

"As far as Mr. Hawkins' testimony goes, he told us he didn't know what the man he saw running from the building stuffed into his pocket. Mr. Hawkins also didn't know whether or not the guy he told us about was responsible for attacking Mr. Jones. There's not any credible testimony anyone other than the Defendant is responsible for the crime. It was a crime committed by the Defendant out of anger and a thirst for revenge. The State asks you to hold the Defendant accountable for his atrocious crime by returning a verdict of guilty in order that justice will be done. Thank you again for your time and attention on this case."

"The closing arguments of counsel are now concluded," announced Judge Brown. "At this time, I will instruct you on the law to be applied in reaching a verdict. When you return to the jury room for your deliberations, a written copy of these instructions, as well as the exhibits that have been received into evidence, will be provided to you. A copy of the jury verdict form to be used will also be given to you."

For the next fifteen minutes, Judge Brown read the instructions on the law to the jury. As Carlos listened to the Court, he wondered if they had already made their minds up. After the instructions were finished, the six primary jurors were taken to the jury room by Bailiff Harrison. Judge Brown thanked alternate juror Jeremy Brooks for his service and excused him from the proceedings. What remained was the most difficult part of the case – waiting for the jury to return a verdict.

37

An hour after the jury began their deliberations, Randolph, Delgado, Williams, Taylor, and Wilbur sat in a restaurant down the street from the courthouse. Everyone, except Carlos, enjoyed his lunch. Delgado ordered only lemonade and wanted nothing to eat. He felt nauseated and couldn't imagine indulging in food when his freedom was on the line. He refrained from sharing his sentiments and was glad his companions were delighted with their menu choices. The talk had been casual and not focused on the trial. But Carlos was about to delve into the topic. He looked at his watch, took a sip of lemonade, and began to speak.

"Okay, Randolph, it's been a little over an hour, and there's been no call on your cell from the courthouse about the jury reachin' a verdict. Is that a good or bad thing?"

Jack answered firmly and without hesitation. "It's a good thing. It means the jury is talking with each other and considering the exhibits in evidence and the testimony. It's what we want."

Delgado rubbed his hand along his chin before posing his next question. "After how many hours with no jury verdict does it become a bad thing?"

This time Randolph was much more deliberate in his response. Besides not wanting to cause Carlos any anxiety if a verdict was lengthy in coming, he knew

John and Josh were closely listening to the conversation. "That's a tough question to answer. I've had cases where it's taken a couple of days before the jury came back with a verdict. Sometimes the result was a not guilty verdict, while other times the jury determined the defendant was guilty. Let's not get too concerned over how long it may take. I'm more concerned the jury carefully considers all the evidence."

"Good advice," chimed in John. "Jack's right, Carlos. Don't get yourself too worked up about how long it takes."

"Okay, I'll accept what was said. How did you two attorneys think the closin' arguments went?" Carlos looked directly at John and Josh.

"I thought Jack did a great job in countering King's points. To me, Jack really hammered home the State's failure to prove beyond a reasonable doubt that you were guilty of aggravated battery on Jones. Hopefully, the jury will see it the same way."

"I agree with John," added Josh. "My feeling, based on what I heard in the closings, is the jury's coming back with a not guilty verdict." Josh smiled at Carlos.

"I sure hope you're right, Wilbur. I can't bear the thought of bein' back in prison."

Randolph quickly transitioned the discussion to another topic. He wanted, as best he could, to help Carlos avoid going into a tailspin. Thirty minutes later, the group headed back to the courthouse. Three hours after they arrived, they were still sitting outside the courtroom waiting for a verdict. Carlos began to pace up and down the hallway and refused to listen to Randolph's instructions to sit down.

"I can't sit down, Randolph. This is drivin' me nuts." Then Delgado turned his attention to his three friends as he momentarily stopped. "You guys don't have to stay any longer. I appreciate all of you being here, but this thing is takin' too long. And I know you all got other things to do."

Before anyone could respond, the courtroom door swung open and Bailiff Harrison came out. "The jury's reached a verdict. Judge Brown wants everyone back in the courtroom before she brings them back in."

Harrison held the door open as everyone filed in. Carlos began to breathe deeply. He was heavily perspiring. Randolph did his best to get him to relax before the jury came out of the jury room. Judge Brown came in to the courtroom and had Bailiff Harrison get the jury. When they walked in, Carlos noticed Jeff Bronson, the CPA, had the verdict form in his hand. As the jurors sat down, they were all stoic. Delgado began to sweat even more as the Judge spoke.

"Has the jury reached a verdict?"

"Yes, Judge Brown," answered Bronson as he quickly rose from his chair.

"Madame Clerk, would you please get the verdict?"

Court Clerk Joanne Murphy hustled over to Bronson in response to the Court's instructions. She quickly brought the form over to Judge Brown who carefully reviewed it. Then she handed the verdict back to Murphy to read aloud. Delgado quivered as he waited.

In a clear and strong voice, Murphy stated: "We, the jury, find the Defendant, Carlos Delgado, is not guilty of the crime of aggravated battery against William Jones."

King sat stone-faced. He did not expect that result, but he would show no disappointment. On the other hand, Delgado was ecstatic. But he was also able to contain his outward appearance, and exhibited only a small grin. Randolph looked at the jury and nodded his appreciation. The gesture was returned with a smile by most. In the back of the courtroom, Williams, Taylor, and Wilbur were all overjoyed. Each of them silently thanked the Lord.

Judge Brown looked at counsel as she asked, "Gentlemen, do we need to address any matters before I discharge the jury?"

Both lawyers stood and answered in the negative. The Court proceeded to wrap up the proceedings with the jury, and they quickly left the courtroom.

After they were gone, Judge Brown spoke again. "Mr. Delgado, based on the jury's verdict, you are free to go. Good luck to you, sir."

Carlos quickly rose from his chair and smiled as he said, "Thank you, Your Honor."

Judge Brown then announced the proceedings were concluded, stood up, and left the courtroom through the door behind the bench. After she left, King approached Randolph.

"Congratulations, Randolph. Good job." King extended his hand as he maintained a stiff upper lip.

Randolph firmly shook King's hand and thanked him. King did not look at or address Delgado as he packed up his files and hastily departed from the room. His slight was of no matter to Delgado. He got what he wanted and was happy to see King vanquished in defeat. Justice was done as far as Carlos was concerned.

After King exited, Williams, Turner, and Wilbur approached counsel table. Then something happened no one would ever expect. Delgado first hugged his lawyer and then each of his three friends. Never had Carlos showed such a sign of emotion. In fact, there were tears rolling down his cheeks as he went from man to man. Each of the four was astounded to see Delgado's reaction. After Carlos regained his composure, he addressed the group.

"I want to thank each one of you for what you did in helpin' me. You first, Randolph, because you did a great job with the case and the trial, and with your help I'm still a free man. And Williams, all the time you spent with me on Sundays getting' me to trust in God, and all your prayers is somethin' I'll never be able to repay you for." Carlos smiled at Robert, who humbly hung his head.

Delgado turned his attention to Taylor and Wilbur. "And you two lawyers. You're both great friends. Thanks for comin' to see me when I was under house arrest and for bein' here all day today to support me and pray for me. There was something else Carlos wanted to say. He struggled to remember what it was. Then a smile crept across his face as he recalled. "Oh yeah, Taylor. Thank you for bringin' me to Randolph to represent me. That was one of the best legal moves you ever made."

"I won't argue with you about that," quipped John.

Randolph packed up his files and all five men left the courtroom. Williams, Taylor, and Wilbur said their goodbyes at the courthouse parking garage. Carlos got into Randolph's SUV for Jack to take him to Randolph's law office where Carlos had left his car. On the way there, Carlos had a proposition for his attorney. "Randolph, I want to take you out and buy you a steak dinner in appreciation for everything you did for me. Not tonight, because I'm way too tired. But next week, for sure, if that's okay with you?"

"That's more than okay with me. You've got a deal."
A giant grin enveloped Jack's face. He was delighted
his client was exonerated and could return to his life at
work and home. There were numerous times when the
jury verdict went the other way.

38

Later the same evening, Robert and Coral were eating dinner at their home. Robert just finished filling Coral in on the trial's outcome.

"This is such wonderful news, Robert. I know you believed Carlos when he told you he didn't commit the crime, but until the jury comes back, no one knows what's going to happen. I'll bet you Carlos will sleep really well tonight."

"There's no doubt about it," laughed Robert. "Not only tonight, but for the next week as well."

Suddenly, their conversation was interrupted by the sounds of a baby crying. Coral left the dining room table and quickly returned with the infant they had temporary custody of while waiting for the final adoption hearing. She sat down with Anthony in her arms. Robert got up from his chair and stood behind the two of them. His voice was filled with joy as he said, "I can't believe what a beautiful little boy he is. God has been so good to us in bringin' him into our lives. And Lourdes and Lydia as well." Robert reached down and gently stroked Anthony's head.

Before Coral could respond, Robert's cell rang. He looked at the caller I.D. "This is our lawyer. I wonder what he wants." He quickly answered the phone. "Good evening, Mr. Andrews. I hope you've got some good news for us."

"I do," replied Andrews. "Today, I found out when the final adoption hearing will take place. I'm calling to give you and your wife the date, time, and location."

"Hold on while I get a paper and something to write with." Robert located a pad and pencil and wrote down the information, but before the call was concluded, there was something else Andrews needed to share. Coral saw a look of concern on her husband's face as the conversation concluded.

"So what was the call about? You seem stressed."

"Mr. Andrews has the date for the final adoption hearing. He called to tell us when and where to be."

"That's terrific. Why do you have a worried look?"

"He also told me the judicial assistant for the judge handlin' the hearing called his office to ask for more information about my prison record. Andrews told me not to worry about it because he would handle it. I thought all of this was taken care of already. I guess it's another example of not knowin' for sure what might happen in the legal system."

"You're right, Robert. We don't know for certain what may happen in court, just like Carlos didn't. But as I know you told him, and I've heard you say many times, it's in God's hands. So relax and let our Lord take control." Coral grinned at her spouse.

"I knew there was a reason I married you. Thanks for the reminder. And now let me put my hands on our precious angel."

About a half-hour later the same evening, the doorbell at Delgado's home rang. He wondered who it was. When he opened the door, he saw Josh Wilbur standing there with a box in his hands.

"Wilbur, didn't you see enough of me today?" asked Carlos in a half-joking manner. Then he stepped back and told Josh, "Come in and tell me what's goin' on."

"I'm sorry to bother you, Carlos. I was on my way home from work when a thought came to me. I know how much you love the chocolate chip cookies from the bakery on Palm Beach. I stopped and got a box of them for you in celebration of your vindication today."

Josh handed the gift to his friend. Delgado gratefully accepted the luscious treats and put them down on a coffee table. "Don't you beat all, Wilbur? This is a welcome surprise. Do you want to stay and have some?"

"Thanks, but no. I know you're tired after everything you've been through. And to tell you the truth, I'm beat too. But I'd like a rain check to come back and have dinner with you sometime in the near future."

"You got it. I'll make dinner, and you can bring a few beers. I'm not about to go to bars anymore, but I wouldn't mind sharing a beer or two with a friend in the comfort and safety of my home. And if you have one beer too many, you're staying here for the night and not driving home. Deal?"

Carlos stuck out his hand. Josh firmly shook it as he replied, "Deal."

"Before I leave, there was one other thing I wanted to bounce off you. If it's not something you want to do, that's fine." Josh appeared hesitant to express his thoughts.

"Just spit it out, Wilbur. If it's somethin' I'm not interested in, I'll let you know." Delgado had his arms folded across his chest as he waited for Wilbur to respond.

"In two and a half weeks, the monthly reunion between the prison ministry team and the inmates who attend our programs will take place at Newtown."

"Yeah, I know. So what?"

"Well, the normal routine is for the inmates to give their testimonies how they are trying to change their lives. I thought maybe we could contact the prison chaplain about you talking to the prisoners about what you went through with the criminal charge and the trial. It might be inspirational and help some of them from making similar mistakes when they get released. What do you think?"

Carlos closed his eyes and rubbed his hands across his face. Then he spoke in a low tone. "You're asking a lot of me, Wilbur. I'm not sure I can or want to do that. Look what happened the last time when Jones heard me, and I know there are other guys in there like him. Whew!"

"Like I said, Carlos, there's no pressure. You're right. There are some inmates who will probably not receive your message in a positive way, but I think there are others who will. It's never easy to be an evangelist for Christ, but that is what Our Lord did for all of us. No matter what the earthly consequences were for Him. He had His eyes focused on eternity."

"Okay, Wilbur. I hear you. That doesn't mean I'll do it, but I'll think about it. Fair enough?"

"Fair enough. Now, let me get out of here so you can enjoy your cookies."

"Good plan."

39

"I can't believe I let you talk me into this, Wilbur," whispered Carlos in Josh's ear. Delgado didn't want anyone else to hear what he said. They were at the monthly reunion of the prison ministry team with some of the inmates at Newtown. Neither Robert Williams nor John Taylor could make the event because of schedule conflicts, but there were fifteen other prison ministers present along with sixty prisoners.

"Don't worry, Carlos," answered Josh in just as soft a voice. "You'll do great. Remember you're doing this for Christ, as one of His evangelists." He winked at Carlos. Before Delgado could respond, the inmate who was the leader of the reunion began to speak.

"Good afternoon, everyone. As most of you know, my name is Larry Blake. I'm privileged to be the leader of this month's reunion. We're going to do something a little different today. Before we hear the testimony of the three inmates who will speak to us, a former inmate, who is now on the prison ministry team, is going to talk to us. Carlos Delgado, please come up here."

Carlos took a deep breath as he walked to the front of the room. Blake warmly shook his hand and then took a seat. As Carlos stood alone at the podium, with all eyes in the room cast upon him, he felt in some ways being in this prison to deliver the message he was about to give was more nerve-wracking than testifying at his trial. But he was determined to do his best to convey what Josh had moved him to share.

"As Larry just told you, my name is Carlos Delgado, and I'm a former inmate at this place. I recognize quite a few faces, and for those I do know, I'm sorry you're still here. I hope you get out soon. For those of you who don't know me, I spent five years at Newtown after being convicted of aggravated battery. I got out a little over three years ago. When I first got out, I was fortunate because I got to live with my mother in Fort Lauderdale and found a good payin' job. So things were pretty smooth for awhile, until my mom died, and I lost my job because business was bad. I relocated to West Palm and found another job, but that didn't last too long because I got blamed for an inventory shortage I had nothing to do with. Being an ex-con didn't help my credibility. I don't want to make it sound like an excuse, but sometimes people get blamed for stuff they have nothin' to do with." Carlos stopped for a few moments to collect his thoughts. He wanted to do his best to impart his message in a way it would hopefully be well-received by many of the inmates.

"I got through those tough times with the assistance of two guys who were inmates here – Robert Williams and John Taylor. And also with the help of one of the men in this room, who hired me to work for him. I'm talkin' about Steve Ramrell. He's been great to me and has treated me better than I ever thought possible."

Cries of "all right Steve" and "way to go Steve" rang out in response to Delgado's statement. Ramrell smiled and called out, "You deserve it, Carlos. Keep up the great work."

"A couple of years ago, I even came in here with the prison ministry team for a four-day retreat. I was asked to give a talk about how I was trying to turn my life around. I thought it went pretty well until I almost got into a fight during a break with one of the inmates who is no longer here. I know some of you guys know him, and I also know some of you are friends with him. I'm talkin' about William Jones."

Carlos looked around the room. There were a lot of interested faces who couldn't wait for him to go on with his story. "I'm not goin' to stand here and say who was right and who was wrong. I'm bringin' my confrontation with Jones up because the next time I saw Jones was in a bar in West Palm after he got out. He was still mad at me, and ended up knockin' me off the bar stool I sat on. I say it was a sucker punch, but he denies it. Whether it was or not isn't the issue. What I came to talk about is the mistakes I made that night at the bar. The first thing I did wrong was even bein' in the bar. I should have just stayed home and enjoyed a couple of beers without goin' to a place where I could get into a lot of trouble."

Carlos saw he had the group's undivided attention. He didn't know how long that would continue, but he hoped for the best. "I made an even bigger mistake after Jones hit me. Jones was thrown out by the bartender. I wanted revenge on him, so I found out where he lived and went to his apartment to pay him back. When I got there, the door was unlocked. I went in and found him on the floor unconscious. I'm not goin' to talk about all the details because we'd be here forever, and that's not the point anyway. What happened was I got charged with aggravated battery on Jones. Because I didn't do it, I wouldn't plead out. So there was a trial. Fortunately, the jury believed my side of the case, and I was found not guilty." Delgado stopped again to focus on where he was headed. He quickly determined what he needed to say next.

"I was really stupid when I went to Jones apartment lookin' for payback. Goin' there got me into a boatload of trouble and could have sent me back to prison. I should have called the Sheriff's Department and filed a complaint. They would have handled it, and I would not have gone through what I did. My mistakes were even worse when I consider how I have struggled to turn my life around, with God's help. Then in a moment of anger, I almost blew it all. I'm very fortunate my case ended the way it did, but from the time I was arrested until the not guilty verdict, I went through hell." Carlos shook his head and grimaced at the thought of what could have happened.

"What I really want to say is that's whether it's in here or when you get back on the outside, when a situation comes up that makes you lose your cool and want to strike back at someone, say a prayer to God for help in not seekin' revenge. Take your beef to whoever's in charge of keepin' the peace, and let them handle it. You'll save yourself from a lot of problems and be glad you did. Thanks to all of you for listenin' to me. God bless and keep the faith."

As Carlos returned to his seat, he received applause from a number of the inmates. As he sat back down next to Josh, Larry Blake came back to the podium and spoke. "Carlos, I want to thank you for your message. It's one I take to heart, and I hope all the men in this room will do the same. God bless you for your testimony and advice."

This time the clapping was even louder and more sustained. Carlos felt goosebumps over his body as he listened to the ovation. Josh leaned over and said to him, "I knew you would be a great evangelist for Christ. He must be very proud of you for speaking to these men."

40

Several months later, it was Robert's and Coral's turn to become enmeshed with the legal system. They were outside a courtroom at the Palm Beach County Courthouse for Anthony's final adoption hearing. Coral held the sleeping baby in her arms, while Robert anxiously watched for their attorney. The proceeding was scheduled to begin in ten minutes. Suddenly their lawyer, David Andrews, hustled down the hallway to both Williams' relief.

"Sorry, I'm late, Mr. and Mr. Williams. There was a huge backlog of people in the security line. The bailiff hasn't been out here, has he?"

"No, he hasn't Mr. Andrews," answered Robert. Then he quickly added, "I know we went over everythin' about the hearin' at your office last week, but is there anythin' else we need to know?"

"No, sir," answered Andrews. "Keep in mind what we talked about. Judge Stackhouse is thorough. He's likely to have a number of questions for both of you, especially for you, Robert. But he's also fair and compassionate. I don't anticipate we'll have any problems with him signing the Final Judgment of Adoption. Listen to his questions and answer them honestly and calmly as the two of you did at my office when we discussed the questions he may have. Okay?"

Andrews' eyes darted around as he waited for his clients' responses.

"We'll do as you ask, Mr. Andrews," replied Coral. Robert agreed.

"Wonderful," responded Andrews. He immediately changed the topic. "Have either of you seen Catherine Walker this morning? She'll be the other person the judge will want to hear from with regard to her preliminary home study and final home investigation."

Before either Williams could respond, Walker came around the corner toward them.

"Here she comes now." Andrews smiled and waved. Walker reciprocated.

"Good to see you, Catherine. How are you doing this morning?"

"Other than waiting twenty minutes in that horrendous line downstairs, I'm doing great. I can't wait to go in the courtroom and tell Judge Stackhouse what terrific parents the Williamses will be for this darling little boy." Walker softly stroked Anthony's cheek. He was still sound asleep.

"It looks like you'll get your wish right now," said Andrews as he watched the bailiff come out of the courtroom.

"Are you folks ready to come in?" asked Bailiff Henry McCurdy.

"Yes, sir," announced Andrews. McCurdy held the door open as the group filed in. Judge Richard Stackhouse was already in the courtroom, as was Court Clerk Mary Thomas.

"Good morning, everyone," declared the Court. "I know Ms. Walker and Mr. Andrews." Looking directly at Coral and Robert, he stated "I assume the two of you are Mr. and Mrs. Williams."

"Yes, sir," answered Robert, "and that's little Anthony in my wife's arms." The baby began to stretch and move around in Coral's arms. Judge Stackhouse smiled as the adults stood behind four chairs that had been positioned by the bailiff behind one of the counsel tables.

"Please take a seat," stated Stackhouse. After they all were seated, he continued. "By statute, adoption proceedings are confidential and held in closed court, so Bailiff McCurdy will go outside the courtroom and make sure no one else comes in."

McCurdy nodded and in a flash was outside the room. Judge Stackhouse then addressed Andrews.

"Mr. Andrews, I've reviewed the file and it seems everything is in order with the birth mother's consent to the adoption, and as I understand it, she was represented by her own counsel."

"That's correct, Your Honor."

"As far as the birth father, the file shows he was personally served with a Notice of Intended Adoption Plan, that a Claim of Paternity form and instructions was attached, and there was no response from the birth father. Is that correct as well?"

"Yes, sir, that is correct."

"Very good. At this point, I've got a few questions I want to ask of Mr. and Mrs. Williams. And of Ms. Walker as well. Let's start with Mr. Williams. Would you please come up to the witness stand, sir?"

Robert quickly obliged. Court Clerk Thomas administered the oath. Robert sat forward in his chair with his hands folded. Although he felt his heart race, he did his best to keep calm and collected, as Andrews advised.

"What I primarily want to ask you about, Mr. Williams, is your felony conviction."

"Yes, sir," replied Robert in a firm voice.

Stackhouse intently studied the court file and then began his questions. "From what I'm looking at, I see it was around fourteen years ago you pled guilty to a charge of DUI manslaughter in connection with the death of an elderly man named William Stevenson."

"Yes, I did, Your Honor."

"Tell me what happened."

Robert took a deep breath and looked Stackhouse straight in the eye as he answered. "The night I killed Mr. Stevenson, I had way too much to drink. It was about a liter of whiskey. Then I made the mistake of drivin' my car. I went only a couple of miles when I smashed into Mr. Stevenson's car. He was pronounced dead at the scene. It was a terrible decision to get behind the wheel. I wish I could take it back." Robert's voice tapered off as he added, "But I can't."

"Why did you have so much to drink? Are you an alcoholic?" Stackhouse closely observed Robert as he waited for the answer.

"I never had a drinkin' problem until about six months before the wreck."

"What brought that on?"

"My seventeen-year-old son was randomly murdered outside a buildin' where he was at a dance. The shooters didn't even know him. They were just lookin' for someone to kill. I couldn't deal with my boy's murder, and started drinkin' heavily to try and kill the pain. Before then, I never had any problems with excessive drinkin'. After my boy's death, I couldn't stop until the night I killed Mr. Stevenson. I've never had another drop of alcohol since then."

"Have you ever or are you now using any kind of drugs that have not been prescribed by a physician?"

"No, sir. I have never used any kind of drugs other than what my doctor told me I needed for my health."

"And what where those?"

"Pills to control my blood pressure and cholesterol level. Nothing else."

"So for the past fourteen years right up to today, you've not consumed a single ounce of alcohol?"

"That's correct, Your Honor."

"Do you foresee a situation where you might drink alcohol again in the future?" Stackhouse once again directly watched Robert as he waited for the reply.

"No, sir. I do not."

"Why do you believe that's the case?"

"Because I've taken it to our Lord and asked for His help never to drink again. I feel with His assistance, I never will."

"Speaking of our Lord, I see in the preliminary home study and final home investigation prepared by Ms. Walker, you are deeply involved in both your church and a prison ministry. Tell me first about your church work."

Robert smiled. Stackhouse saw the sincerity and love shining in this giant of a man as he answered the question. "First Baptist Church in Pahokee is a wonderful, God-honorin' church which has been a true blessin' to me and many others. Pastor Gilbert is an incredible minister, with a tremendous heart for those in need. He's been an inspiration to me, and he's gotten me to be a volunteer at the church – first by fixin' up the buildings and grounds and then, and more importantly, by leadin' a Bible study every week. My church and the congregation are a key part of my life."

"That's very admirable, Mr. Williams. Now tell me about the prison ministry you participate in."

Once again, Robert's beautiful grin surfaced. "While I was in prison, for the first five years, I didn't want to have anythin' to do with God or anyone on this planet. Slowly but surely, with the help of some good men I came back to the Lord. After I did, I started to get involved with the chaplain's office. I helped to run a number of faith-based programs and Bible studies which were intended to assist inmates in overcoming their past mistakes and turning their lives over to Christ. We weren't always successful with everyone, but the important thing was we tried our best to be evangelists for Jesus with men who were in dire straits."

Robert stopped momentarily to collect his thoughts. He didn't want to be verbose or appear prideful. "Anyway, when I got out of prison, I felt in my heart I wanted to continue to minister to the inmates in the best way I could, so a couple years ago, I joined a prison ministry team, and we go into Newtown Correctional Institution on a regular basis and offer different programs to inmates who want to participate. On one Sunday every month, we have a reunion between the inmates and prison ministers. The prisoners are in charge of the program and do a great job. The bottom line is I enjoy being part of the prison ministry team."

"Thanks for answering my questions, Mr. Williams. I have one last one. Why do you want to adopt this baby?"

Robert looked over at Coral. He wanted to be honest in his answer, but at the same time, he didn't want to say anything which might cause the Court to rule adversely. "At first, the movin' force behind the adoption was my wife. She met the birth mother at a prayer service goin' on near an abortion clinic. One thing led to another, and eventually the birth mother chose to have the baby and give it up for adoption rather than to abort the child. Praise the Lord for that! Afterwards, my wife kept feelin' God was callin' us to become the adoptive parents."

Robert swallowed hard before he went on. "When my wife first approached me about adoptin' the baby, I was uncertain about what to do. The reason was the feelin's I still have about losin' my son. Eventually, with a lot of prayer and her encouragement, I realized adoptin' this child was what God wanted us to do. Since Anthony's lived with us, our life has become more blessed than it already was. At this point in my life, I can't imagine bein' without him. I can't wait to teach him how to throw and catch a football."

Robert stopped talking and looked at Judge Stackhouse. He appeared to be touched by Robert's statements. He cleared his throat and said, "Thank you for your testimony, Mr. Williams. Those are all the questions I have for you. Please return to your seat."

Robert went back to his chair. After he was seated, the Court looked over at Coral. Before he could address her, Anthony started to cry. Coral quickly pulled out a bottle of milk from the diaper bag beside her and began to feed him with it.

Judge Stackhouse smiled and then addressed Coral. "It looks like you've got your hands full, Mrs. Williams. I've got some questions to ask you, but please remain seated where you are. The Court Clerk can swear you in right there."

Thomas hurried over to Coral and administered the oath to her. After Thomas finished, Judge Stackhouse began to speak to Coral.

"How long have you and Mr. Williams known each other?"

"It's been a little over three years."

"Where did the two of you meet?"

Coral looked over at Robert and laughed. He did the same. Then she turned her attention to the Court and said, "I'm sorry for laughing, Your Honor. It's sort of a funny story."

"You can tell me. I'm all ears," responded Stackhouse.

"We met at a landscaping supply store in Belle Glade. I was buying these large bags of fertilizer to use on the lawn at my house. When Robert saw me struggling to put them in my cart, he came over and asked if he could help. I said yes, and he ended up not only putting the bags in my cart and then my trunk, but he followed me home and unloaded them. We hit it off really well, and he came back the next day and put the fertilizer on my lawn. From there, one thing led to another. We started dating and then got married."

"And I see from the file I have the two of you have been married for a little over two years."

"Yes, that's right."

"And I assume you've been happily married to each other?"

"We certainly have," replied Coral in a convincing tone. "We're truly blessed."

"I'm glad to hear it. Now let me change topics." The Court's demeanor became more serious as he asked, "Have you ever seen your husband drink any alcohol or use any drugs other than what a doctor prescribed?"

"Absolutely not, Your Honor. Robert doesn't drink alcohol or take any non-prescription drugs."

"Do you drink alcohol, Mrs. Williams?"

"Not at our home. Occasionally, when we go out socially, I will have a glass or two of wine, but that's it."

"Do you feel your husband will be a good father for Anthony?"

"Robert will be an absolutely wonderful father. He will raise Anthony to be a man after God's heart and will love him dearly."

Coral looked at Robert. He put his right hand under his eyes to catch the tears he was moved to when he heard his wife's words.

"Tell me why you want to be Anthony's mother, Mrs. Williams?" Judge Stackhouse watched Coral with keen interest as he waited for the response.

"I love children, but was never able to have a child of my own as a result of a hysterectomy I had years ago. Because of my feelings for kids, I've been a preschool teacher for ten years. I care for all of them, but it's not the same as having your own child. When the opportunity came up with the birth mother to adopt her baby, I felt God was calling us to become his parents. Since this precious baby's been with me, I've loved him with every ounce of my being. I always will." Coral pulled a tissue from her purse to wipe off the tears rolling down her cheeks.

Judge Stackhouse was deeply touched by Coral's devotion to the infant she held. He quietly said, "Thank you, Mrs. Williams. I don't have any more questions." The Court immediately turned his attention to Catherine Walker. "Ms. Walker, please come to the witness stand so I can ask you some questions."

Walker was sworn in and sat down. Both Walker and Judge Stackhouse simultaneously grinned at each other. "How many times do you think you've testified in my courtroom, Ms. Walker?"

"At least a hundred."

"Minimum. I know about Ms. Walker and her background, so I'm going to direct my questions to the preliminary home study and final home investigation she prepared, which is part of the court file. My first question relates to Mr. Williams' conviction for DUI manslaughter. I've read your reports, and they're extremely thorough, but I want to hear your opinion of Mr. Williams' fitness to be the child's father, and the basis for the opinion."

Walker put her head back and pondered the response. She was a pro in the courtroom, but still concerned the answer would convince the Court of her position. "As you know from reading my reports, Judge Stackhouse, I interviewed a number of people about Mr. Williams. One of them was the pastor of his church, Anthony Gilbert. Pastor Gilbert had nothing but glowing things to say about Mr. Williams. He couldn't emphasize enough how much good Mr. Williams had done for him and the congregation. In fact, I even went and spoke with a few people who attend the Bible study Mr. Williams leads. They all spoke highly of him." Walker was on a roll and didn't want to lose momentum. She quickly and expertly changed gears.

"Besides speaking with people connected with Mr. Williams' church, I interviewed one of the assistant volunteer chaplains at Newtown Correctional Institution. His name is Dennis Davis. He's been a volunteer chaplain there for fifteen years and has known Mr. Williams ever since he was first incarcerated at Newtown. He talked to me extensively about how Mr. Williams turned his life around from when he began to serve time in prison. According to Mr. Davis, for a number of years after Mr. Williams began his confinement, he was difficult to get along with. Basically, he wanted nothing to do with anyone for the first five years or so of his time in prison. But then, he gradually began to change and became a very positive influence on the other inmates as well as the penitentiary employees. By the time he left, Mr. Williams was a role model for the prisoners and completely turned his life over to God." Walker took a deep breath before she went on.

"Mr. Davis also told me Mr. Williams has continued to be an excellent role model for everyone at the prison after his release. He's been part of a prison ministry team, which regularly goes into Newtown. Mr. Davis additionally said Mr. Williams has positively influenced many inmates and Newtown is fortunate to have him continue to interact with the inmates. I also spoke with several longtime prison employees who had similar things to say about Mr. Williams."

As he listened to Walker's testimony, Robert felt humbled but proud to serve his Lord and Savior in the way Jesus moved him to act. There was certainly no financial remuneration associated with his service, but there was a much more important focus and goal – one that was eternal and led to the ultimate treasure in Heaven, not only for himself, but also for the men whom Robert served. It was all of theirs for the asking.

"In addition to the people I've already mentioned, I talked with several business references Mr. Williams gave me. They spoke highly of him, and said he was fair and honest in his business dealings with them. Based on my investigation, Mr. Williams is doing well financially in his construction business, and Mrs. Williams is also gainfully employed. As far as I can determine, there are no financial security issues to be concerned about."

Walker was about to change topics once again. Her eyes lit up as she delved into this new subject.

"As part of my investigation, I made three visits to the Williams' home. One time before the baby was placed there and then two visits afterwards. The home itself is lovely. It's spacious, well-decorated, and spotlessly maintained. The baby's bedroom is beautiful. Mr. and Mrs. Williams renovated the room to look like a sports arena, but at the same time they kept a religious design with the room. There are crosses and other spiritual items which match beautifully with the sports theme. It really is neat. The bedroom and home are a great living environment for the child. Those are the highlights of my investigation and form the basis of my opinion as to Mr. Williams being a fit and proper parent."

"Your investigation and both reports are very thorough. Now tell me what your opinion is." Judge Stackhouse already knew the answer based upon the documents Walker prepared, but he also wanted to hear from her verbally while under oath.

"My opinion is Mr. Williams would not only make a fit and proper parent, but he would and will be a wonderful father to the child. I believe Mr. Williams will be a terrific role model, and the baby will be fortunate to have him as a father."

Coral squeezed Robert's hand. The two of them were grateful for Walker's testimony, and hoped it would cause Stackhouse to overcome any concerns he might still have about Robert's past conviction.

"And I assume your opinion regarding Mrs. Williams is she would not only be a fit and proper parent, but also a wonderful mother to the baby?"

"Absolutely, Your Honor. Not only did I see Mrs. Williams interact with the child at their home, but I also went to the preschool where she works. I observed how well the baby was cared for by the staff members who are in charge of the infants. I also saw Mrs. Williams at work with her toddler class. There are ten children she is in charge of, and they love her. She does a marvelous job with them. She will be a super mom for the baby." Walker looked over at Coral and smiled. Coral nodded in appreciation.

"That concludes my questions, Mrs. Walker. Please return to your seat." As Judge Stackhouse waited for her to leave the witness stand, he glanced at some additional paperwork he had been given by Andrews.

"Mr. Andrews, I've reviewed the proposed Final Judgment of Adoption of Minor which you provided me. I understand that the name to be given the child is Anthony Williams."

"That's correct, Your Honor."

"It's the Court's determination that both Mr. and Mrs. Williams will be fit and proper parents for Anthony Williams and it is in his best interests for the adoption to take place. Therefore, I'm going to sign the Final Judgment."

With the stroke of a pen, Robert and Coral were now the proud parents of the baby whose life had been spared by his birth mother. Neither of the Williamses could hold back the tears of joy overcoming them.

"Thank you very much, Your Honor," said Robert as he stood up. "This is a tremendous blessing for the three of us and for Anthony's birth mother as well." Coral nodded her head in agreement.

"You're welcome, Mr. Williams. I wish all of you the best, but we're not quite finished. There's one more thing before we conclude."

"What is it?" Robert nervously asked.

"If it's okay with the two of you, I'd like to hold Anthony." This time Judge Stackhouse smiled ear-to-ear.

"Of course it's okay," laughed Coral.

Stackhouse practically flew off the bench and stood in front of Coral. She carefully handed him the baby. The Judge took him like the expert father he was and rocked him back and forth. Anthony was now wide awake, and when he looked at the Judge, a tiny grin crossed his face. Everyone in the courtroom saw the reaction and was delighted by it.

"Mr. and Mrs. Williams, Anthony is a beautiful boy." Judge Stackhouse looked directly at Robert as he also said, "You're right, Mr. Williams. All of you have been blessed by God with this child."

41

"All right, darlin', tell me what I can do to help. We've got to get rollin'. The baptism is supposed to start in half an hour." Robert slipped his suit jacket on as he stood in Anthony's bedroom watching Coral finish dressing their child.

"The best thing you can do, Mr. Williams, is to stop standing over me, and get the air conditioning running in the car. We'll be ready in a few minutes."

The tone of his wife's voice, coupled with her referring to him as "Mr. Williams," was Robert's clue he needed to do as instructed. He quickly complied. The inside of the car was ice cold when Coral fastened Anthony into his car seat. As they pulled into the parking lot of St. Juliana's Catholic Church in Belle Glade, they were amazed at the number of vehicles already there.

"My goodness, Robert. I knew we were going to have quite a few people here, but this looks like a lot more than we thought were coming. It's a good thing we bought two of those giant cakes. I was afraid they were going to be too much, but now I'm concerned we may not have enough."

"It's a good thing the Taylors, Carlos, and Josh volunteered to be here early to get everything set up for the party after the baptism. In fact, there they are." Robert waved at his friends as he pulled into a parking space. They all came over to the car. Each of their faces was covered with a smile as the Williams' family exited their vehicle.

"Hooray, the guest of honor is here," called out John Taylor. "How is the little guy doing this morning?"

"He's been as fussy as I've ever seen him. I had a hard time bathing him, and then getting him dressed was a real adventure." Coral let loose with an exasperated sigh. "Which is why we're running late. Sorry, everyone."

"There's nothing to be sorry about," answered Anna Taylor as she looked at her watch. "We have five minutes until the baptism is supposed to begin. The church hall is set up and ready to go. Wait until you see all the food your guests brought with them. It's amazing." Anna laughed and shook her head.

"Yeah, and that's nothing compared to the number of presents the little guy is getting," added Josh. "There are two tables full of them."

"Oh, my gosh," answered Coral. "We asked people to contribute a dish to share, if they could, but not to bring any presents."

"Don't worry about it," said Anna. "No one ever listens to those requests when a baby is involved in the celebration."

Coral looked around. She noticed the Taylor children were not here. "Anna, where are your kids?"

"They're home with a sitter. There was no way we were bringing them when we needed to get the hall set up. It would have been a fiasco with them running all over the place."

"I'm sorry we won't get to see them," replied Coral.

"There will be plenty of other times when we all get together," chimed in John. "Today its better they're

home driving the sitter nuts, rather than Anna and me."
Everyone laughed.

The group walked into the church where they were
greeted with a roar of applause. Both Robert and Coral
were overwhelmed when they saw the size of the crowd.
At least two hundred people were present. Father
Anderson immediately came over to the Williamses. He
was followed by Sister Agnes, who was instrumental in
arranging for the use of the facilities and helping with
the invitations.

"Welcome everyone. Now that our guest of honor
has arrived, we can begin the ceremony." Father
Anderson grinned as he said, "Let's move over to the
baptismal fount."

Lourdes and Lydia stood directly behind the
baptismal fount. When Coral saw them, she headed
straight to the sisters. "It's good to see both of you."
Coral kissed each of them on the cheek. Then she
handed Anthony to Lourdes. The sight was Heavenly to
behold. An infant whose life had been spared was being
caressed by his biological mother, who cared enough
for her baby to be present at his baptism ceremony.
There wasn't a heart in the building that remained
untouched by this wondrous scene. Robert knew Jesus
was present with them and pictured Him standing to
the side watching everyone with pride and joy.

"Are we ready to begin?" asked Father Anderson.

"Yes, we are," answered Coral. Lourdes gently
handed Anthony back to Coral.

"I understand the godparents are John and Anna
Taylor."

"Yes, we are, Father," responded John.

"The two of you please step here to the side of
Robert and Coral."

The Taylors positioned themselves as requested by the priest. Father Anderson began the baptism ceremony. Anthony fell asleep at the beginning of the baptism and he remained sleeping until Father Anderson carefully poured water over his tiny head. Then he quickly awoke and let loose with a blood-curdling scream. Most of the crowd couldn't contain their laughter, particularly when Father Anderson declared, "I have a way with children, haven't I?" Ten minutes later the baptism was concluded and the church was filled with joy and laughter. The ceremony was a beautiful one, and another celebration now waited. They slowly made their way to the church hall, delighted by Anthony being brought into the Christian faith.

As Coral and Robert sat at their table, they were in awe of the number of people present and the amount of food brought to the party. All of the clergy and laity who attended the meeting at First Baptist Church in Pahokee nearly a year ago when Maria Rodgers made her presentation for Choose Life Pregnancy Care Centers were here today, along with their families. Many of the people who participated in the prayer chain at the abortion center in Wellington also came with their families. Before everyone started to partake in the bountiful feast, Pastor Anthony Gilbert said a prayer of thanksgiving. When he finished, the guests began to enjoy a tasty assortment of dishes. Lourdes, Lydia, Anthony Davis, and Father Anderson sat at the table with Robert and Coral. Anthony Williams was again sound asleep in his stroller.

As the crowd finished their food, and before the cakes were cut, Robert went to the front of the room where a podium was located. He picked up the microphone and began to speak.

"Coral and I want to thank everyone for bein' here today and sharin' with us this blessed time. Our precious baby has now been brought into the Lord's family. We especially want to thank Lourdes Castillo for makin' the decision to bring Anthony into the world. If she hadn't been so compassionate and selfless, Anthony wouldn't be here now nor would any of us." Cheers and applause erupted in the room. Lourdes blushed and grabbed Lydia's hand. Then she waved at everyone. When the noise subsided, Robert began to talk again.

"I hope all of you don't mind, but I'd like to share a prayer I wrote in thanksgiving for Anthony's birth. It won't take too long for me to read it." There was dead silence in the room as Robert started to read what he had written.

"The Priceless Life of A Child"

Dear God, we humbly come before You and thank You for providing us with the ability to create life. Please help us never to forget how priceless and beautiful the infants born into this world are.

Help us to keep Your words and treasure Your commands, so we may always respond with gratitude and thanksgiving when a new life is ready to enter this world.

Guide us in Your ways of wisdom and lead us along straight paths so we may put aside all personal concerns or worries about a child being brought into this world. Help us to recognize how precious a child is so life over death for the child is chosen. In those instances where it is not possible for parents to personally raise the child, provide them with the strength,

compassion, and mercy to choose life and
adoption for the baby rather than abortion and
death.

Assist us to walk in Your light so we may
always see and honor the need to treat our
children with love, dignity, and respect.

Help us to appreciate our children as being
crowns of glory bestowed upon us by You.
Regardless of any trials or difficulties we may
endure, may we never lose sight that a child is
one of the greatest blessings You have given
us. Please always be with us and provide us
with the grace needed to overcome any adverse
situation which we may face with our children.

In Jesus' name we pray. Amen.

"Amen" rang out the rambunctious response. The
room once again came alive with applause. The cakes
were cut. None was left, but everyone received at least
one slice. The day was a Heavenly gift for all those
who had come to witness a baby baptized as a child of
Christ.

Later that evening, the Taylors, Carlos, and Josh
were at the Williams home. There were so many
presents they couldn't all fit into Robert's car. The back
of the Taylors' van was used to transport many of the
gifts. Everyone sat in the living room. Anthony was
now wide awake and the center of attention. He was
spitting and sputtering to everyone's delight.

"Man, this kid is really wound up." Delgado
laughed as he continued, "Williams, I think you're
really goin' to be in for it as this boy grows up. But
he'll help you stay young, right?" Carlos grinned and
clapped his hands as he posed the question.

"I sure hope so," answered Robert. "I'm counting on it. And I'm glad to see you in such a good mood. We never had a chance to talk much today. How have you been?" Everyone in the room had a close connection with Carlos. Robert didn't think Delgado would mind answering the question. He was right.

"I've been great. Sorry I haven't been out to your church the past few weeks, but we've got this major project goin' on at work, and I've had a ton of overtime. We'll finish the job this week. I'll be at your church and Bible study class next Sunday."

"Glad to hear it," said Robert.

"And so you know, I've been readin' the Bible every day. I'm stayin' out of trouble, and I intend to keep it that way with God's help. I haven't gone to any bars and won't."

"All that sounds terrific, Carlos," answered John. "You seem like you're on the right track."

"I am, Taylor, but there's one thing I've got to admit." Carlos looked slyly over at Josh. The two of them started to laugh.

"What's going on?" John grinned as he waited for the response.

Josh couldn't help cutting in and answering the question. Delgado didn't mind. He bit his lip as Josh began to explain. "A couple of weeks ago, I went over to Carlos' home to have dinner and watch a ball game. I brought some beer with me. We were having a good time. So good, I didn't want to drive home. Carlos put me up for the night in his guest bedroom. Neither of us should probably have had as many beers as we did, but it was fun at the time."

"It sure was, Wilbur. And Williams, before you start lecturing us, that's not somethin' that we do often. So don't worry about us becomin' drunks."

"I wasn't goin' to give a lecture, and I'm not worried about Josh or you becomin' drunks. I'm glad you guys didn't go to a bar, and nobody drank and drove a car. I don't want to see either of you repeat my mistake."

"Or mine," added John.

"We won't," replied Carlos. Josh agreed. Carlos held out his hands as he said, "Now pass the boy to me, Williams. I haven't held him yet. I think it's time I did."

"No problem." Robert gingerly handed Anthony to his friend. The room lit up as Carlos cradled the infant and softly talked to him. It was a side of Delgado that none of them had ever seen. Anthony was already making a positive impact on others in his brief existence. He was able to because of his birth mother's decision to choose life over death.

42

"Lourdes, please hurry up," called out Lydia as she knocked at the bathroom door. "We've got fifteen minutes until we leave, and I haven't been able to get in there yet."

The door flew open and out stepped Lourdes. Lydia took two steps back as she admired her sibling's appearance. "Wow, aren't you the fashion model? I can't believe you're my little sister."

"Do you really think I look okay? There's supposed to be a lot of people at the church." Lourdes paused, and then added with a smile, "Including Anthony. In fact, he should be here any time now to pick us up."

"I've already told you how good you look. Now please get out of the way so I can try my best to be ready when your boyfriend gets here."

Lourdes felt the irritation in her sister's voice and quickly moved. As Lydia closed the bathroom door, there was a rapping at the front entry to the apartment.

"Is that you, Anthony?"

"Yes, it is. I'm here to take two of the prettiest ladies in Belle Glade to church."

As Lourdes opened the door and Anthony saw her, he was speechless. It wasn't the reaction Lourdes hoped for. "What's the matter? Don't you like the way I look?" She had her hands on her hips as he came into the apartment and closed the door.

"I love the way you look. I've never seen you so dressed up." Anthony gulped.

"Well, if I'm going to speak to a bunch of people at a church about choosing to have my baby adopted instead of aborted, I want to look my best. So, I splurged and bought a new dress and tried some different makeup."

"Well, you look great, and I think everybody there will feel the same way."

Suddenly, Lourdes frowned. Then she vigorously waved her right hand in front of her face in order to fan herself. Anthony was puzzled as he watched her reaction.

"What's wrong? All of a sudden you look stressed out."

"I am feeling pressured. Unlike you, I've never spoken to a big group in public. You've been through this several times already. I hope I can get through it and do half as good as I've seen you do."

Anthony saw the anxiety in Lourdes' eyes. He gently took her hands into his. "Lourdes, I have no doubt you will do a terrific job. You've already gone through the hard part in making the decision to have your baby instead of aborting him. Look what happened. A handsome boy came into the world, and lives with great parents, and you're still an important part of his life. If Jesus helped you through all of that, don't you think He will be with you today?"

Anthony's beautiful smile emerged. Lourdes kissed him on the cheek and then hugged him. Lydia came out of the bathroom, and playfully admonished them. "Okay, you two. Both of you have work to do. Let's get going."

"Yes, ma'am," replied Anthony. "I'm ready to drive both of you to Loxahatchee." He bowed low gracefully, opened the door, and stuck out his hand for the two sisters to leave before him.

"Now, that's more like it," Lydia chuckled on the way out.

When Anthony and the Castillo sisters arrived at St. Peter's Lutheran Church in Loxahatchee they were greeted with a parking lot full of cars. Lourdes looked around nervously as she exclaimed, "Wow. I didn't think there would be this many people here!"

Before anyone could respond, they saw Maria Rodgers standing next to the space Anthony pulled into. She waved excitedly, and her face lit up with a big smile. As the three of them got out of the car, Maria hugged each one.

"I'm glad the three of you are here," said Maria. "Lisa Long and John Carroll are both inside. Now we're ready to go. The church is packed."

"I see that," replied Lourdes. "I hope I make it through my talk."

Maria saw how concerned Lourdes was. She put her arm around Lourdes' shoulder and quietly said to her, "I know you will do an awesome job, Lourdes. Like you did in our practice sessions. Keep smiling. By the way, you look beautiful."

Maria's words bolstered Lourdes. She walked into the building with more excitement than anxiety. Pastor Paul Demus saw the group and immediately went over to them.

"Welcome, everyone. It's wonderful to have all of you here." His eyes sparkled as he spoke. "The congregation is looking forward to hearing from our guests about the success of adoption in your lives. What I've decided to do is have our speakers make their presentations first. Then we'll have our services later. All are welcome to attend and greet the members of our church afterwards. We've got a lunch prepared for everyone. I hope you will stay."

The response was unanimous and in the affirmative. Demus was delighted. He led Anthony and Lourdes to the front of the church where Long and Carroll were seated. After Lourdes and Anthony sat next to them, the pastor approached the podium. Although the room was still noisy, as he reached the stand, it became very quiet.

"Good morning, everyone. It's a blessing to have you here. We are in for a special treat today as many of you already know. We're privileged to have four speakers who will talk to us about how adoption has made a wondrous impact on their lives. Before we start our services, we'll listen to what they have to say. After the services are concluded, we'll be having a luncheon in the church hall. Our speakers will stay and be available to answer any questions. I also want to mention in addition to our four speakers, we have Maria Rodgers with us as a guest. Maria is the Program Administrator for Choose Life Pregnancy Care Centers. Choose Life is a wonderful organization which helps pregnant women in Palm Beach County choose life rather than abortion. Maria will also be available at the luncheon to answer any questions."

Demus stopped for a few moments and cracked a big smile. "By the way, Choose Life can always use more volunteers and donations as well. Hopefully we'll be able to help her out with those needs today." Maria grinned at Demus as he concluded speaking for the time being. "Now it's time to hear from our speakers. First up is Lisa Long."

Demus sat down as Long approached the podium. She made the same presentation as the one given earlier in the year at First Baptist Church in Pahokee. After she finished, Carroll and Anthony gave similar testimonies as they had at First Baptist. Then, it was Lourdes' turn. She had overcome her anxiety and confidently began her talk.

"My name is Lourdes Castillo, and I live in Belle Glade with Lydia, my sister. Last year, when I was eighteen, I became pregnant. The biological father wanted nothing to do with the baby. In fact, he wanted me to have an abortion. I didn't know what to do. My sister and I had no other relatives in our family. Mom had passed away, and our father had left our family years before. We weren't ready or able to raise an infant together, so I went to a women's center out in Wellington to find out information about having an abortion." Tears began to well in Lourdes eyes as she continued.

"On our way into the center, we passed a large group of people who were praying. They had big signs. I remember one of the signs said to choose life, not abortion because there were options available. After we got the information from the center and were driving back past the group praying, I asked my sister to stop the car. A woman came over to me and talked with us. Then she gave us some brochures. Her name was Coral Williams, and she gave me her cell number. Eventually, I called her as I was trying to decide what to do about my pregnancy. I was so conflicted." Lourdes stopped and took a deep breath. As she looked out at the congregation, she saw she had their total attention.

"Ms. Williams was a volunteer at one of the Choose Life offices in Pahokee. My sister and I went out there one Saturday to get more information about options to abortion. Both Ms. Williams and Ms. Rodgers were there. They gave us a lot to think about, and they were both kind." Lourdes looked over at Maria and smiled. The gesture touched Maria's heart. How thankful she was for being able to help Lourdes in her monumental life and death decision.

"They also asked us to attend a church service at First Baptist Church in Pahokee the next day to hear three speakers talk about adoption. We decided to go and listen to them. And guess who the three were?" Lourdes turned around and waved her arm at Long, Carroll, and Anthony. Her words and gesture were greeted with both laughter and applause.

"Each one of their talks touched Lydia and me deeply. Afterwards, the two of us met with Anthony to ask him some questions. I started to become more and more convinced I should meet again with Ms. Rodgers and Ms. Williams. So Lydia and I did. I had an ultrasound at Choose Life's offices. We were able to see some awesome pictures of the baby, and we found out my child was a boy. After the ultrasound, we got more information about the adoption process from Ms. Rodgers. I decided to put the baby up for adoption rather than have an abortion."

The congregation was overjoyed. Applause and whistles permeated the air. When the room quieted down, Lourdes was smiling brightly as she continued. "I haven't told you the whole story yet. I don't want to go on for too long, but I want to share with you about the actual adoption. I really felt a bond with Ms. Williams, and she did likewise. She is married with no children. One thing led to another, and it was Mr. and Mrs. Williams who ended up adopting the baby. We have an open adoption where I am able to see my son on a regular basis and be a part of his life. As part of that open adoption, I was at my son's baptism ceremony, which took place a few weeks ago."

The church was once again engulfed with clapping and excitement. After the sound subsided, Lourdes announced, "One last thing. The baby was named Anthony in honor of Anthony Davis for the inspiration he provided about going forward with the adoption. Anthony Davis and l are now dating each other. That's all I have to say."

This time the entire assembly rose from their seats and loudly voiced their approval over what they had heard, not only for what Lourdes had shared, but also for the other three speakers as well. The messages of life over death, and adoption over abortion, had been well-received. The speakers' testimonies would long be remembered by those present.

After the services were concluded, the church members and their guests were in the hall to partake of the delicious lunch. Lourdes left her table to get a piece of the chocolate cake which looked so good she couldn't resist it. A young woman came up to her and asked if they could go outside to talk. Lourdes agreed, and the two of them walked to a quiet part of the parking lot where no one else was present.

"Thanks for coming out here to speak with me, Lourdes. My name is Julia McDonald. I'm not a member of this church, but my friend Denise McKenzie is. She knew the four of you would be talking today about adoption and brought me here to listen." Julia bowed her head and then bit her lip before she continued.

"I'm in a situation much like you were. I got pregnant a couple of months ago and am trying to decide what to do with the baby. I'm only nineteen and single. The father wants nothing to do with the child. I live at home with my parents and haven't told them about it. I don't know what I should tell them because I don't know whether I should have an abortion or not, but from what you talked about, it seems like I should choose life for the baby, and give him or her up for adoption. What do you think?"

Lourdes saw the fear in Julia's eyes. She remembered it well. She also recalled how the anxiety was overcome with the help of a number of people. She thought it was her turn now to pass those good deeds on.

"Of course, I can't tell you what to do. But you asked for my advice, so I'm going to give it to you. I think you should tell your parents about the pregnancy and what you heard being discussed here today. Then you should see Ms. Rodgers and Mrs. Williams. They will be able to give you a lot of information about adoption and the many good things which come from it. Maybe after you talk with your parents and meet with Ms. Rodgers and Mrs. Williams and get their input, you'll decide to keep the baby. One thing I can tell you for sure, you will never regret sparing the child's life and allowing the baby to be born and loved by many people. I hope what I said helps you." Lourdes looked sincerely and sweetly at Julia.

"You've been a tremendous help and have given me a lot to think about. Thanks for talking to me."

"You're welcome. I wish you the best."

Now it was Julia's turn to make a life and death decision over the fate of an unborn child. Lourdes fervently hoped the same choice for life would be made by Julia.

43

"Come on, you precious little girl, tell me how old you are." Coral smiled as she continued to coax the answer from Laura Taylor. Laura put up four fingers from her right hand.

"You're four," said Coral.

"Yes. I'm a big girl now." Laura looked over at her brother, Jean. She was waiting to see what he would say.

"No, you're not," Jean emphatically declared. "You're still a baby."

"I'm not a baby," protested Laura in an angry tone. "I'm in preschool."

"All right, children. That's enough from both of you. Jean, apologize to your sister right now." John Taylor stared at his son as he waited for Jean to follow his instructions.

"Sorry, Laura." Jean had his arms folded across his chest as he begrudgingly did what he was told.

"Robert and Coral, aren't the two of you glad it's only Laura you're taking care of while we're away? Imagine if Jean and Renee were both here as well. Then add Anthony into the mix. Wow!" John laughed as he considered such a scenario.

"Sorry, John," joked Robert, "but we're not that good of friends."

"Robert," answered Coral, "how can you say such a thing?"

"We know he's only kidding," declared Anna. "At least, I think he is." This time it was her turn to giggle at the bantering. The rest of the adults quickly joined in the merriment.

After Coral stopped laughing, she changed the subject. "Okay, so we know Laura is four, and in preschool. Jean, how old are you and what grade are you in?"

"I'm ten years old, and I'm in fifth grade," proudly declared Jean. "But I'm not in my mother's class because she said it would be a conflict. Mrs. DeRosa is my teacher."

"And what about you, Renee?"

"I'm eight years old, and I'm in third grade, Mrs. Williams." Renee went and stood in front of Coral. Then she jumped into Coral's lap. Coral kissed her on the top of her head.

"I've got to say all of you Taylor children are growing up so fast." Coral shook her head in amazement. "I'll bet our little Anthony will grow up just as quickly."

"Where is Anthony?" asked Renee. "We haven't seen him since we got here."

Coral grinned at Renee. "Honey, you just got here ten minutes ago. Anthony is in his bedroom sleeping, but I don't think it will be too much longer before he wakes up and you can see him."

"Laura will see him when he wakes up," interjected Robert, "but I've got to get goin' with the rest of the Taylors' if they want to catch their plane in Miami."

John glanced at his watch. "You're right, Robert. We do need to get moving so we're at the airport on time."

"But, Mommy, I want to go too," cried out Laura. She grabbed Anna's legs. Anna gently picked her up and spoke to her in a soft tone.

"Laura, Mommy and Daddy have talked to you about how you're too young to go on the trip to Haiti with us. We won't be gone very long."

"But I want to go," argued Laura as she cut her mother off, but Anna still had another card to play.

"Besides that, you have to stay here and help Mrs. Williams take care of Anthony. Remember?"

"Laura, I need you to stay and help me with my baby. Okay?" Coral looked with mock angst at Laura.

Laura was unconvinced despite Coral's plea. Suddenly, there was a piercing cry from Anthony's room. He was now wide awake and looking for attention.

"Let me down, Mommy. Anthony's calling me." Laura practically jumped from Anna's arms. She raced to Anthony's bedroom, followed closely by Coral.

As Coral rounded the corner from the living room to the bedroom, she looked back, waved, and said to the rest of the Taylor family and her husband, "You better get out of here while that little girl is occupied. Have a safe and blessed trip."

"Thanks, Coral. See you in five days." Anna motioned for everyone to follow her as she hurriedly went out the kitchen door. They all quickly filed into the Taylors' minivan for the two-hour trip to the Miami airport.

"John and Anna, I have to tell you what a wonderful thing I think you're doin' by takin' Jean and Renee to Haiti to visit their uncle and his family. I'm sure they can't wait to see them, and the two of you as well. God bless you both for takin' the time and makin' the effort." Robert was clearly moved by the Taylors' actions.

"We told Mr. Baptiste the last time we saw him at our home we would bring Jean and Renee to Haiti when they were older," replied John. "And now was a great time to go. I've got a lull in my court hearings and trials, and school's closed for a mid-term holiday Monday and Tuesday. It's only Wednesday the kids and Anna will miss."

"I've got a substitute lined up for Wednesday," interjected Anna. "We were all able to work the trip into our schedules. Although Mr. Baptiste didn't have the room to accommodate all of us where he lives, the Haitian lawyer who represented us in the adoption of Jean and Renee is letting us stay at his home. He has a couple of extra bedrooms available because his two children are in Florida on a college work/study program. Everything came together for us to go."

"It's something we really need to do for a number of reasons," added John. "Mostly because the children need to see their relatives. Both Jean and Renee were very young when they left Haiti and don't remember much about it at this point in their lives." John stopped and took a deep breath.

"Honestly, Robert, both Anna and I need to experience firsthand what life in Haiti is like. We know from the news and what you've told us about your time there it's a very poor country with many people still suffering from the earthquake in addition to the poverty. I think it will help us to greater appreciate what blessings we have in America and to see what programs in Haiti we might be able to help out financially."

"Those are all great reasons to make the trip," replied Robert. "You need to be prepared to see some very dismal livin' conditions. But there is hope, especially with the number of relief workers from different countries who come and try to make things better for the Haitian people. While you're there, make sure you check out the orphanage which I helped rebuild after the earthquake. Your attorney can take you there. It is an inspirational example of how things do change for the better."

"We'll make sure we visit there, Robert," said Anna. "We know the place means a great deal to you."

"It sure does. After you see it, you'll understand why. Clearly, the Lord is at work there."

"The Lord has been at work in many ways this past year, hasn't He?" John was deep in thought as he continued. "Look what happened to Carlos. He was exonerated of the charges against him and has grown closer to God. And Coral was one of the people who were instrumental in Lourdes' decision to not abort her baby and instead give him up for adoption. Then the baby is adopted by our two great friends while Lourdes still has the opportunity and desire to be a part of Anthony's life. How awesome is that?"

"Really awesome, Dad," answered Jean.

John turned around and looked at his son. He smiled as he told his boy, "I should have known you were listening to us. You never miss anything do you?"

"Nope," answered Jean.

"I don't miss anything either, Daddy," called out Renee. "And I think God is at work in all of us by our going to Haiti, both for our good and the good of the people we meet."

"Out of the mouths of babes," declared Robert.

Acknowledgments

I want to thank my editor, Adele Brinkley, for her invaluable assistance in helping to make this book a better one. Bob Modini, my friend and fellow prison minister, was a tremendous asset with his suggestions and revisions, and I am indebted to him for his time and effort. I also greatly appreciate my publisher's, Cathy Teets, confidence in this story to undertake its publication.

Although this book is a work of fiction, much of the pro-life theme came as a result of my daughter, Carolyn, deciding several years ago at the age of 18, to choose life for her unborn baby after she became pregnant. As a result, we now have Tyrell, a precious 4-year-old grandson, to share life with. Some of the best times in life come when Tyrell is with Aaron, our other 5-year-old grandson, who is the child of our daughter, Diana and son-in-law, Jeffrey. The love which these two boys have for life, and the positive impact both of them have upon so many people, is a gift from God.

My wife, Katherine, continues to be my biggest supporter in many ways. Our 40 years of marriage has flown by, and I give thanks to God for having brought the two of us together as husband and wife.